# A POUND OF FLESH

*Also by the same author*
A MIDSUMMER KILLING

# A POUND OF FLESH

## Trevor Barnes

William Morrow and Company, Inc.
New York

For Alison Halford
Assistant Chief Constable
Merseyside Police

*Age Quod Agis*

First published in Great Britain in 1991 by New English Library Hardbacks

It is the policy of William Morrow and Company, Inc., and its imprints and
affiliates, recognizing the importance of preserving what has been written, to
print the books we publish on acid-free paper, and we exert our best efforts to
that end.

Library of Congress Cataloging-in-Publication Data

Barnes, Trevor, 1955–
    [Dead meat]
    A pound of flesh / Trevor Barnes.
      p.  cm.
    ISBN 0-688-11048-7
    I. Title.
    PR6052.A6688D4   1993
    823'.914—dc20                          92-35811
                                                CIP

Printed in the United States of America

First U.S. Edition

1  2  3  4  5  6  7  8  9  10

Wenn ich einmal soll scheiden,
So scheide nicht von mir!
Wenn ich den Tod soll leiden,
So tritt du dann herfür!

Be near me, Lord, when dying,
O part not Thou from me!
And to my succour flying,
Come, Lord, and set me free!

Extract from text of Elgar/Atkins edition of Bach's *St Matthew Passion* reproduced by permission of Novello and Company Limited

## Acknowledgments

If the legal background to this novel has any authenticity, it is due to the generous help of Roger Finbow and John Watson – both partners in the City firm of Ashurst Morris Crisp – although it should be noted that any resemblance between Ashursts and the fictional partnership portrayed in this book is purely coincidental; (Acting) Chief Inspector Tom Millest of the Metropolitan Police again saved me from errors in police procedure by casting his sharp eye over the typescript – the ones that remain are solely my responsibility; Dr Elizabeth Gaminara provided some invaluable information about poisons; Faye Webb, our nanny, has provided me with the tranquil atmosphere at home essential to writing by looking after our daughter so well. I would also like to thank my agent, Heather Jeeves, publisher, Clare Bristow, and editor, Carolyn Caughey, for being their usual pillars of strength – especially when their author pressed the wrong button on his word processor and despatched five chapters into the ether. Last of all, a special word of thanks to my wife, Sally, for her constant patience and support.

# 1

Most of the neighbours slept soundly through the night. The clouds rolled over in waves and the necklaces of street-lights twinkled through the hours of darkness. The police were most discreet. It was only the stupidity of one detective constable who drove into the road with his horn screeching at two o'clock in the morning that shook a handful from their slumber. Most swore under their breath, listened to the comforting patter of rain on their window and drifted back to sleep. A few of the more curious twitched back their curtains and saw a line of police cars drawn up outside number forty-three. Men flitted like shadows under the harsh sodium light from the street-lamps. The curtains were held back in murmured amazement for a few minutes before curiosity soured to boredom and the neighbours wandered back to bed. Until dawn clawed its way across Clapham Common, none knew the angel of death had passed over Rosebrooke Road.

A small crowd gathered in the strengthening light. They stood in animated knots of twos and threes behind the luminous tape, some huddled under umbrellas, a couple of older women in transparent plastic headscarves, others simply bare-headed. A white Rover nosed into the street and spurted through the puddles towards them at a potentially lethal speed. Behind the wheel was a handsome black man in his late twenties, beside him a slightly older woman whose lips were tight with disapproval and alarm. 'Slow down, Dexter, for God's sake,' she hissed. 'One murder is quite enough for today.'

The driver braked and skidded to a halt a few yards short of the first group of onlookers. He hooted imperiously and they eddied to either side with a murmur of discontent like a herd of grazing cattle.

A uniformed constable ambled towards the car with a scowl and wiped the beads of water from the rim of his helmet. Detective Sergeant Dexter Bazalgette wound down the window and flourished the leather wallet that contained his Metropolitan Police warrant card. 'We're from AMIP,' he said.

The constable nodded. He had been told to expect the Area Major Investigating Pool.

'I've got the Detective Super with me,' continued the sergeant. 'Where's the detective inspector?'

The constable bent down to look into the car and raised his eyebrows when he saw the superintendent was a woman. He pointed towards one of the terraced houses about thirty yards ahead. 'Inspector Thomson? You'll find him inside.'

The crowd, swollen by inquisitive commuters, closed behind the car. 'You'd have thought half an inch of rain would've kept them indoors, wouldn't you?' grunted Dexter.

Blanche Hampton smiled wearily beside him. 'Everyone wants to see a body. Especially if a government minister's involved.'

The superintendent narrowed her heavy eyelids against the drizzle and strode towards number forty-three. Her face was rounded, with a nose that the uncharitable might describe as stubby, and a firm chin. In another woman these features would have resulted in plainness. And indeed Blanche's face fell easily into sadness and had a faint masculine air. But the superintendent was far from plain: her eyes were blessed with long lashes and an enquiring sparkle, and her skin with a glowing clarity. Men found her attractive without quite knowing why. She was a tall woman and well-fleshed, forever wishing she were thinner, although she had little fat to shed. Her hands were hidden in the pockets of her Burberry raincoat which flapped intermittently to reveal the navy blue business suit beneath. She was a little knock-kneed and had a tendency to walk with her feet splayed outwards. This imparted a swaying motion to her busy, rather ungainly, lope which she always preferred to a run.

Rosebrooke Road was one in a grid of anonymous streets to the west of Clapham Common. The road-markings were broken where the tarmac had been lifted for repairs. Puddles lay in the potholes like newly minted coins. Behind Blanche the two-storey, red brick terraces stretched away into the suburbs of south London, prosperous and smug in their Edwardian gentility. Ahead, the houses melded into the mist of the Common, intersected by the black branches of plane trees. Even if she had not been told the number, the superintendent would have recognised the house from the mêlée of policemen at the front door. The front garden was a rectangle of damp dirt, the boundaries marked by a privet hedge and what she guessed in summer would be a stunted hydrangea. Water dribbled from the eaves above and slapped onto the tiles beside her.

Detective Inspector Thomson from the divisional CID stood in the hall puffing a cigarette. 'It's like a fucking butcher's shop,' was all he said at first with a distant Liverpudlian lilt, screwing up his face with disgust and nodding towards the stairs which led up to the flat. His teeth stood out like matches from a cribbage-board. He looked up suspiciously at Dexter: six feet two inches tall of black detective sergeant wearing an expensive wool jacket in a bold check set off by an even bolder purple tie. Dexter's face was a handsome mask of chocolate skin, his hair trimmed short, marred only by an enormous, spongy nose – the result of a juvenile rugby accident. The sergeant held Thomson's glance and returned it with a good-natured smile. There was nothing retiring about the detective sergeant. It was his very impulsiveness and theatricality, allied to intelligence and hard work, that had enabled him to survive in the Force. He made a good pretence at least of looking people straight in the eye, for beneath the calm self-confidence lurked insecurity and violent swings of mood fostered by his homosexuality.

Thomson turned back to Blanche, his nose seeming to crinkle under the weight of Dexter's aftershave. He nodded to the stairs which led up to a dim landing. 'She's up there. The pathologist got here about twenty minutes ago.' He was younger than he looked, Blanche decided, examining the scarlet flush on his cheeks and tousled black hair.

'What have you found out so far?'

'Not much – apart from her name. Patricia Hoskin. Single. Lived here alone. Aged thirty-two. And daughter of a Home

11

Office bloody minister.' He flicked a shrewd look at the superintendent. 'Perhaps that's why my guv'nor called you in so quick, ma'am.'

Blanche Hampton nodded. Perhaps he was right, she thought. Murder was always a priority for the Force, but more so when someone of influence was involved. There might have been some bleary-eyed phone calls in the early hours between neighbours or golfing partners, ending in her car radio squawking half an hour before with the message from the local chief superintendent. She was to take charge of the case immediately.

Blanche liked Thomson. He treated her like any other male detective superintendent, neither softening his language nor whispering sexual innuendo behind her back. It was only after he had been speaking to her for a while that he seemed to remember her sex and superior rank and marked it with the word 'ma'am'. Blanche disliked the term for its associations with royalty but was proud to hear it used nonetheless: 'ma'am' symbolised her petty triumphs over an institution and culture inimical to women.

The inspector drank at his cigarette. 'She got found early this morning. Just after midnight. She was supposed to meet a friend of hers at some arty cinema in the West End and didn't turn up. The friend got suspicious 'cos Patricia apparently was a reliable girl – never missed her appointments.' He spotted a man walking by outside. 'Jeff!' he barked, 'anything turned up yet?'

The man stopped for a second, shook his head like a terrier emerging from a swim, and trudged on.

'Anyway, to cut a long story short, this girl, Dinah Lynn, gets highly suspicious. She comes round and persuades the people who live in the flat to help her knock the door down. That's where I came in.'

And stayed all night, thought Blanche, scrutinising the inspector's raw eyelids. But he would never whine to her, a woman and a superior officer from the Area Major Investigating Pool. Bleating was confined to the police canteen and drinking with colleagues off-duty.

'I got our Crime Squad together first thing,' Thomson explained, 'and they started the house-to-house enquiries at seven o'clock.' He glanced down at his ritzy watch, a circle of silver and gold studded with numerous dials. 'About an hour ago. I wanted them to catch the locals while they were still stuffing cornflakes down their gullets.'

Blanche wanted to take over the case as soon as possible but did not want to offend Thomson by being too brusque: she sensed a faint hostility emanate from the Liverpudlian. Sections of the Force sometimes resented one of the Area Major Investigating Pools taking charge of a case. Others, like Thomson's chief superintendent, seemed to welcome the AMIP as a way of reducing the work of his own division. Blanche ordered Dexter to help Thomson's officers in interviewing the neighbours and the young couple who lived on the ground floor.

When the house had been split into two flats, the builders had encased the bottom of the stairs with varnished plywood, creating a small and depressing vestibule. The emulsioned chip-wallpaper around the light switch was grey from endless finger-marks. Thomson tossed the butt of his cigarette into the gutter outside and the superintendent followed the inspector's crumpled raincoat through the open door and up the stairs.

They emerged onto the landing, covered in an oatmeal carpet. A few prints of landscapes in pine frames adorned the walls and a dusty fern lolled in a ceramic pot on the floor. Through an open door to the left, Blanche took in a rumpled double bed and rectangle of grey window looking onto the backs of terraced houses. Straight ahead was a small kitchen. It was decorated in the 'country cottage' style that Blanche instinctively disliked, every square inch veneered in oak to give an impression of warmth and homeliness. The effect, in the confined space, was the opposite. In the gloom of the early November morning the kitchen looked dark and oppressive. They passed by the bathroom to the right and entered the sitting-room at the end of the landing. So far the flat had been unremarkable. It was decorated with feminine homeliness but without either much taste or expenditure and was typical of a certain type of working woman, Blanche thought, with little interest in domestic chores. She realised with a jolt that it reminded her of her own maisonette in west

London, where she had lived alone since her divorce. Her flat though, she reflected with pride, was always free of dust and furnished with better taste.

The curtains of the sitting-room were still drawn but the room was far from dark: arc-lights erected by the police photographer shot fierce pools of illumination onto the floor and walls. The sharp contrast of light and dark reminded Blanche of the theatre, with the spotlight on the corpse at the centre of the stage. For a moment, she simply studied the interplay of brightness and shadow, and forgot that she was investigating the murder of a human being with all its ensuing pain.

'I see what you mean about the butcher's shop,' said Blanche, in her well-articulated voice, taking in the black pools of congealed blood around the body. The murdered girl – there was already little doubt that it could be anything else but murder – lay face down in front of the sofa, arms by her side. Her trousers and panties were round her calves and her bloodstained blouse had been dragged to the top of her back. All Blanche could distinguish of her face was a stain of congealed blood.

A man in his fifties knelt in front of the corpse with his back to them, dictating into a miniature tape-recorder. A few yards away was his open pathologist's case. As soon as he heard Blanche's voice, Dr Ruxton swung round his head and gave a suppressed smile of recognition. 'Ah, Superintendent Hampton. Good to see you again.' He was dressed in his usual tweeds, the balding head and heavy eyebrows emphasised by the savage lighting. At his full height, Ruxton still stood a head below Blanche. The superintendent, at almost six feet, looked down on many men. Years ago, she had been embarrassed. Now she was proud of her height, even convinced that it had helped speed her promotion. Yet she had never lost one mark of those years of timidity and of desire to meld into the crowd: rounded shoulders and a tendency to stoop. 'A rather grisly case, I'm afraid,' Ruxton continued with the macabre enthusiasm of a connoisseur. 'The tip of the nose and the lips have been cut off.'

The superintendent pressed on. She trusted Ruxton completely despite his eccentric manner. He was one of the best

Home Office pathologists in the country. 'Was that anything to do with the cause of death?'

'Probably not. I think she was strangled first. There are some classical *petechiae* spots around the eyes – you know the little haemorrhages.' Blanche pushed her tongue to the front of her teeth; she had forgotten how sometimes the pathologist's lecturing manner grated. Ruxton turned back to the corpse and drew in his receding chin for another burst of didacticism. 'You know of course that "asphyxia" comes from the Greek word for "pulseless". You have to go through several stages of asphyxiation before it's fatal.' Ruxton stood up and gestured to the dead girl's head. 'Also it looks as though whoever did it cut off a lock of her hair – you can see the scissor mark.' He sighed. 'I'm just about to turn her over to see if I can find out whether in fact it *was* strangulation that killed her.'

With a delicacy that Blanche admired and a look suddenly full of the knowledge of sorrow, he flipped over the body. A sigh of horror rustled in their throats: not only had the girl's lips and nose been mutilated but the tips of her breasts and the insides of her thighs had been sliced off.

'So much for that steak I was planning for dinner,' whispered Thomson with a face as hard and expressionless as a paving-stone.

Ruxton's mind was not so easily distracted by the awesome butchery. He leant forward over the dead girl's neck. 'Yes. I thought so. Strangled by hand. Finger "blob" bruises on the neck.'

Blanche's heavy eyelids peeled back automatically when the body of Patricia Hoskin rolled over. She ran a hand through her straight brown hair and readjusted the clip that held it in place as an excuse to look away. In the hierarchy of crimes she, like most policemen, did not necessarily think murder was the worst. Most stemmed from domestic quarrels or beatings fated to go awry. Rape, incest and buggery more frequently made her clench her fists to still the burning anger. But the mutilated corpse of Patricia Hoskin squeezed the breath from her lungs. The blonde hair was clotted with blood and the wounds to the nose and mouth transformed a face that before might have looked almost too scrubbed, too

15

clean, into a mask of horror.

'Was she raped?'

The pathologist shrugged his shoulders. 'Quite possible. But I won't be able to say for certain until the swabs have been analysed.'

'How long has she been dead?'

'Somewhere between twenty-four and forty-eight hours, I'd say. The body temperature actually goes up you know when someone's strangled, but this poor girl's is right down now.'

Even though she had seen several victims of murder before, Blanche gagged at the sight of this butchered cadaver. She did not know why this particular corpse should touch her so powerfully, except to make her tremble with the idea of it happening to her own body. But she knew she could not afford to start showing weakness now: all the men would turn to each other if she staggered out of the room and smile conspiratorially. 'Despite her reputation, she's just another "plonk" like the rest of the women,' they would say. She closed her eyes for a moment, swayed and respired deeply. But she need not have worried. When she opened them again, Thomson was already scurrying out. Two of the Clapham detective constables smiled to each other. 'Gone to throw up, ma'am,' explained one. 'The DI can't stand the sight of blood.'

The inspector's sudden departure was a welcome distraction for Blanche, and she turned back to the pathologist who was scrutinising the bruises on the girl's neck, below the exposed and bloodied teeth. 'So I can assume all this . . . mutilation was done after she was dead?'

'Yes, yes, of course.' He looked vaguely irritated by the question as he turned to look at her. 'But once you're dead, what does it matter?'

He turned back to the body to examine the fingernails for scrapings from the attacker's face or body. From his manner, Blanche knew he had nothing else to say for the moment and it would be foolish to disturb him. She would have to wait for the results of the full post-mortem and forensic results for more details.

The scenes of crime officer – a quiet, fair-haired man with

16

a stutter – introduced himself to the superintendent. The SOCO confirmed he had found many fingerprints but had not yet taken a set from the corpse for the purposes of elimination. Holding a glass vase against the light to check for further fingerprints, he told Blanche that the flat looked as though it had been 'turned over': drawers had been pulled out of chests in the bedroom and clothes strewn over the floor, and in the sitting-room someone had searched through the bureau. Whoever it was, he said, may have been wearing sheepskin gloves because some of this material had been snicked by a splinter on the front of the bureau where it folded down to form a desk.

'Any evidence of a forced entry?' asked Blanche. She squinted through her brown eyes and twisted her head to one side: her typical gesture of concentration.

'Not so f-f-far,' replied the SOCO. 'I've b-been round the f-flat thoroughly. All the d-doors and w-windows were OK.'

Except the one downstairs of course, thought the superintendent. Thomson had limped back into the room, his pale face even whiter. Blanche turned to him with a smile which she hoped would not be interpreted as patronising. 'What state was the door in downstairs when you arrived?'

'Just like it is now of course,' snapped Thomson, as though the question were an affront to his efficiency. He *did* think the smile was patronising, considered Blanche. 'If you're thinking the girlfriend of Patricia Hoskin and the couple downstairs smashed the door down together, ran up the stairs, strangled the girl and then carved her up like a side of roast beef, I agree it *is* a possibility, ma'am.' He now laid mordant stress on the last word, as if he were using it sarcastically. The superintendent gave him a bleak stare for a moment and then gave him another, more open smile of apology. It was her way of saying, 'Of course, I understand, I've been imposed on you. You're tired and fed up, and would prefer to be getting your local Murder Squad together rather than standing here and answering my silly questions.'

To her relief, the inspector smiled back, the moment of tension past. 'Yeah, it's a puzzle isn't it? It looks as though she let the murderer – and presumably the person who sorted through her stuff – in through the front door. Now why should she do that?' He looked up shrewdly, as if posing a riddle to which he knew the answer.

Blanche shook her head with mock modesty. 'God alone knows. Yet.' She turned back to the SOCO and asked if he had found the girl's handbag.

'I hadn't, as a m-m-matter of f-fact.'

The superintendent assumed the killer had taken it. She paused and squinted with concentration again. 'Have you found bloodstains anywhere else, apart from round the body?'

'There are a few d-drips that look as if they've c-c-come from the bits of f-flesh. They're n-next to the body. And there's an angled stain on the c-carpet next to the sofa, like a t-tupperware box.' Presumably what the murderer placed the shreds of flesh in, Blanche thought. The SOCO added that there were also some blood smears on a couple of knobs on the kitchen units, and traces of blood on the door to the flat and on the front door. A pattern emerged in Blanche's mind – a murderer who wore clean gloves when he searched the flat for valuables, and understandably bloodstained ones after the mutilations. Yet the butchery puzzled as well as disgusted her. It was clearly not a botched attempt at dismemberment. Equally, the calm and neat way in which the pieces of flesh were cut off and removed argued against the mutilations being carried out in a frenzy of sexual revenge.

Thomson had sat down on a chair and his eyelids creaked wearily into life again as Blanche wandered across. 'I don't suppose you've had time yet, but I wondered if you've had any luck on the boyfriend front?' she asked.

'According to the Dinah Lynn woman, the dead girl didn't have one. Apparently, she broke up with the last one a few months ago.' Blanche made a mental note to interview the friend herself and also to find the most recent boyfriend. 'As for Patricia Hoskin's work, I phoned 'em up first thing this morning. The boss said she didn't go in yesterday but did the day before. So it looks as if she was murdered the night before last, Tuesday.'

Blanche nodded. She was impatient to look around and sense the personality of the victim. From her experience the successful investigator of murder has to plunge into the

18

world of the dead – whether it be the brittle wealth of Kensington, the petty snobberies of Streatham, or the stale suspicion of housing estates in Leytonstone. And then fate intervened. 'If a murder ain't solved in four days,' a wrinkled detective inspector had told the graduate high-flyer on her first murder case ten years before, 'you know you've got a sticker.'

She glanced round the room and took in two original, but third-rate, Victorian paintings in battered frames, a yucca plant and Habitat furniture that now needed replacing. The seams of the sofa were starting to split. But the room was still cosy and clean. The superintendent ran a manicured finger-nail along the spines of the paperbacks which lined one wall: a wide range of novels, leavened with cookery and travel. Every object sported a skin of dust and so a faintly neglected air. Her eyes were suddenly snared by the red light on the stereo. 'This was switched on when Dinah Lynn and the others broke in, I suppose?'

The SOCO shrugged. 'S'pose so. There's a b-bloodstain on the plastic cover over the t-t-turntable and on the p-pick-up arm.'

Blanche's forehead creased with puzzlement. She thought she had worked out a coherent picture of the killer, only leaving bloodstains where he needed to on his way out of the flat. But now, it seemed, he touched other things after the mutilation.

She twisted her head to read the record label: side seven of Bach's *St Matthew Passion*. The boxed set lay open on a book-shelf above that sagged with the weight of records. The dead girl had catholic tastes, from the classical composers to pop records that dated from her youth.

Blanche wandered into the bedroom and surveyed the tangled web of clothes and shoes on the floor. The doors of the fitted wardrobes still stood open. The drawers lay on the floor like ships tossed on a stormy sea. It looked as though the SOCO had done a thorough job: for a murder Blanche knew the division would have called in one of their best men. For some reason, the bedside table of varnished oak still stood upright and in its usual position. In an automatic ges-ture of curiosity, the superintendent pulled open the cupboard section. Inside was nothing but a towel and, beneath the towel, a desolate packet of condoms. It was unopened, still virgin in its plastic wrapper. A cautious girl, thought Blanche. And a hopeful one.

The superintendent heard the rustle of clothing behind her. The SOCO stood beside her holding out a small diary. 'I f-f-forgot to mention this, s-s-superintendent. I found it under the b-b-bed.'

Blanche took the diary gingerly, as if it were a sheet of thin ice. By the grey morning light, she flicked it open to the title page and confirmed it belonged to the dead girl. Then she moved on to the present week in November. There were three entries in a chaotic scrawl. For the previous night, Wednesday: '7.30 p.m. Dinah Lumière Cinema.' The appointment she missed. And for Tuesday, the day that mattered, Blanche told herself: '12.30 Staff lunch. 8.00 p.m. Helen Rowe meets Michael Drayton!'

Blanche called in Inspector Thomson and showed him the diary. He said no one so far had mentioned Helen Rowe or Michael Drayton. She stood by the window and the damp, suburban gardens were reflected on her pensive eyes. Somewhere there, she hoped, secreted among the bare apple trees and handkerchiefs of lawn, might lurk a reason why the murdered girl chose to end her diary, and end her life, with an entry about someone else that closed with an exclamation mark.

# 2

David Parker traced the start of his problems to the viewing of the body. Until then, David considered, he had been normal enough. He had not wanted to examine his dead mother again particularly but felt the hushed expectation of the undertaker and his assistant like a fist under his chin, forcing him to look up. David wished he had resisted harder, turned his muscles to unrelenting steel, and just walked away from the coffin. But he had not had the strength – strength of will, his mother would have suggested, David thought with a shiver of guilt – to resist them. He had looked up, and since then occasional but terrifying panics had seized and released him with the capriciousness of a schoolboy's erection.

He glanced round the church with what he hoped was a disguised sneer of disdain, not only for the building but for most of the mourners. The county of Suffolk is celebrated for its churches, but not the one at Kirsham, David reflected: an undistinguished Victorian pile which merited only four lines in Pevsner. The nave and chancel were one, the whitewashed walls peeling in places with damp, the only object of interest the octagonal font, with the four Signs of the Evangelists. The congregation sang as raggedly as they looked. He stood in the front pew with Auntie Iris, his mother's younger sister, and her husband Jack, along with their grown-up children. Behind them were clusters of more distant relatives, as well as villagers who had known his mother. Among them was her closest friend in Kirsham, Mrs Goddard.

David thought her a pious and abject lump of seriousness, who disapproved of his godless, London ways and who had leeched off his mother for the past two decades. Mrs Goddard used to call in to see her every Monday, Wednesday and Friday, as well as on Sunday morning to accompany her to church. Over the years she had become a sort of unpaid companion, running errands and nodding dutifully in agreement while his mother whined. Her husband had been killed in 1944 in the Normandy landings and Mrs Goddard had lived ever since off her widow's pension and the generosity of his mother. Well, no longer, David thought to himself. When Mrs Goddard had called round on the Sunday morning after his mother died, he had been there waiting to meet her on the doorstep. He was determined not to let her in the house again. He gave her the news of his mother's sudden death and watched her face crumple. She mumbled something about it being a terrible shock and stood motionless in the porch for a full ten seconds before she let out a groan and began to sob. She showed more emotion over the death, David remembered, than he ever had. He only wished he could have shed some tears for effect. Embarrassed and annoyed by the old lady's weeping, David bundled her into his car and drove her to the church, breathing a sigh of relief as he watched her totter along the flagstones to the south door.

David had been disquieted by the prospect of meeting all his clucking relatives at the funeral and making all the tedious arrangements – the will, sorting through his mother's junk, selling the bungalow. He considered he had nothing in common with the past. He had sloughed it off and did not want to return. He was now a successful tax lawyer in the City and had nothing in common with the little village where he had been born outside Ipswich. What few friends he had, for David was a loner who relished his own company above that of others, were ones he made at university. He would sell the bungalow and perhaps return to Suffolk with his fiancée, Pamela, for the occasional weekend at a country house hotel. A senior partner in his firm of solicitors knew a good place near Aldeburgh. He wanted to package the past and forget it.

The doctor had handed over the death certificate on the Saturday morning, confirming that Mrs Parker had died suddenly of a combination of influenza and a heart attack the night before. She had probably passed away with little pain, he said, and there was nothing that David could have done. The son tried to simulate grief and thanked the doctor for coming. He was relieved when he heard the crunch of gravel on the drive and the doctor disappeared down the Kirsham road. He wanted to be left alone to think.

That evening he had telephoned Pamela to tell her what had happened. They had become engaged only a fortnight before his mother died. David had always kept her away from his mother and family because he was faintly ashamed of them. His instinct for their mutual dislike was confirmed when Pamela had insisted on accompanying him home to Kirsham for a weekend. He had not dared tell his mother that Pamela was coming so no beds were prepared and Mrs Parker was taken completely by surprise. David's mother spent the whole weekend baiting Pamela while his fiancée kept complaining about the shabbiness of the bungalow and the lack of heating. David had driven back to London early before Sunday lunch. The weekend had been a disaster and Pamela said she never wanted to go to Kirsham again. David had nonetheless proposed to her a few weeks later. Although he was thirty-six years old, she was his first serious girlfriend and he yearned for the companionship and respectability that marriage held out.

When he had telephoned that Saturday night, Pamela had expressed her sympathy coldly. She was unable to suppress completely the note of relief in her voice.

Back in London, his firm was very understanding and agreed to the necessary leave to enable him to make the necessary funeral and probate arrangements. David resented the time he would have to spend away from work because he had a particularly heavy schedule at the time, advising one major company on its tax structure and another on how to assemble funds for venture capital. Both were valuable new clients it was important to keep and David was always reluctant to delegate work. He believed many of his colleagues were lazy and stupid. He only trusted himself.

He had driven back up the A12 to Ipswich in his sparkling new Mercedes the next day. Every time he came to see his mother, and he did about once a month, David felt himself travelling back down a tunnel of memory. He marvelled yet again at how much the road from London had been transformed since he was a child. First a loop of road had been coiled around Colchester, then a bridge thrown across the

23

river Orwell and finally a dual-carriageway built to leave Chelmsford no more than a smear in the distance. Once in Ipswich, he rushed around the town, from his mother's bank, to her solicitor, to Auntie Iris. In retrospect, David thought, he unconsciously had left his mother until last. Auntie Iris insisted that her nephew made the 'arrangements for the funeral personally', by which he knew she meant write out a cheque to the undertaker.

The son had sat in the reception of the funeral parlour for ten minutes while, as the owner phrased it, his mother was 'got ready'. David stared out of the window at the grey slab of October sky, the damp roofs of slate belonging to the red-brick houses along the Rushmere Road, and at the cars which rolled along at such a sedate pace compared with those he was so familiar with in London. The window was decorated by two vases of plastic flowers which had been bleached of colour by the sunshine of distant summers.

'If you'd like to come through now then, sir?' The under-taker's voice was heavy with the diphthongs of the Suffolk accent which David had lost completely. He surprised David by his youthfulness. He was about forty, with a sponge of blonde hair, heavy features and a hesitant smile that revealed a chipped front tooth.

David followed him through the sliding door of varnished plywood, down a short corridor and into a room lit by two fluorescent bulbs and the light from a sash window. He had kept his eyes trained on the floor, scrutinising the scratches on the white plastic tiles. He sensed the oak coffin on the two trestles, the assistant standing behind with a vacant look in a suit that was several sizes too small.

David had not wanted to look up. But he felt obliged to. It was what normal people did and he did not want to arouse suspicion. His hands trembled and he sensed the skin all over his body tingle, like the feeling when blood streams back into a limb that has gone 'dead' because of a constricted blood supply. He had wanted to say something banal like, 'she looks as if she's just fallen asleep,' or 'she looks very restful,' and then walk out, without looking up. Just as he was about to do so, David saw the undertaker's feet, clad in burgundy moccasins, shuffle closer, as if he feared David might faint. It was

24

that movement that alarmed him, jerked his chin up, and made him look at the woman in the coffin.

She had lain there without the threat and menace he had expected, probably because her eyes – those hard, unforgiving eyes whose approval he had always sought – were closed. He remembered her dead in her bed, dressed in her blue, brushed-nylon dressing-gown, her hands clutching the same eiderdown he remembered from childhood, her grey hair brushed back from her forehead. Her wide, blue eyes were closed then as well, thank God. If they had been open, the doctor or the undertaker would have had to fight to draw them down, like recalcitrant window-blinds. Now they were shut. Shut forever, he had realised. She *did* look as though she had fallen asleep. She looked younger than her seventy years. The harried look he knew had fled and her cheeks looked fuller and redder. He took a step forward and realised the appearance of youth was partly due to the discreet application of cosmetics to the high cheekbones and flat nose. The thick lips had been drawn down over the prominent teeth. The undertaker could not suppress a smile of satisfaction at his handiwork. 'She do look at peace, don't she, sir?'

David nodded vaguely, fascinated by the waxy mask in front of him. He felt disembodied, as if he was not there, but floating outside himself, looking on as a spectator. What are you feeling? he had asked himself. You should be feeling grief, perhaps faintness. Your throat should be crammed, your eyes brimming. You should be feeling *something*.

'David! Are you alright? David,' Auntie Iris hissed into his ear, with a flourish of breath that smelt of polo mints. He was still on his knees on the red prayer cushion. Everyone else had raised themselves and was back sitting on their seats, waiting for the vicar to begin his address. Several glanced at him and whispered to their neighbour. David flushed with annoyance at his stupidity. These vacant moments had only begun after he had seen his mother's body. He told himself once again that he must pull himself together.

He hated being the centre of attention. Not that he was particularly ugly. His face was firmly sculpted with a strong nose and wide but delicate mouth. Harsh, steel-rimmed spectacles hooded his grey eyes, which sometimes shied away

25

from the glance of others with a jagged movement. Although he enjoyed dressing in clothes of quality – like the made-to-measure pinstripe suit and the wool overcoat he wore at the funeral – David carried with him an air of eccentric disregard for appearance. He rarely combed his straight, mud-coloured hair, which often hung down into his eyes or straggled over his ears. His slight stoop was common to many lawyers like him in their mid-thirties who spent a lot of time at their desks without compensating exercise. David, how-ever, was not fat. He enjoyed food but there was a suppressed nervous energy about him that swallowed up the calories that in others would have turned to flab.

The coffin was closed now, of course, and decorated with several wreaths. But when he had shambled out of the fu-neral parlour into the drizzly evening just over a week ago, after viewing the corpse, David had been haunted by the face within. He had jumped into his car and driven home to London in a frenzy, jumping traffic lights, overtaking on the inside lane, cutting into lines of traffic waiting at junctions. He gripped the wheel so intently his muscles ached and yet he could not relax. When he finally arrived back outside his elegant but empty house in Islington, David had slumped over the steering-wheel and stared for a full quarter of an hour at the specks of rain glistening like beads of mercury on the outside of the car window. One drop resolved into the image of his mother's face, grew larger and larger and larger, until it filled the whole of his vision. The eyelids flickered, before they sprang back to reveal the accusing eyes beneath, blazing with disgust and anger, the same eyes as when . . . David had woken up in a panic, starting back in the car seat, his back chill with sweat. His watch showed a quarter past seven: he had travelled the hundred miles home in an hour and a half and then must have fallen asleep for a few min-utes. David was conscious of breathing out heavily: he was lucky to be alive.

David staggered into the office in the following days, battling to regain control. He thought he was very cour-ageous and his application seemed to pay off. His ability to concentrate returned to what it had been before. Pamela invited him round to dinner to discuss arrangements for their wedding and they went out to the cinema. Everyone treated him with a new warmth at first, realising what had happened. David received their sympathy with pleasurable embarrassment but found it faded fast and that people returned to their usual, respectful distance.

The return of David's self-confidence in the period leading up to the funeral was spoilt only by bouts of agonising anxiety: after a moment or two of nothingness, the pit of his stomach suddenly dropped away, leaving his limbs devoid of all strength and his body racked by a restless pain beyond words. These moments of anguish lasted a few seconds and disappeared with the unexpectedness with which they had arrived. But they worried David deeply: he had never experienced anything so dreadful before.

The pall bearers raised the coffin to their shoulders. The vicar led them down the aisle, his grey hair plastered with brylcreem. Feet shuffled down the pews and the mourners followed, buttoning up coats in preparation for the chill wind already gusting through the west door. The vicar's surplice flapped up like a frightened seagull as he passed outside and plodded towards the graveyard. David looked back at the church: the walls of flints set in concrete, the roof of red tiles, the spire of blackened wood which culminated in a fluttering wind-vane in the form of a cockerel. They passed between mossed gravestones and along a bank topped by thrashing yews. The east wind, that Suffolk wind frozen by its passage over the grey waves of the North Sea, whipped them to their places around the pile of newly-dug earth. The soil was sandy and crumbled easily in the hand, staining it like saffron.

The graveyard fell away to a valley and rose up into a field, pricked with winter wheat sprouting up through the drills. The field flattened out to become the horizon, lined with solitary oaks. Some of the graves were well tended and splashed by colour – chrysanthemums and lilies. Others were marked by long grass and their only tribute was the yellow sycamore leaves whisked by the wind.

David had only ever before attended one funeral, that of his father, who had died suddenly twenty-seven years before. He remembered seeing that body too in an open coffin, and thinking that he was asleep and needed a shave. Despite the funeral it had been several months before he came to accept that his father would never come back.

David tried to concentrate on the service but could not. Instead he was distracted by the way the trunks of the pine trees seemed to glow in the fitful light and how slabs of cold sunshine scurried across the valley towards them. The next thing he recalled was Auntie Iris nudging him as the knot of mourners was breaking up. The grave-digger was just about to finish his work. 'Are you *sure* you're alright, David?' she screamed into the wind, her handbag grasped in one hand, while the other pressed against her hat, which reminded her nephew of a black turban.

He nodded. 'Fine. I'm alright.'

She stared at him disbelievingly. Uncle Jack hovered at her shoulder, with a good-humoured smile of false teeth. 'Would you like to pop back home with us for a cup of tea? There's a spot of dinner on as well . . . nothing special. But you're welcome to stay.' Some other friends of his mother would be there as well, she added.

David knew by 'dinner' she meant 'lunch', and by 'a spot of dinner', a lozenge of over-cooked meat garnished with two watery piles of vegetables. With a covert sneer, he imagined them all sitting round the table in Auntie Iris's front room, holding the Sheffield knives and forks that were only deployed for special occasions, mouthing compliments about the food. Uncle Jack, with a wink, would ask him, as he always did, how his 'courting' was going, and David, as he always did, would squirm with discomfort. 'No, thanks. I'm afraid I've got to get back to London. I've a big job on at the moment.' David only wanted to be left alone. He tried to inject a smile into his clean-shaven face.

A silence fell between them like a wall. Iris's eyes, behind winged spectacles, reminded him of his mother's in their intensity. He knew she was not deceived by his excuse. She smiled nonetheless, tugging back her powdered cheeks and rouged lips. 'I was wondering about . . . well, Mabel's things. I know she left you everything in the will . . . but . . . ' David saw Uncle Jack look away with embarrassment, his eyes chafed red by the wind. 'Well, there are a few odd things of Mabel's that I'd love to have – for memory's sake.'

David tried to imagine what she could have wanted. There was nothing of his mother's he wanted to keep, except possibly some of the family photographs. 'You can have whatever you like.' Iris smiled with relief and, her nephew perceived, just a hint of greed. 'I'll give you a call some time and we'll go round the bungalow together.'

Leaves flurried across the graveyard as David drove off. He wanted to escape, escape from his relatives, escape from the funeral, escape from the past. Kirsham was a small village that lay a few miles out of Ipswich to the east and, without any conscious purpose, he took the lane into the town. He was soon on the Felixstowe Road, and headed down towards the docks. Ipswich he often thought had lost its individuality since his childhood. It was no longer special but just another, rather ugly town. Cars clogged the roads, rather than men on bicycles whirring home like a plague of locusts from the engineering companies. Part of the docks, he saw, were being redeveloped into some sort of marina, the maltings into flats for young professionals like those he worked with in the City.

A few streets away, in what had once been the medieval centre of the town, he suddenly remembered the newsagent where, as a youth, he used to buy 'girlie' magazines. His curiosity aroused, he drove there through a tangle of one-way streets. It was still there, brooding under the jutting eaves: the same name, 'Gipping News', painted in black on a white board. The interior was much smarter now, but behind the counter stood an elderly man with wispy hair and red cheeks. David thought he looked distantly familiar. Notices were written on postcards and sellotaped to the inside of the window; the racks of magazines stood on the right with the pornographic ones on the top. David ran his tongue over dry lips, aware that his breathing had suddenly accelerated. He had recognised the man: it was the same proprietor who had served him all those years before. As an adolescent, he used to circle the shop, plagued by guilt, assembling the courage to push open the door. Once inside he imagined the eyes of the same man drilling into him as he shambled to the rack, and flicked through as many magazines as he dared, before selecting one or two with the sort of photographs he preferred: buxom girls with big breasts. As a teenager, he had been

29

terrified of being seen in the shop by someone who recognised him, a relative or friend who might have come into town. But the terror also excited him, a cocktail of adrenalin and sexual excitement. He had bought the occasional 'girlie' magazine ever since. He liked to pore secretly over the available flesh, the contours sharpened by black stockings and suspender belts, aroused by the models' smouldering glance. Unlike the girls he met in real life, these ones did not pose a threat. And, as he stood chuckling in front of the newsagent's that cold November day of his mother's funeral, he discovered these girls still aroused him. David wished to prove to himself that he had grown up, no longer felt guilt about his arousal, no longer feared an ambush when buying a pornographic magazine.

He strode into the shop and found himself in front of the magazines, some in plastic covers, others not. He plucked one out and, as he was about to peruse it, a dumpy housewife waddled in towing two spotty children. One stood beside his mother at the counter staring at him unblinkingly. David's ears burned. He closed the magazine, snatched another at random and slid them under a copy of *The Spectator*. The woman plodded out.

David wondered whether the elderly proprietor would recognise him again – the successful City lawyer, outwardly so different from the callow schoolboy. As he approached, the man rested his cigarette on the edge of the counter, blowing out smoke through the side of his lips. He added up the cost of the magazines and slipped them into a white plastic bag. Their eyes met for a second when David handed over the money but the man showed no sparkle of recognition. David had become just another new customer.

It was almost three o'clock when the tyres of David's Mercedes scrunched to a halt on the sparse gravel of the drive leading up to his mother's bungalow at Kirsham. The building was eighty metres back from the south side of the Kirsham road, behind a tall hedge. It stood prominent and alone, the roof tiles green with lichen, the blue paint peeling from the window frames, in three acres of land. The nearest house was three hundred yards away, to the west.

David sat down in the kitchen and nursed a cup of tea. He

mused on the home-made cupboards, their paint worn and scratched, the table topped with green formica, the cold, lustreless Aga in the corner and the tea-cloths hung up to dry from a frame on the wall. The golden hands of the electric clock on the wall still hummed round: no one had yet bothered to cut off the electricity. He told himself, as always, that he had to hurry. He had things to do. But what? The office and the whirl of activity which sustained him seemed so distant and unimportant suddenly. No, no, they *are* important, he told himself. You are still in a state of shock after your mother's death. Do not be dragged down. Go and do something. He walked through to the back door and stood on the concrete patio.

The wind had softened, as though to allow the clouds to curdle into a cream film that stretched across the sky. To the right stood a small apple orchard, to the left ploughed fields, whose flatness ended in the dark band of a pine wood, brooding in the fading light. Down the middle of the rough lawn, more clover than grass, ran a path of bricks which led to a dilapidated shed. It was his father's tool shed, built of wood, with a mineralised felt roof and two windows like empty eyes. It seemed to lurk at the bottom of the garden like a savage animal under the protection of two apple trees and a lilac, blown bare by the autumn wind. The structure stirred a memory David had spent his life trying to forget. Even now, the sight of the shed caused him unease. He had never wanted, and hardly dared, to enter it since that distant summer.

He turned back to the house. Of course, he thought, the property was his now. He could do what he wished and have the shed dismantled, razed to the ground like the ancient cities he had read about in history books. The prospect pleased him, cheered him more than anything else since the death of his mother. He would be able to return to normal. He had not had a panic attack for three days and he had been sleeping well.

In the kitchen, he washed his hands in the freezing water. As he was about to lock the front door and drive back down to London, David sensed a powerful desire to wash his hands again. It rose up and surged through his muscles, tensing them, making them hard as wood and as restless as the clouds earlier in the day. It was ridiculous, he told himself, you washed your hands only a moment ago. He stood wavering on the doorstep for several moments, in thrall to the desire, before locking the front door with a decisive click. He really had to get the removal of that shed organised.

# 3

David's desire to wash his hands became obsessive in the days that followed the funeral. He repeated to himself that it was neurotic behaviour but the wish still remained. The tension built up over an hour or so and had to be satisfied. If it was not, David found his feet started to tap more and more restlessly on the floor and his concentration fragmented. It was embarrassing to visit the bathroom several times during a business lunch, theatre performance or dinner party. David developed various ploys to control what was happening. Before going into a long meeting or starting lunch, he would wash his hands assiduously and relish the pleasure of the warm water sluicing away the soap from his skin, and during the event itself he would consciously 'ration' his visits to the bathroom or lavatory. But as soon as it was over, he found himself rushing back to the basin to wash his flaking skin.

Apart from the obsessive hand-washing, which he came to accept and integrate into his life, David continued to have panic attacks once or twice a week. They worried him but he preferred, as ever, to keep the concern locked in himself. Work had always been the centre of his life and other activities peripheral. He had a small circle of acquaintances rather than friends – mostly male and in legal circles. He had never had a really close friend, even in childhood. People were best kept at a distance. So after the funeral, to try to forget his worries, David worked even harder than before. He thought Pamela seemed pleased at first, as if his excessive energy were confirmation that his mother's death had affected him less than she feared. As it continued, however, she grew irritated.

They had met six months before at a dinner party given by an old school friend of Pamela. The friend enjoyed matchmaking and, knowing that Pamela had just finished an unhappy affair with a merchant banker, asked her husband whether there were any eligible bachelors at his solicitor's firm. He replied that he knew only one of the right age and that was David Parker.

David had dressed for the dinner with the apprehension known by all who are not naturally gregarious. He had developed over the years a mask of social self-confidence that only occasionally slipped, when for example he became excited and forgot to keep his mouth closed when eating, called a napkin a serviette, or simply became bored and was deliberately rude. He was charmed by Pamela's demure plumpness. As he watched the candlelight ripple along her bare forearms, he wanted to pick her like a ripe pear, sinking his teeth into her succulence. She in turn was intrigued by David's wolfish good looks. The angularity of his bones and smoothness of his skin attracted her – she hated bearded men – as did his eyes, alert, grey and veering away from hers through shyness.

David had never had a serious relationship with a woman before. He was awkward in their company and, at the age of thirty-six, had been a virgin until he met Pamela. While an adolescent he had been strongly religious and his distrust of pre-marital sex lingered into adulthood. He had had a few friendships with women, but whenever they threatened to come too close, threatened his privacy, he sheered away. He was ashamed of being in thrall to his emotions. Once the friendship was over, David was overwhelmed by regret. He reverted to a corrosive loneliness which he fought off by working harder and drinking harder. But with Pamela it was different.

Almost all her friends were married, and, aged thirty-four, she wanted a husband and children. Her proper and guileless exterior hid a sharp mind. Using the excuse of her being a fellow solicitor and devotee of the cinema, Pamela extracted David's telephone number and a few days later invited him to the National Film Theatre. They both enjoyed the evening and started to go out together. Pamela welcomed David's diffidence about sex and his courtesy. David in turn found himself enmeshed, watched over by a woman who was sensitive to his peculiarities and, much to his surprise, he did not resent it. He floated along on the stream of respectability

34

and, a few weeks before his mother died, found himself proposing marriage to a radiantly happy Pamela over a pizza one lunchtime in the City.

Parents seemed the only problem. Pamela's, who owned a large house outside Harrogate and another in Kensington, found David shy and boring. Their cut-glass politeness made David more insecure than outright hostility. In turn David's mother abhorred Pamela from the moment they first met during the appalling weekend at Kirsham. She said Pamela was arrogant and unfriendly; Pamela in turn had no time for a 'bitter and shabby' retired primary school teacher.

In the days after the funeral, David sometimes slipped out of himself and examined the familiar with what seemed new insight. He sat at the table in the kitchen of Pamela's house in West Hampstead, scrutinising her with unblinking eyes. She was babbling on about the wedding again, how they must not invite *too* many guests to the tiny church, how the arrangements would be *much* easier now that David's mother had died, how the tables *must* be arranged in the marquee for the reception, and where *on earth* all her relatives were going to stay. As her rouged lips fluttered, David wondered why he had not noticed before Pamela's exaggerated stress on particular words in order to make what she was talking about sound more dramatic.

'David, have you been *listening* to what I've been saying?'

Her voice grated, reminding him of the egg-slicer he had chanced across in his mother's kitchen after the funeral: taut, silver wires cutting through the air. David grunted and offered to pour her another glass of wine.

'I don't want any more wine, thank you, David. I want your attention. For once,' she snapped, pushing her chair back, and folding her napkin with icy venom. She ran her well-manicured finger up her forehead and through her dark brown hair. 'I just don't know what's got into you recently . . . '

David did not look up. He raised one hand to the wine bottle and started to pour himself another glass, his sixth.

'You've had enough wine. You don't want any more.'

The bottle hovered for a moment, while he considered what she said. Then he continued to pour. He wanted to annoy her. 'Stop going on, will you?'

35

'God, you're so rude! I can never tell you anything.'

He sipped the claret and let its sharpness prickle his tongue. 'On the contrary. You're always telling me lots of things. Most of them pretty boring!' He spoke coolly, his mind calmed by alcohol. He shrugged with disinterest. He was thinking whether he really wanted to marry this woman after all. He saw the route ahead as clear as a motorway at five o'clock in the morning: endless trips to Peter Jones and Harrods to stock the new house in Hampstead Pamela wanted to buy; frigid family weekends up in Yorkshire; children; work and more work; and all the time Death approaching on tip-toe, so silent one never heard its foot-fall.

Pamela's face had always been peculiarly attractive to David: thick lips, a mole with four hairs growing from it to the left of her bulbous nose, and wide, beautiful eyes. She was always well-groomed, her hair shaped as if she had just returned from the coiffeur, her cheeks scrubbed and powdered. But since his mother died some of her characteristics had started to irritate him. Her English reticence and good breeding became blandness. Her concern with etiquette turned to snobbery. Her interest in his affairs verged on intrusion. Her unwillingness to do as he wished became stubbornness.

He had finally, and clumsily, lost his virginity to Pamela soon after their engagement. David had always cherished a fantasy to make love to a woman on the floor of a well-lit room – like one of the sets used by the glamour models in the magazines he sometimes bought. But Pamela had resisted on that first night, led him upstairs to the bedroom and then, only when all the lights were extinguished, encouraged his advances to continue. She enjoyed making love, she said, but only in the dark. This furtiveness made David angry: he wanted her to overcome his distrust of sex rather than encourage it.

Pamela sat in her kitchen, still smouldering over his remark. Sometimes these silences froze the air between them, David thought, the same silence as fell between him and Auntie Iris at the funeral. He knew he would end up apologising. That was always the way. It was weakness on his part, but David had never been able to bear conflict between himself and another. He was always ready to apologise, always ready to seek reassurance. He despised himself for it. 'Do you really want to marry me, Pamela?'

She tossed her head back, and by the harsh light of the tungsten lights in the ceiling, David saw that her eyes glistened with tears. She gamely tried to smile. 'Of course I do . . . of course.' David smiled inwardly. It was the answer he wanted to hear, the answer he expected to hear. She gulped. 'It's just that sometimes, I wonder whether I'll ever be able to tell you anything without you being rude to me.'

David gulped down the last of the claret. He stood up with a sureness of purpose he had not known for several weeks. He stood behind Pamela and slipped his hands down the front of her blouse. She looked up with a mixture of irritation and pleasure. 'David, you know I . . . '

He felt suddenly masterful, the desire throbbing, impatient for satisfaction. Her lips lay under his, passive and unresponsive, the lipstick greasy. His hands, questing down the buttons of her blouse, met resistance. 'No, David, no. Not here, *please*.' The same bleating, David thought, through the fog of his lust, the same bleating. Her hands tried to push him to one side but he pulled her bra up to expose her chest. He kissed and then, in a frenzy, bit her right breast. She gave a muffled scream and dropped panting to the kitchen floor, her skirt rucked up.

David's eyes flickered over the expensive, cream kitchen units and onto Pamela, her body quiet now, no longer writhing, except for her bare chest heaving with anger, her right breast marked by his teeth, her eyes closed, her lips sewn shut in a grim line. A victim, he thought, resigned to sacrifice. She had deliberately laid out her body, white and cold, like a fillet on a fishmonger's slab. With alarm, he sensed his desire fade. He tried to ignore what he took to be Pamela's indifference. He closed his eyes and prodded at Pamela ineffectually for a minute or two. With tears of frustration brimming at his eyes, he sensed the blood seep away. It was of no use.

Her eyes flickered open. They stared at him, welling with disdain and contempt. David looked away. He had never been impotent with her before. Never. It had never been a problem. Why had it happened now?

He wanted Pamela to comfort him, ring him with her arms, and kiss away the tears he felt still prickling his eyes. Instead she dragged herself away and sat with her back against the wall, staring at the kitchen tiles, the lights making harsh shadows beneath her breasts. 'You've ruined that blouse,' was all she murmured.

David breathed in shallow gasps, angry and gulping back the tears. He could think only of his limpness, how his body had betrayed him.

'After all that excitement,' Pamela said with an uncharacteristic sneer, 'throwing me on the floor, you couldn't even manage to finish it off.'

Her words scorched his heart. 'I didn't know you cared. You were frigid enough.' He zipped up his trousers with trembling fingers. The muscles in his face tightened.

Pamela raised herself. Her eyes blazed with contempt as she patted down her skirt. 'You know I hate it like that – under the lights, like a public performance.' Her femininity had been insulted too: perhaps his impotence meant he no longer found her attractive. 'It's never happened to me before. Even when things were going wrong with other men and we were about to break up, we always managed to make love.'

'I *wanted* to, for Chrissake,' screamed David. 'But it's no good when you're lying there like a dead animal on the road.'

'Well, you're hardly Casanova!'

'At least I try and show some interest when we're making love. A little loving kindness.'

Pamela snorted. 'Like tonight, I suppose.' She picked up her shoes and disappeared through the kitchen door, her eyes glazed. He heard her climb the stairs and slam her bedroom door.

David sensed the panic attack a long way off, like the rumble of an underground train passing under a London theatre. His stomach fell away, breathing rasped, chest pumped madly. It was a waking nightmare of helpless falling, of unimaginable anguish. His muscles tensed and relaxed, as if someone were shooting an intermittent electric current through his body. Just when he thought the pain would

38

never stop, it released him and David sank exhausted into a kitchen chair.

He sat panting for several minutes. The attack was Pamela's fault of course. She had brought it on by making him impotent and then mocking him. He grimaced with the pain of the memory. He would have revenge. She did not know what she was doing, who she was dealing with. She probably thought he was as bone-headed as some of those public school types he had met at lawyers' drinks parties. Stay patient and calm. Calm and patient. Wait for the opportunity. In the meantime, he would force himself to act as if nothing had happened.

He washed his hands thoroughly in the basin in the downstairs lavatory before climbing the stairs. He knocked on Pamela's bedroom door.

'Go away, David. Just go away.'

He paused and held his ear close to the white paint. He detected suppressed sobs. 'I'm sorry, darling.' He heard more sobs and repeated his apology. David's thin fingers grasped the brass-plated door-knob and turned it. He pushed but the door did not give way. Pamela had locked it.

'I can't talk to you, now,' she said, her voice strangled by tears. 'You know I can't. I'm still too upset.'

'I'll give you a call in the morning. OK?' He listened intently and made out a murmur of agreement. David swayed with indecision outside the bedroom door, looking at the numerous family photographs that lined the wall beside the stairs. 'I'm sorry,' he said for the last time, attempting to inject more sincerity into his voice.

David turned and scampered down the thick stair-carpet, a smile tugging at the margins of his thin lips. He had decided. He wanted to find a new woman – whether to replace or supplement Pamela he was uncertain as yet. And he had remembered a way of finding one.

# 4

A couple of weeks later David left his office in the Broadgate centre in the City to go home to Islington. He walked down to Bank underground station at eight o'clock in the evening and took the tube from there up to the Angel. He preferred to arrive early and leave late to avoid the absurd overcrowding at rush hour. The grey panoply of cloud that had blocked the sun earlier in the day had disappeared to leave the November sky above clear and dark. The sulphurous glare of the street-lamps however blotted out the stars, and lit the way for the stream of cars nosing their way up City Road. David sniffed the chill air and turned left into Colebrooke Row. He stopped to glance down at the black lozenge of the Grand Union Canal and when he opened the door of his elegant Victorian terrace house a few minutes later, the envelope was waiting for him on the mat.

It was reassuringly anonymous: A4 size, made of commercial brown paper with a faint grain, his name and address typed onto a white sticker. The only sign that it was out of the ordinary was the letter X hand-written on the top left-hand corner followed by the numbers 427. The box number, David recalled. Thank goodness his tenant had left three months before. Bob, an Australian whose physical fitness was matched only by his inquisitiveness, might have asked some embarrassing questions. David would not even have been surprised if he had tried to steam open the envelope to discover what was inside.

Trembling with excitement, David felt the urge to wash his hands again. Afterwards he massaged cream into the flaking skin, a habit he had formed over recent weeks.

Up in his study, strewn with law reports and papers, David gulped down two gin and tonics and then remembered his pet. In the bay-window, on the floor, was a glass box whose interior was bathed in the mellow light from an electric bulb. An Indian python about five feet in length slithered its lazy way about the terrarium. David watched with quiet pride as it immersed itself in the water basin, where it lay, only its nostrils protruding from the water. Pamela had been nagging him for weeks about the need to sell or destroy the snake before their marriage because she would refuse to live with it, but David had procrastinated successfully. It was yet another thing she did that had begun to annoy him.

David was reassured by the thickness of the envelope as well as its anonymity. He had feared there might be no replies at all. He wondered what the magazine did in such circumstances. Just send on an empty envelope or include a cyclostyled apology? 'We received no replies to the advert you placed in the lonely hearts column of *London Life*. This means you appear unattractive to your fellow human beings.' David quivered with nervous anticipation as he sliced the letter-knife along the flap of the brown envelope.

He spread the eight envelopes he found inside over the desk. Most were white, although two were blue and one pink. Before, all he had done was send replies to some lonely hearts adverts in one particular issue of *London Life* about eighteen months before. He had never thought of placing one himself. Those replies had ended unhappily, for he became obsessed with one woman he met who had no interest in him whatsoever. It had been a hurtful experience and in quiet moments the humiliation still rankled. Perhaps his luck had changed.

The most obvious difference between the letters was that five of the eight had the box number only written on the envelope. These were the girls who had sent replies to several adverts. Hedging their bets, David considered with a dry smile. The other three had the full address of the magazine: either these girls had more money and did not mind the cost of posting individual replies, had answered only his advert, or were clever enough to understand the psychological advantage of sending a reply which *appeared* individual. The City solicitor was pleased with his own cleverness. He was stimulated by the psychology of lonely hearts.

He took the letters out and laid them beside their

41

envelopes. Two he rejected immediately. They were both from box-number envelopes and were photocopies of a typewritten letter which the women had obviously sent to several men. 'Can't even be bothered to write a short letter. Think of themselves as too busy. Don't want to make any commitment,' thought David. A third letter was from a hospital porter. Two paragraphs into the letter David shuddered: the porter had misread the advert and thought it was for a gay lover. He had even included a photograph of himself sitting on a bed wearing a pair of bathing-trunks, the eyes albino red from the flash on the camera. David was filled with a mixture of disgust, as though the youth had accosted him in a public toilet, and irritated laughter – after all, had he not put 'seeks woman' in his advertisement? He tore up the letter and photo and tossed the fragments into the rubbish bin.

He also rejected the women who seemed to be living on the margins – an actress who was 'resting', and a twenty-eight-year-old art student. That left three. He went down to the drawing-room and poured another gin and tonic, rehearsing imaginary conversations. Clutching the top letter, he dialled the telephone number. He was surprised to see his hand shaking. He ran his tongue over his lips, which had suddenly gone dry, and gulped. A girl answered. 'Hello?'

'Is that, er . . . ' He cursed and quickly checked the Christian name from the letter, penned in round, regular handwriting. 'Isabel?' He wondered whether he should disguise his voice, make it deeper, more articulated. His voice was not naturally deep and resonant. Perhaps, in his nervousness, he sounded high-pitched and effeminate. But it was too late now. He had already spoken.

'No. She's not in just at the moment.' The girl sounded classless and indifferent.

'Do you know when she'll be back?'

'Probably around midnight. Do you want to leave a message?'

David had not considered the possibility that the girl he wanted to speak to would be out and that the telephone would be answered by a friend. It had not happened with the previous advert. 'No, that's OK. I'll phone some other time.' He laid the telephone back in its cradle. If he left a message,

David would need to leave a name, and the name would mean nothing without an explanation. He did not want the embarrassment of explaining to a stranger the circumstances that had led him to phone her flatmate out of the blue at a quarter to ten on a Thursday night. He might phone again but an instinct whispered not to. It told him to prefer women living alone, so avoiding all these problems, and to use a false name at the beginning. One of the women he telephoned might know a friend of his . . .

David found the right girl straightaway with his second phone call: the thirty-three year old who used pink note-paper.

'Yes, that's right,' she said uncertainly, as though he was not right at all. 'I'm . . . Helen.'

A pause ripened on the line before David plunged ahead with his patter. He began with his false name. 'Hi! My name's Michael Drayton. You replied to the ad I put in *London Life* the other week.'

'Oh, yes.' She laughed gently.

'Anyway, here I am . . . I thought I'd give you a call and introduce myself. Not that there's much more to me than's in the advert!' He wondered whether his hearty tone was appropriate. He grimaced at his own awkwardness and abruptly changed the subject. His tremulous hand held her letter. 'Thanks very much for your letter. So you work for *The Times* do you, doing telephone sales?' He hoped he did not come across as patronising.

She sounded very cheery and relaxed. So much more lively, he thought, than Pamela's restrained voice. Helen confirmed the details in her letter: she was born and brought up in Norwich, had studied English at Oxford, had worked as a teacher for a while but now owned a flat in Clapham and ran a section of *The Times* telephone advertisement department.

After they had chatted merrily for ten minutes or so, David suggested they met for a drink somewhere. 'If we get on alright, perhaps we could go on to dinner.'

'Sounds good to me,' she chirped. They compared diaries and fixed on the following Tuesday. 'I know a good wine bar near here. You said you lived in Islington, could you bear to come all the way over here to south London?'

David did not relish the thought but agreed nonetheless. 'So where would you like to meet? At the wine bar?' It occurred to him that he had no idea what she looked like. He only had the description in the letter: five feet five inches, medium-length blonde hair and green eyes. He could dress distinctively. 'I could wear a college scarf and have a copy of the *Daily Telegraph* under my left arm,' he murmured.

'What do you mean?'

David had forgotten that he had not given her the linking thought. Until then, he had been amazed how relaxed and controlled he had been. 'I was thinking out loud. Working out how to make sure you could recognise me.'

She giggled. 'I'm sure we'd get by. But, look, just to avoid all that, why don't you come round to my flat? Just press the buzzer and I'll come down.'

David agreed readily. She had omitted her address from the letter and so gave him the details before ringing off. It was a much better arrangement than one or the other sitting in a wine bar alone nursing a half-empty glass and casting shifty glances across people coming in through the door, David considered. He felt exhilarated by his own coolness. He must have made a good impression, otherwise Helen would not have agreed to meet him. He was filled with a sense of power as he gathered up the letters on his study desk. If he had placed just one advert and received all these replies, there must be hundreds of lonely women in London waiting to meet him. He opened the blind and looked out into the night towards Shoreditch, across the dim gardens, the slate tiles, the lighted windows. Each light, he thought, was a beautiful girl, like the ones in the magazines, waiting to be seduced by him. Girls who did not make the same demands as Pamela. Girls who did not think sex belonged to the night. What appealed to him about meeting Helen was the lack of emotional commitment, the impersonality of the whole operation. None of his emotions risked bruising from placing the advert – although of course he had been lucky and had replies. It had cost him nothing except the amount he wrote on the cheque.

Pamela rang later the same evening. David had telephoned her soon after the incident in the kitchen to apologise, and when they next met David pretended that what had happened was not important. He heard himself repeat his excuses, empty words necessitated by convenience. How easy it was, he considered, for men and women to be weighed down by the inertia of relationships and keep the peace, rather than tell the truth and risk loneliness. David had acted as though their relationship had returned to what it was before. But in his heart, he knew it could not: he had been impotent since that night in Pamela's kitchen and he had placed the lonely hearts advert the next day in revenge. He guessed this was how a husband feels who regularly visits a prostitute and then returns home to sport a mask of normality with his wife.

So when Pamela telephoned that night, David made the effort to chat about the tedium of the day. He wanted to continue the pretence that he still loved her.

'I tried to ring you several times before, but you were always engaged. Who were you chatting to for so long?' she asked. David told himself that her query could not be based on any evidence of betrayal. Her tone was not suspicious, just inquisitive.

'Sorry, darling. It was one of the new guys at work. He had a problem with a company merger we're handling.'

Pamela did not query what he said. So trusting, David thought with contempt.

'Listen, David,' she continued in her gentle way, 'I was talking about your hands to Di today – '

' – For Christ's sake,' he shouted, 'how many times have I told you not to go around telling everyone about it. They'll think I'm weird or something.'

'Well, it's hardly normal is it? Having to wash your hands thirty times a day! Besides, I *haven't* been going around telling everyone. As a matter of fact, Di was the first – '

' – Oh, she was the first was she? I told you not to tell *anyone*.'

'By the way, how *are* your hands now? Are they any better?'

David breathed in deeply. 'Fine, darling. Fine. Definitely getting better. And they'd get better even faster, if you weren't going around whispering about me behind my back to all your friends.'

'David! Just listen for a second. Di was wondering whether

you ought to see a psychoanalyst – '

'Look, I'm not seeing any bloody psychoanalyst!' David was pale with anger, gripping the telephone like the handle of a dagger. He told himself to calm down and speak more slowly. 'I just want to be left alone.'

'Well, if you don't want to talk about it, let's leave it.' She went on to ask whether he was free next Tuesday night, because she had just been phoned by an old school friend who had invited them round for a 'quiet supper'. It was the night he had agreed to meet Helen.

Suddenly, David could only think of his hands. They seemed slimy and greasy and sweaty. Even as he listened to Pamela, the urge quivered within him to slam the receiver down and rush to the nearest wash-basin. He examined his right hand, the palm creased by scarlet runnels, the bony fingers trembling. He could no longer think clearly.

'David? David?'

'I was just thinking. I . . . can't make it.' What on earth could he say? What excuse could he make? What did husbands say who were meeting a mistress? 'That was part of . . . what that phone call was about.' After the hesitant start, the words began to flow more easily. 'The clients are thinking of launching their bid towards the end of next week. There's an important meeting on Tuesday night at their offices about the tax implications and I've got to be there. Sorry.'

She was unhappy but accepted his excuse.

David gritted his teeth as he ran to the bathroom. As he rinsed his hands under the tap, David reflected on how well he had taken to lying. Admittedly Pamela was gullible, but one still needed a certain skill. The events of the evening filled him with a certain frisson. He felt exhilarated by the risk, the danger. It reminded him of a rainy afternoon when he had driven home to London after seeing his mother. It had been several years ago, and he was on the old Chelmsford by-pass at dusk. He was in a hurry and started to overtake a slow lorry. Just as he drew level with the driver's cab, David suddenly saw with horror that a car was in the opposite lane and flashing towards him through the drizzle, hooter wailing. How he missed it, he had no idea. The lorry was still thundering along beside him, a blank wall offering no es-

46

cape. David stamped on the brakes and watched as though in slow motion as his car eased into a skid and swung through a complete circle, coming to rest a few yards in front of the bumper of the oncoming car. He had survived. But throughout the odd second or so of the skid, David believed he was living at a heightened level. There was exhilaration at seeing every object around him — the windscreen wipers, the steering-wheel, the glove compartment — with unparalleled clarity. He also felt strangely invulnerable. He believed he was safe and nothing could hurt him. And David repossessed the same feeling on the night he arranged to meet Helen.

# 5

David was nervous. He had never betrayed a girlfriend of his before because there had never been a proper relationship to betray. The nervousness was because he had stepped into unknown territory. He had often told himself that it was fear of loneliness that drove him to women, but, as he sat in the car garnering his courage, he wondered whether loneliness was not preferable to being squeezed in the vice of an approaching marriage that he did not have the strength to break. Why, he wondered, were women not more like his snake – passive and undemanding, giving back only as much warmth as they received?

David felt uncomfortable south of the Thames. He had always lived in north London and easily became lost among the anonymous streets of Clapham, Brixton and Battersea. It had taken him a little longer than expected to find Rosebrooke Road but he had set out early to allow for this. He always hated to be late. He parked round the corner and walked along the line of terraced houses until he reached number forty-three, passing no one. Drizzle pricked his cheeks.

The gate had disappeared from the gap in the low wall which marked the boundaries of the front garden. Above he saw a rectangle of warm light glowing through bamboo blinds: Helen's flat. Water dribbled from the eaves above and slapped onto the tiles beside him. The bricks above the porch were green with damp. The house had an unkempt and lonely air which contrasted with the girl's manner over the telephone. He pressed the bell for flat two and heard it ring far away in the depths of the house.

David breathed in and drew himself up to his full height as the light in the hall was switched on and the square of stained glass in the door flashed into a whorl of bottle greens and burgundies.

'Hello,' she said. 'You must be Michael.'

'Yes, yes,' he stammered, remembering the false name he had given her over the telephone. 'I'm Michael Drayton.' He touched the cold, limp hand that she self-consciously extended to him. It felt like a damp leaf.

She was already dressed in a raincoat and erected her umbrella with a snap. 'I thought we'd go to this nice wine bar I know – at least I think it's nice. It's only a few streets away. Just over there.' She pointed to where the Common lay, sodden and dim, down at the end of the street.

David found he did not need to talk. Helen chattered away as they sidled to the wine bar, apprehensive of pauses. Her voice had an attractive, throaty quality. She was rather beautiful, David considered. She was of medium height for a woman and walked with an elegant sway. Her blonde hair was artificially bedraggled and imparted a hint of the untamed to what might otherwise have looked too scrubbed, too clean a face. Everything about her was wholesome: the rounded cheeks, white teeth, even the chubby eyelids. The eyes themselves were green and almond-shaped, their animation emphasised by a frame of discreet make-up.

In the wine bar, he found it impossible to concentrate on what she was saying. He kept thinking of interesting things to say but when an opening swung open in the conversation, he forgot what it was. Instead, he alternated between staring into her face with a vague smile, like a foreigner who did not understand the language, and scrutinising irrelevant details of the wine bar. A series of reproductions of classic black and white photographs hung on the walls. He took in every detail of one by Frank Horvat: a man reclining on a bench in the foreground, arms and head thrown back, with the serried towers of Manhattan rising up behind on the far side of the river. He examined the potted plants in the window; the young couple at the next table; the spelling mistakes on the blackboard menus, offering 'moules mannière' and 'river trout ammandine'.

'Am I boring you?' Helen asked suddenly, sipping her glass of Muscadet.

'No. Why do you say that?'

'Well,' she said, looking down at her glass, 'you seem very interested in what's going on round about.'

David smiled an apology. He was attracted to her – her plump body swelling into the white blouse and tight black trousers – and wanted to impress her. Yet he knew he was not doing the right things. He had done them before: crack jokes, keep eye contact, ooze self-confidence. But he seemed to have forgotten the lessons. 'I'm sorry. I'm a bit distracted tonight. It's terribly rude.' He gulped. 'I've just got to go to the loo, and I'll explain when I get back.'

He sensed his confidence return like a rising tide as he dried his hands on the roller towel. 'Relax. Enjoy yourself,' were the orders he issued to his body. 'You've nothing to lose. Tell her a version of the truth. Win her sympathy.'

David repeated his apology as he slipped back into his seat. She looked up, fresh as a flower. 'You see . . . I'm still terribly upset. I was going out with my fiancée for the past year. We just drifted apart. But she's damaged me. She was cold, deep down. Heartless. Selfish.'

'I know how you feel,' she said, leaning forward, her eyes moist. 'It's like what I was telling you about John.' David remembered vaguely from her chatter that John was her last serious boyfriend and that she thought David looked a little like him. She related the end of their relationship four months before in words selected with what David considered almost mendacious care, wanting to emphasise her availability and desire for love. He felt like an angler whose fingers on the rod sense a fish nibbling at the bait.

'She scarred me forever,' David continued, looking into her eyes. 'You see . . . I don't think . . . I'll ever be able . . . '

Helen leant forward. One of her hands brushed against his like a sigh of hot breath. 'Don't tell me if you don't want to. I understand.'

The chairs next to them erupted into a clatter as the couple to their right stood up to leave. The woman, dressed in a denim shirt strapped down by a pair of scarlet braces, glanced at them with curiosity. David admired how her firm breasts were emphasised by the braces. He turned back to Helen, and allowed his eyes to drool over her cream skin, sensing the crutch of his trousers grow tight for the first time

50

since his last, abortive attempt to make love to Pamela. He suggested they should eat together. Helen agreed.

They crossed Battersea Rise to an Italian restaurant run by an English couple. It was self-consciously superior, with minimal decoration on the walls and white tables and chairs. David felt he was eating in a hospital operating theatre, using the knife like a scalpel to prise apart his veal. He was confident now in the belief that Helen pitied him and so was attracted to him. He forced himself to become good company. The clenched tension melted from his limbs to be replaced by aching sexual desire. David paid the bill in cash with a flourish and said he would escort her home.

The wine and the excitement made him animated, even loquacious. They strolled up the road, past a snooker club, and then a string of brash, opulent shops – delicatessens, wine merchants, boutiques – symbolising the gentrification of the area. David was so intent on Helen that he only glanced up at the Common as they passed: the children's playground forlorn and sodden, the trunks of the plane trees sporting white wounds where the bark had peeled away, car headlights strobing far away between the trees. Each time a car whooshed by in the drizzle, his desire sharpened, like the second hand of a clock moving inexorably on.

Outside the flat, he detected her moment's hesitation before she invited him up for coffee. He watched her body sway up the staircase in front of him, the hips rolling.

'I live alone,' she explained, taking his damp cashmere overcoat. 'I used to have a tenant but prefer my privacy. I like to get up in the morning and not have to talk to anyone.' A harried smile twitched on her lips as the coats she held dripped onto the carpet. David wanted to take her in his arms and throw her on the sofa at that moment. But she quickly turned away. 'I'll go and make some coffee.'

The sitting-room of the flat was cosy and clean. The furniture was all bare wood and straight from the Habitat catalogue, although now a little scruffy. The seams of the sofa he sat down in were starting to split and one of the legs wobbled. He wanted to say something but nothing came to mind. The silence was filled by sounds from the kitchen – the ring of cups against saucers and the rumble of an electric kettle.

Outside rain water gurgled through the drainage pipes.

'Do you take milk or sugar, Michael?' Helen's throaty voice curled round the kitchen door.

The name fell empty of meaning on David's brain. 'Michael? Who's Michael?' Then he remembered. All evening he had pretended to be someone else, a man called Michael Drayton. Sitting back in the sofa and kicking out his long legs, he now regretted that he had invented the name. It was a barrier between himself and Helen – a symbol of his lack of confidence and his willingness to lie. There were enough barriers between them as it was, he thought, without constructing more. Once a lie was in place, one had to live it. 'Er, nothing please. Just, just black,' he stammered.

David wondered where she would sit. If she decided on the sofa, it would be a sign in his favour. Helen's well-manicured fingernails however placed the cup on the coffee table beside him and he watched her step over to the stereo on the bottom case of the bookshelves. 'You said you liked classical music. Is Bach OK?'

He nodded.

'Bach can be so sad. But he's also so beautiful.'

She sat down in an armchair next to the television set and sipped her coffee. The strains of the *St Matthew Passion* swelled faintly into the room. David knew it well from his childhood. Bach was one of his mother's favourite composers along with Mozart.

David wondered what his strategy should be. Her retreat from the sofa was a symbolic rejection, the eight feet of oatmeal carpet yawned between them like an unfordable river. Mad schemes floated into his mind: crawling across to her and nestling his head against her feet like a cat; perhaps he should slump to the floor and pretend to faint. He wanted her sympathy and pity. Yet David felt unable to do anything or say anything. His muscles hardened with anxiety, fluttering with spasm. All he was aware of was his sexual excitement, his attraction to the comforting body sitting opposite by the television, legs crossed, lips forming words that made no sense. His skin tingled, goosepimples rumpling the surface.

'Michael? Are you alright?' His eyes were still locked in

fantasy on the armchair. They quickly focussed on the shape three feet in front. She stood above him now, green eyes boring into his, a look of perplexity furrowed into her brow. Her hands were on the bottom of her thighs, the line of her bra a ghost beneath the blouse. 'Michael. Are you OK?'

Without thinking, he looped his right arm out behind her neck and tried to draw her lips down to his. But by the time his mouth came into contact with her skin, Helen had twisted to one side and his lips bit into her cheek. His left arm clamped round her waist. He had the full, arousing sensation of her warmth against him. He burrowed his face in her hair and pumped his lungs full of the heady perfume. Still muffling her face on his shoulder and pressed on by the weight of his arousal, David dragged up the back of her blouse and slid his hand up the ridge of her backbone until it was stopped by the strap of her bra. A sharp, agonising pain clutched at his neck. She was biting him. He suddenly realised she was struggling frantically to be free, her left hand trying to pummel his chest, her right tugging at his hair.

David threw her to his left onto the sofa and swung his right leg over her feet. With horror, as though in slow motion, he watched her lips draw apart and a scream spring forth that split his ears. His left hand smothered her mouth. His right jumped to her throat and he pressed as hard as he could, using his left arm to protect his face from the flailing of her nails. Her body writhed, her chest struggling and labouring beneath his weight. Her eyes peeled back and began to bulge, her tongue protruding between her teeth, her face suffused with blood.

David was engorged with the sense of power, of control. He felt he was standing on a high cliff, able to see for miles and miles with a clarity he had never experienced before. He sensed his erection, thicker and more powerful than he had ever known it, replete with blood and desire for this woman who dared to resist him. She would be ready for him in a moment, this Helen he had known for only a few hours, this Helen who had provoked him and then proved frigid. In a moment, she would see sense and understand him, sympathise with him, be tender, show a burning passion for his body, take the initiative, do scandalous and outrageous

53

things, speak the obscenities his mother had slapped him around the head for when he was young, speak them in a throaty hiss, pinioning his body against hers.

When he looked down again, her eyes had closed. He occasionally felt her body twitch beneath him. David slowly removed his hands from round her neck and, as he sat back, the sense of throbbing power that had been coursing through him only seconds before ebbed away into the night.

Someone was breathing heavily in the room. Who? He jumped backwards. The girl, Helen, of course. But when he looked again, she was completely still. The respiration, the hoarse dragging in and out of breath, belonged to him. It was what separated him, alive, from the dead girl on the sofa. A few drops of blood trickled from her right ear, blood that to his eyes only seemed to sharpen her beauty.

David told himself that he had not intended to kill her, only pacify her. He wanted time to tell her that he loved her and found her sexually attractive, that she aroused him. It was her fault. She had worn make-up and tight trousers and an alluring blouse. She had invited him into her flat for coffee. Then she – the woman with whom he was no longer impotent – had refused him. It was her fault.

The sight of Helen, sprawled and vulnerable on the sofa, no longer stimulated him. The idea of any form of sex with the dead was disgusting. Instead, he fell to his knees and crawled across to her left arm, which lay outstretched almost touching the carpet. David rubbed his head against her hand as though she was stroking him. He closed his eyes.

He was seven or eight years old. He sat on the carpet in front of the television, the green carpet his mother had laboriously woven at home, the black and white screen flickering like fog. His father sat in one armchair, balding and relaxed, his eyes twinkling with mischief. His mother sat in the stained wooden armchair beside her husband and behind her son. He felt again her fingers trickle like water through his hair. He would turn and smile at her. And she, in turn, would smile at him and then at his dad. Not the smile of the past quarter of a century – pinched and obligatory, wan and rare, the caricature of a smile – but a radiance that spread through her whole face. That smile died away to a look of

54

serenity and peace, the look borne always by Jesus in the Sunday School books at Kirsham church.

His eyes flickered open and he thought he detected the same expression on Helen's face: a look of love and forgiveness that calmed him. It also made him realise for the first time what he had done. He had killed another human being. He remembered the sense of power with satisfaction. He had exercised the right to decide when and how another human being should die, had held life between his hands like an injured bird. At the moment David had selected, he had squeezed life out of another's body, extinguished the girl's spirit.

David listened intently. Helen's scream might have alerted someone. But the only sound was the tinkle of the rain in the guttering and the *St Matthew Passion* on the stereo. He walked through to the hall and took the gloves from the pocket of his coat.

He had to remove any clues, perhaps try and make it look as though a man had broken in. Now, he told himself, if you were a burglar, what would you be looking for? Jewellery. Money. He strode through into her bedroom and ransacked the cupboards and chest of drawers. He found a couple of necklaces, a brooch and bracelets. He had no idea of their worth.

What about her desk? He stumbled back into the sitting-room and pulled down the top of her bureau, finding it difficult with his thick, sheepskin gloves. He took two building society books and discovered in a small drawer three adverts cut out from the lonely hearts column of *London Life*. One was his. He could almost recite the words by heart.

'SUCCESSFUL LAWYER, mid-thirties, cultivated, attractive, Cambridge-educated, interest in food, cinema, classical music and books, seeks mature, understanding, sexy woman, thirties, for caring, sharing relationship.'

He had thought hard about including the word 'sexy'. It sounded hollow and cheap. But he knew what he wanted it to signify: a woman who wore make-up and high-heeled shoes, even stockings and suspenders, rather than Pamela in her petticoats, flat shoes and dowdy clothes. And Helen had understood. She was a 'sexy' woman. He placed the adverts in an empty envelope and placed them in his jacket pocket.

He went back and knelt down beside Helen again. She *was* a sexy woman. She was so beautiful. He took off his gloves, unbuttoned her blouse and ripped open the flimsy bra. He brushed the tip of his forefinger around the faint knobs at the outer edge of the nipple and then edged it in across shallow cracks in the skin to the nipple itself. His lips were drawn to it, down, down to death. And as he kissed it an idea burst into his mind, so deep and dark, that he could not admit that it was his own at first, but an alien transplant. The idea calmed him, relaxed him. He walked to the kitchen to find a knife.

# 6

The couple who lived beneath Patricia Hoskin sat together, hollow-eyed on their sofa. The man, rather than husband – for they were unmarried – wore a look of suspicious irritation and kept rubbing the palms of his hands over the knees of his brown corduroy trousers. The woman had crumpled like a paper bag and an occasional ripple of sobbing would shake her body. The man's name was Colin, and the girl's Susan. Dexter Bazalgette, Blanche's detective sergeant, was sitting opposite them when she strode in. The flat was dingy and over-furnished, with every shelf and table groaning with ethnic ornaments: painted elephants, lacquered boxes, sandalwood Buddhas.

Dexter intercepted the superintendent by the stripped pine door and gestured with a roll of his eyes that they should talk outside.

'What are they running in there?' Blanche began, with amused curiosity. 'A branch of the Victoria and Albert Museum?'

Dexter dropped a chocolate eyelid. 'I think that's why the guy is so pissed off with us being here. He says he runs an art import business on the side.'

'About which presumably he thinks the Inland Revenue should remain in a state of blessed ignorance? Like good Catholic girls knowing nothing about contraception.'

The superintendent knew Dexter was the sort of Catholic who sported his religion like a flag of convenience and would not take offence. The detective sergeant knotted his brow in mock irritation for a moment before breaking into a cocky smile: natural teeth that reminded Blanche of the White Cliffs of Dover in their perfection.

The jesting over, Dexter scampered through the significant parts of their statements. Blanche listened with her

57

characteristic squint of concentration. The couple had said they had not seen anything suspicious in the last few days. They were not on particularly close terms with Patricia, just meeting her every now and again on the stairs and saying hello. Then yesterday morning, when Susan had done some shopping, she noticed the curtains of the upstairs flat were still closed. She had not been especially suspicious about this and assumed Patricia had gone to work and forgotten to open them. Last night, they had stayed in and watched television. About half past eleven, there had been a ring on their bell. They were reluctant to answer it since they were already in bed, but in the end, Colin had staggered to the door in his dressing-gown. On the doorstep was Dinah Lynn, Patricia Hoskin's friend who was so worried about her she had driven all the way over to Clapham. Colin and Susan both thought she was over-excited. But in the end her hysteria wore them down. What made Colin agree to break down the door was the sight of lights being on in the flat, but there being no reply when they called out. Inside, in the sitting-room, they had found the body and called the police.

Colin looked up with a renewed glower of suspicion as Blanche entered the room again. The woman pushed a stone carving of a man with an elephant head to one side on the varnished coffee table and plucked a Kleenex from the box. She dabbed her eyes. Blanche, as a result of a tour of India as a student and a retentive memory, recognised the sculpture as one of Ganesh, the Hindu God of Learning. Sometimes she regretted not remaining a student. Her history degree from Cambridge was good enough for her to have stayed on to do postgraduate research but was of no use in the Metropolitan Police. She was a 'flyer' – a graduate entrant who in the eyes of many had risen too fast for her own good – and a woman. She found it was often best to keep her learning to herself. The paperback copy of *The Tales of Hoffmann* she was reading weighed heavily in her pocket. She was intrigued by the schizophrenia of Hoffmann – a civil servant during the day and at night a writer of macabre stories – but found his tales too clotted with Romanticism for her taste.

'What time did you get home the night before last please?' Blanche enquired.

Colin sighed and ran a hand through his black, greasy hair. He licked his lips and gazed at the ceiling to aid his memory. 'I suppose it must have been around a quarter past eleven.'

'Did you see anyone outside? Cars drawing away?'

He shook his head slowly. 'All I saw was the old woman who walks her dog late in the evening. She goes round and round the block almost every night.'

Blanche and Dexter exchanged glances. Colin said she lived somewhere in the neighbourhood, although he was not sure where exactly. Dexter made a note.

'And as you came in, did you notice anything suspicious? Had the front door to the house or the door to her flat been left open?'

'No. They were both locked.'

'Did you hear anything upstairs?'

'Well, we got ready for bed. I didn't hear anything.'

'I did.' The woman's words sizzled on the damp air of the room. 'I heard the front door slam.'

Blanche turned to her: a bundle of mousy hair and pale skin who looked as though her skeleton had been melted away by tears. The superintendent had to tell herself to wait. Even by her mid-thirties she found the wisdom of patience did not always come naturally.

'It was just after we got in. I was tidying up in the front room and for some reason just listened.' She shrugged. 'I heard someone hurry down the stairs. And whoever it was slammed the door behind them.' She glanced up in explanation, running a hand encrusted with jewellery through her ginger hair. 'It's quite stiff, you see, the door. You have to pull it hard to make it shut.'

'What time was that?'

'God knows. Just after we got in. Say twenty past eleven. Five and twenty past,' she said with the airiness of someone for whom time was not important. 'But that's not all.'

The man crossed his arms and looked away from his girl-friend with a pout of discontent. Blanche guessed he did not want to be involved in any way at all and his girlfriend was breaking the vow of silence.

'I carried on listening for a few seconds and heard music. It was up above, quite faint but I could still make it out.' She looked at the sculpture of the elephant and studied it like an old photograph, redolent with memory. 'Classical stuff. Depressing. Choir singing. Not my scene, I'm afraid.'

Blanche rested her elbow on the arm of the chair, and flopped her rounded chin on a cupped hand. It was one way to describe Bach, she supposed, remembering the *St Matthew Passion* she had seen on the turntable upstairs: 'classical and depressing, with a choir singing'. Roger, the husband from whom she had separated, used to make comments like that to irritate her. He wore his philistinism like a medal ribbon. Not that there was much room for Bach in the Metropolitan Police, Blanche reflected. To reach her present exalted position as a detective superintendent in the Central Area Major Investigating Pool, she had had to pretend she was not an intellectual, learn not to blush when jokes were told about women's 'minges', drink hard, forswear tears and laugh off the lunging lips of fellow policemen while on patrol in dark alleys.

'If we played you the piece of music, do you think you'd be able to spot which bit you heard?'

'Sure,' interrupted Colin, who had obviously decided that now the taboo had been broken it was best to appear cooperative. 'Sue's really musical.'

Blanche ignored him and waited. The woman said she might. Blanche had noted that side seven of the *St Matthew Passion* on the turntable upstairs lasted twenty-two minutes and ten seconds. And since a corpse could still not manage to put a record on by itself – despite the technological leaps of the Japanese – the music must have been started just before the murderer had arrived or while he was still in the flat. Colin and Sue had missed the killer by minutes.

She asked them about the cryptic entry in the diary for Tuesday night about Helen Rowe meeting Michael Drayton. Both gazed back blankly. The superintendent paused. 'What about boyfriends?'

Colin puckered his dark cheeks as a gesture of ignorance. 'God knows what went on in that department. There was one guy who I met on the stairs a while back going in or out, called John something. I never knew his surname. He looked like a regular boyfriend but I haven't seen him for the past couple of months. Occasionally we'd also see another man at the door or on the stairs. But she didn't seem particularly close to any of them.'

The superintendent raised her recently plucked eyebrows. 'Did they stay overnight?'

The man looked uncomfortable and then sniggered like a schoolboy. 'John did. I used to hear the bedsprings creaking in the middle – '

'Oh, shut up, Colin,' snapped the girl suddenly. 'The poor girl's been murdered!'

Colin rolled his eyes to the ceiling in a gesture of hopelessness.

Blanche was about to ask another question, when a constable scurried in and said her chief's office had just called from New Scotland Yard. They wanted her to contact Commander Spittals urgently. The superintendent ordered Dexter to start trying to find the old lady who exercised her dog late at night in the neighbourhood, while she strode up to Patricia Hoskin's flat to use the phone. On the stairs she brushed against Inspector Thomson, who asked whether it was OK now for the body to be removed. Blanche nodded.

'Ah, it's you, Blanche. About bloody time.' The voice of Commander Brian Spittals, her former chief from the Serious Crimes Squad, was brittle with irritation, his Mancunian vowels softened but still distinguishable.

'What's the matter, sir?' Blanche said patiently, starting to count the droplets of water on the window in front of her.

'"Grief" is the matter, superintendent. Some trouble I wanted to let you know about. I had a call half an hour ago from the Assistant Commissioner's office, saying you're investigating the murder of this Hoskin girl.'

'That's right, sir. I started first thing this morning. I've already given orders for a Murder Squad – '

' – I know, I know, it's all under control. I'm not phoning up about your administrative arrangements. I'm phoning up just to check that you know who this girl's dad is.'

'Paul Hoskin, sir. A politician, and quite an important one.'

'So far, so good. But I bet there's something else you don't know.'

She toyed with being arch and replying 'How can I, sir,

61

when I don't know it?' But she knew from past experience that such banter goaded Spittals to fury. 'What's that, sir?' she enquired at her most meek.

'He's an old friend of the Assistant Commissioner. Like they go on holiday together, play golf together. The Assistant Commissioner wants results. And he and the dead girl's dad want them fast.'

Dinah Lynn seemed as much in mourning for herself as for her friend. An air of neglect hung about her expensive flat in West Kensington – the furniture drooped, the house-plants mourned, the books appeared to gather dust even while Blanche watched them. Although the same age as the dead girl, thirty-three, Dinah seemed much younger, a pixie in a woman's body.

'I'll never forget it. As long as I live,' she sobbed, her lips pulled into strange shapes by facial muscles of which she was no longer the mistress. Her hair was cropped and dyed the colour of rust. Her exotic ear-rings, shaped like silver crescents, shook as she wept. Both helped to fill out a face that would otherwise have appeared too thin and pinched. Dinah sat by the window of her ground floor flat, the afternoon light drizzling onto her puffed features. She was petite and self-aware, hands on knees clasped together in a pair of green trousers. She wore a red checked shirt and scuffed white shoes, the brightness of her clothes heightened by her wan skin.

Dinah plucked a paper handkerchief from the box on the coffee table. 'When we walked into the flat . . . The sight of Pat just lying there, all covered in blood. I'll never forget it to the day I die.'

Blanche glanced out of the sash window at the buildings opposite: a grubby, stucco-fronted terrace, transformed like the one she was visiting, into flats. Flights of steps led to identical mock Georgian front doors, each decorated with a silver vodaphone box and a square of bubbled glass like those in shops illustrated by Arthur Rackham or Anton Pieck. The rain had halted but bequeathed a film of leaden cloud that was already strangling the afternoon light.

To Blanche, Dinah seemed a highly intelligent woman with

a good heart, interested in events and people, but perhaps ill-starred in love. She was not married and, the superintendent suspected, like many women with brains who had not found a partner by their thirties, had perhaps begun to despair of ever doing so. A sparkle lurked in Dinah's swollen eyes and a nervous energy galvanised her fingers to clutch at and release her trousers. Her voice had a tone of cracked imperiousness: a teacher who was endearingly not quite sure of her authority.

The dead girl's best friend had already given a chaotic, but Blanche thought essentially accurate, account of what had happened on Wednesday night – fifteen or so hours before – when she had insisted on breaking into the flat. 'The people below – a pretty drippy couple I always thought – were reluctant, and understandably so, to help me break in. But I knew something was wrong.' She sat further forward on the edge of the armchair, wringing one hand through the other. 'I just knew it. Pat always, but always, kept her appointments. She was a stickler for punctuality and would never let one down. Even if she were ill, she would always make the effort to come to a dinner party or something.'

Dexter slouched, relaxed but alert, on a chair next to the superintendent, ball-point poised in case the interviewee uttered anything of significance. Dinah occasionally vouchsafed him a patronising but nervous smile, like a missionary in the bush singling out for praise the model pupil in a class of young cannibals. She did not meet many blacks, Blanche concluded, and was uncomfortable in their presence.

'I don't suppose Patricia told you what she was intending to do on Tuesday night?' asked Blanche. 'That's the night we think she was murdered.' Dinah did not just twist her neck but rolled her whole head from side to side in an eccentric gesture of denial. It was a strange head, Blanche reflected, with a wide forehead that narrowed almost to a point at her chin, like a cyclamen leaf.

'She didn't mention anyone she was going to meet?'

Dinah rolled her head again.

Blanche prodded on. 'It's just that there's an entry in her diary for Tuesday. For eight o'clock in the evening it has "Helen Rowe meets Michael Drayton!"' Blanche paused.

Dinah, she guessed, might savour the possible importance of what she was about to say. 'She wrote it with an exclamation mark.'

Dinah made a noise which would have been a sob if she had not tried to smile at the same time. Her teeth were small and neat like a doll's. 'She was a strange girl, Pat. Full of high jinks and jokes.' She scrutinised her hands intently, picking hairs – real and imaginary – from her trousers. 'We were at school together you know. People wondered what we had in common. They called us Beauty and the Beast. Patricia was the Beauty of course, with the blonde hair and English Rose good looks. I was the Beast – not very good-looking but brainy.' She glanced up, seeking reassurance, and the detective gave her a cracked smile. Blanche was saddened once again by the number of clever women who cripple themselves through self-pity.

'So what *did* you have in common?' Dexter asked gently.

A crease folded itself in Dinah's brow, as if forced to consider the question for the first time. 'For a start, Pat was an anarchist like me. But deep down, I don't know, to be honest.' She pasted on a self-mocking smile. 'Lack of a husband possibly. Neither of us had much luck with men. And then there was the cinema, books, theatre. A sense of humour.' She flopped her head to one side with a sigh of recollection. 'We just got on terribly well. Friendship, I suppose.'

Blanche nodded so as not to appear unfeeling but scratched at the surface of the question again. 'So you can't explain that diary entry?'

Dinah glanced up, her face suddenly bruised again by grief. 'Neither of those names mean anything to me.'

'What about the exclamation mark?' Blanche knew that morsel of punctuation was becoming an obsession but had to ask nonetheless.

'Pat was highly literate, if that's what you mean. A full stop did not mean the same to her as an exclamation mark – unlike a lot of people these days.' She made the last comment with a grunt of cynical contempt, as if referring to the loss of a sense of God rather than punctuation. But, Blanche reflected, the sprightly woman opposite had every reason for cynicism: she taught English at a London polytechnic. The sparkle rekindled itself in Dinah's lustreless eyes. 'It sounds to me as if she was playing some sort of game. Pat was keen on games, keeping one guessing, having a joke.'

Blanche had already been thinking along the same lines. She was convinced the diary entry was in some form of code. Its tone was like a crude poster for a wrestling contest. There was also a strange objectivity about the entry, as though Pat was watching the event scheduled for eight o'clock as an outsider, a spectator at a play. The exclamation mark sharpened the sentiment of drama and expectation 'So the names mean absolutely nothing?'

Blanche reflected on whether she should dye her hair like Dinah. Although still safely in her thirties, the detective had plucked out the odd grey hair in the past few months. She wondered whether radical action was required.

Dinah tugged back the ends of her lips as if amused by an irony in what she was about to say. 'You see . . . we both knew a Helen Rowe from school . . . that's Roedean where we both were.'

'So why did you say the name meant nothing?' Blanche asked, her voice grating with irritation.

'The thing is . . . I didn't think the name could mean anything in Pat's diary – that it was some sort of sick joke.' The dead girl's friend lifted her left hand to her brow and squeezed the bridge of her nose between forefinger and thumb as if she had a headache. She sighed. 'We both kept vaguely in contact with Helen after school. But about four years ago she married an Australian and went to live in Sydney. I sent her a couple of letters but heard nothing more from her. Then about a fortnight ago, the old school magazine came through our front letter-boxes.' She flopped the hand from her forehead and began to pluck at her trousers thoughtfully. 'There was one of those anonymous little announcements inside. The same size as the one about the hockey team or the drama society's production of *The Critic*. It said that three months ago, Helen Rowe was killed in a road accident in Australia.' Her bloodshot, grey eyes glittered with the irony of life.

Blanche crunched through the implications of what she

had just heard. The school magazine – Blanche could imagine it, just like the one she still received once a year from her private school, printed on glossy paper and crammed with articles of compulsive irrelevance – would have dropped onto Patricia's coconut doormat at the same time as on Dinah's. The announcement would have blown a surprised chill into her heart. And since Helen Rowe could meet nobody three months after her death on a stretch of Sydney tarmacadam, except perhaps a stray Antipodean cherub or seraph, in her diary Patricia took the name of her dead acquaintance to denote someone else. Perhaps herself. And if 'Helen Rowe' *were* Patricia's *nom de plume* – or perhaps *nom de guerre* Blanche thought with an inward smile – who was Michael Drayton? And why did she want to disguise her own name in her own diary?

'Michael Drayton, on the other hand, means absolutely nothing to me at all,' said Dinah with a firm snap of the lips.

The superintendent believed her and asked about the men in Patricia's life.

Dinah blinked and gazed out of the window, as if grasping for the right words: criticising the dead, especially friends, should be done with reticence. 'She always seemed popular with men. Probably because she was vivacious and opinionated. Sometimes it was just exhausting being with her. She wasn't even classically beautiful. She was always trying to lose weight – unsuccessfully for the most part.' Dinah, in a spasm of conscience about finding fault with her murdered friend, laughed for comfort. 'Anyway, she married – very unsuitably – when she was twenty-four. Her parents, I know, were very much against it. He was an actor and it turned out six months later – God knows why it took six months because I could tell as soon as I met him – a gay.'

Blanche saw Dexter's pen start to quiver on the page and then her detective sergeant tauten his cheeks in a vain attempt to suppress a giggling fit. Suddenly he exploded into laughter – great, heaving cackles inspired by Dinah's mischievous face. Dexter was only too aware of the irony because he was homosexual himself.

Although equally puzzled, and amused, by the delay in the discovery of the former husband's homosexuality, Blanche glued her face into a mask of sympathy. 'Shut up, Dexter,' she murmured. 'Show some respect for the sacrament of marriage.'

Dinah laughed convulsively as she spoke: an eccentric over-reaction, Blanche thought. 'Presumably the poor chap couldn't get it up for six months and it took that long for Pat – never the brightest as I said – to reason it out. Pat anyway could never understand men.' Thin fingers, pale fingers, Blanche noticed, the nails so short they must be gnawed. 'So Pat quickly got a divorce. And she's had a number of boyfriends since.'

'How many?'

Dinah pursed her lips – whether through disapproval, jealousy or to aid memory Blanche was not sure. 'A few.'

'And did she have one at the time she was murdered?'

Dinah narrowed her eyes at Blanche before looking away. 'No. She didn't as a matter of fact.'

'The people downstairs said there had been a boyfriend called John something. Do you know his surname?'

Her glance swung away from Blanche to the window and she hooked her thin legs under her body onto the sofa. Dinah's face pondered on the stripped floorboards. 'Do I have to tell you? I mean is it relevant?'

'It may well be,' murmured Blanche.

The girl sighed and caressed one of her ear-rings. 'His name's John Hebden. He's a journalist and,' she paused for a moment for theatrical effect, 'married.' She hesitated for a moment as if to think and then sighed. 'But he couldn't have had anything to do with this.'

'What makes you so sure?' asked Dexter. 'They'd broken up. Perhaps he'd met her again to make up and there'd been a row that ended with him murdering her.'

'I hardly think that's likely,' she replied coolly. 'John's a passionate man but not the sort to go round to a former girlfriend's and kill her.'

Blanche stared at her. 'How do you know?'

Dinah plucked an invisible hair from her trousers. 'He's just not that type. Too gentle.'

The superintendent looked round the flat. The floorboards were bare and varnished, and the white walls were hung with small abstracts in aluminium frames. All three of them – Dinah, Dexter and herself – sat in expensive, black leather sofas while Dexter flicked ash from his cigarette into what looked like a coffin of blue glass on the coffee table. Dinah, the superintendent concluded, had private means to be able to afford all this aggressive modernity, even if she could not be bothered to maintain it. Every object in the room that was not in daily use was powdered with dust, and every corner was crammed with papers and junk.

'So why *did* John Hebden break up with Patricia Hoskin?'

Dinah pushed her shoulders back and sniffed. It was her attempt to look wise. 'The usual story, I'm afraid. He was married. Patricia wanted him to leave his wife. He refused. She wasn't satisfied with just a warm body in bed.' She recited the explanation like a credo.

Blanche nodded indulgently, remembering she had in small measure benefited from a man's matrimonial loyalty – her errant husband had returned to her after an affair, only for their marriage to splutter out in a separation. She still met Roger occasionally for a drink and one evening they had even ended up in bed together. But she regretted it afterwards and their relationship was now wholly platonic.

As a woman Blanche had always felt isolated inside the force, and as a police officer she felt isolated outside it. She had rejected the Met's 'canteen culture' long, long ago – her self-respect had always been more important than easy acceptance and going out with a different policeman every night of the week. After her separation, she had simply come to accept it was almost impossible to be a single policewoman and have a normal social life. Many of the available men were either divorced or widowed, perhaps wanting another family, while others found it difficult to accept a woman like Blanche, self-confident and used to wielding authority.

She had played the lonely hearts game a few times, her guarded advertisements stimulating replies from a motley collection of men – including teachers, insurance salesmen, bankers, a lawyer, a doctor and a Nigerian businessman who said in his letter he was searching for a 'beautiful wife' to accompany him back to Africa. Blanche met the lawyer once for a meal, did not like him, and thought she made it clear by her lack of enthusiasm that she did not want to see him again. But the lawyer proved difficult to shake off – phoning Blanche's ex-directory number until she changed it. The divorced doctor on the other hand was intelligent and congenial. Blanche embarked on an affair with him which foundered on the superintendent's irregular hours. The doctor never seemed to understand when Blanche was forced to cancel a visit to the theatre or cinema because of the pressure of work, even though he did the same himself. They broke up after a few months. Blanche recognised she had found a new spouse without realising it, a domineering husband who resented her spending time with other men: the Metropolitan Police. It was an arranged, but not fulfilling, marriage. Blanche still cherished the hope of finding love elsewhere but not through the lonely hearts columns.

The superintendent dragged her mind back to the investigation. 'But why exactly did Pat and John break up?'

'Pat lost patience with him. She wanted to get married, have children and so on. John didn't. He just wanted a mistress.'

'And would Hebden have a motive to cause her harm?'

Dinah narrowed her eyes like lock-gates. 'No, of course not. I'm sure he was very upset at the time but nothing to make him want to murder Pat. The very idea is disgusting.'

'You don't think this Michael Drayton was some new man in her life?'

'God knows. All I do know is that my best friend is dead.' Her chirpiness cracked over the last few words and she picked imaginary hairs from her blouse for a moment or two before billowing out a sigh of hopelessness. 'Look, superintendent. Despite our differences, I always counted Pat as one of my best friends, one of my closest friends. She told me most things, I think, but not everything. I didn't tell *her* everything I've done.' She paused and glanced towards the window again, as if recalling some trespass against her murdered friend. 'There were certainly things about her relationship with John that she didn't tell me.' She glanced patronisingly at Dexter. 'People are a bit like their desks. They always keep a couple of the drawers locked.'

As she walked away from the flat, the detective saw herself

once again, as she had at moments in previous murder cases, like an archaeologist, piecing together the shards of a broken life, listening to murmurs from the past and trying to amplify them into a coherent story. Blanche squinted in meditation on the serried rooftops. She sensed the murderer could not have been far away when the couple downstairs returned to their flat: the *St Matthew Passion* was being played as a requiem, footsteps scurried down the stairs and the front door was heard to slam. She had to find Michael Drayton and discover whether he was the same person as John Hebden quickly.

The sun was already setting on the first day of her murder investigation. An Assistant Commissioner was watching her progress and she only had two or three days more in hand before the case threatened to become a 'sticker'.

# 7

The snake stirred. A moment before only its black nostrils were visible in the water basin. But now the python raised its head silently into the sultry air of the terrarium. The scuffling vibrations from the cardboard box in the study had roused the serpent from its sleep.

David sat at the pedestal desk, his grey eyes meditating on the hairs on the flank of his right hand. He held the letter from Helen Rowe, the pink rectangle of notepaper that had lured him to take her life. He scrutinised the hand once again. The skin was soft, yet cratered and pitted by wrinkles. His fingers looked weak, certainly not powerful enough to squeeze the life from a young woman. It was all a dream, some gauzy fantasy, that would evaporate when he awoke. The problem was that he was already awake, his hands quivering, his lips chapped by the winter cold. And on the desk was further proof of what had happened three nights before: a copy of Thursday afternoon's *London Standard*. The newspaper was folded back at page five with the headline, 'Minister's Daughter Strangled'. She had lied to him about her name as he had lied to her about his – an equality of deception that he now found amusing. He had not intended to kill her of course. It was an accident precipitated by the girl herself. She had invited him up to have coffee in her flat and flirted with him. David had simply responded in the way any normal man would, and it was her screams that had alarmed him. He had only wanted to quieten her so that he could apologise for the misunderstanding and leave in a civilised way.

David glanced affectionately across at the terrarium. The lights inside cast warm shadows across the carpet. They burned for fourteen hours a day, summer and winter, to maintain the daytime temperature at around thirty degrees.

He padded across to the glass box in time to watch the python slither effortlessly out of the porcelain water basin and coil itself in a corner.

David had decided to buy the snake eighteen months before. He had been invited round to a client's house to discuss the tax position of a company he was planning to set up. At the end of the interview, the man had insisted on showing off his pets. The solicitor was content to view them through the glass, watchful and uneasy. Suddenly the client whipped out a baby Indian python and, chuckling, draped it over David's arm. His initial fear was overcome by the affection that humans feel for the young of almost all other living things. David was entranced by the animal's exotic beauty as it pulsed up his arm and onto his shoulder, a throbbing rod of muscle about two feet long. The scales against the delicate skin at the side of his neck were not slimy but smooth and dry, reflecting back the same heat they absorbed from David's blood. While the client babbled on inconsequentially, David concentrated on the thrilling sensation of the snake against his body. In the space of half an hour, he decided to buy one of his own.

It was partly, David thought, as he gazed into the terrarium, through pride at overcoming his own fear. It was also the sense of peace he experienced when holding a snake. The animal was passive. Unlike human beings, it demanded no affection from him and gave none in return. The creature was simply alive, stimulated only by the occasional craving for food.

The python had grown to four feet since David had bought it, shedding its skin carelessly like lingerie around the cage. The snake lazed away most of the daytime in the water basin, only stirring towards the evening when the heat in the terrarium was allowed to cool. During the hours of darkness it would slide over the newspapers lining the floor and crawl among the damp rocks that formed its retreat.

Every fourth Friday, in the evening, the snake was fed. Its muscular body lay bunched at the back of the terrarium now, the wedge-shaped head thrown elegantly over the outer coil. The ground colour was a rich cream, the skin brindled by khaki blotches which terminated in a stain on the head shaped like a tuning-fork. David had read stories that *Python*

72

*molurus molurus* attacks and eats human beings but knew they were almost certainly apocryphal. The legends imparted an aura to the snake that David relished and the creature seemed to have divined the role it was supposed to play. It refused from the beginning to eat dead rodents, even ones heated in the microwave, and so David had always fed the python live flesh. The pet shop in Islington stayed open until late on Fridays and once a month on his way back from work David stopped by with his cardboard box to buy a mouse.

Following the ritual he had developed over the past months, David picked the white mouse up by the tail and gently lowered it to the floor of the terrarium. He was fascinated by, even enjoyed, what followed, hoping to snatch from the demise of a mouse some clue to the mystery of life and death. The animal stopped squeaking as soon as its claws touched the newspapers, its pink nose twitching on the balmy air. It seemed oblivious to any danger and scuttled around the glass perimeter of the cage, almost brushing against the python. The snake was motionless for a moment and then its head slid forward, the tongue flickering towards the spot where the mouse had passed. David knew the python's tongue was carrying scent molecules to its mouth, tasting the smell of its victim.

The serpent almost imperceptibly loosened its coils. The rodent squatted on its haunches, whiskers quivering, before it scampered forward.

In a blur of speed that David could not follow, the snake entwined the wretched creature with two knots of its body. The movement was so swift, so lethal, that the air was crushed in an instant from the lungs of the mouse, whose mouth lolled open in a voiceless cry of despair. David narrowed his eyes, alert for some token of the moment of death. But, as usual, there was nothing. Only a nervous twitch of the victim's ears.

Fascinated, David watched the python release its prey a few minutes later. The snake seized the mouse by the nose and advanced its teeth up its snout, first on one side and then on the other, in a methodical, plodding motion. After a few minutes, the lower jaws displaced themselves to accommodate the head. Silver dribbles of saliva glistened on the

73

mouse's fur. The python's eyes bulged with the effort, the scales on its neck straining apart. From time to time the snake rested but eventually the rodent disappeared completely between its jaws. The python yawned three times and slithered away to digest its meal, the mouse no more than a bulge in its neck. David's marionette theatre of death was closed for another month.

His eyes were troubled as he sat down at his desk again. What he had just seen reminded him of what had happened on Tuesday night. The story in the newspaper said the police had not yet arrested anyone and were appealing for witnesses. A warm sweat of panic prickled over David's body. The article was already a day old and he had done nothing to destroy the evidence of the killing still in his house. A lethargy had stolen over him since Tuesday night, and David had found it impossible to think clearly.

He ran downstairs and shook open a black dustbin bag. He bundled together all the clothes he had worn three nights before — overcoat, gloves, trousers, shirt, socks, black leather brogues — and thrust them inside. The shirt and trousers were stained with blood, and with a grunt of despair David wondered why he had not thought of the need to do this before. He had wasted three days.

It was almost ten o'clock when David heaved the plastic bag over the front step. The chill November night slapped his cheek. A white mist hung in the street, softening outlines to a uniform blandness. The road was deserted apart from two youths in leather jackets who strode away laughing from the pub, their shadows slithering over the cracked pavement. David had lived in the same house for six years now and had probably been to the pub as many times. When he drank alcohol it was either alone, at parties, or in a wine bar in the City, not in a drab public house inhabited by people with skin like dough and hair powdered with dandruff.

David remembered a skip outside a house that was being renovated a few streets away. He threw the plastic bag into the boot of the Mercedes and drove there, his headlights cutting like knives through the mist. When he arrived the skip had disappeared. The solicitor cursed. On reflection he sighed with relief. It was folly to dump incriminating evi-

74

dence so close to his house: he should travel to an unfamiliar stretch of London.

Marylebone Road was a stream of pinpricks of light – blood-red, orange and white – all made hazy by the mist. David drove with exceptional caution just in case he was seen by the police and stopped for a road traffic offence. The only sounds he heard as he rose up onto the elevated section of the Westway were the heightened whine of his engine and the swish of tyres as other cars passed him. When the road descended again to ground level at Shepherd's Bush, David took a turning to the left. The road stretched ahead, lined by stunted trees, litter and row after row of post-war council flats. They were stolid dormitories of brick, pock-marked with balconies. At the margin of the estate in a side street, David glided past two skips pressed together under the sulphurous flare of a street-lamp. He parked nearby in a road of terraced houses. The street was deserted. David took the bag from the boot and walked up the road that debouched almost opposite the two skips. Just as he arrived, a man loped out of an alley on the far side of the road and stood under the street-lamp. He wore creased trousers, a thin anorak and an expression of drunken bemusement. He looked resentfully at a spot behind the skips and lit a cigarette before stumbling off up the road.

David skulked in the shadows to check no one was watching. A car drove past, a furry toy clinging to the back window by four sucker feet, reggae music thumping the night air. The skips were oozing with detritus – plasterboard, twigs, broken cupboards, newspapers. David hurried forward, his shoes clicking on the tarmac, and heaved the plastic bag up onto the top of the heap. It rested there for an instant, tumbled a couple of feet and wedged between some branches.

David had turned and was about to stride away into the safety of the night when a man's voice rang out: 'Hey, what do you think you're up to?'

David's stomach dropped away and nausea clotted his throat. His heart fired like a piston. From behind the skip stepped the unmistakable profile of two policemen, black and solid in their overcoats, the silver badges on their helmets glistening in the lamplight.

The policeman on the right was in his late forties and spoke again with the same distinctive mixture of authority and contempt. 'People pay good money to hire one of these skips. And then people like you come along and fill them up with your crap without paying a penny.' His face was an impenetrable blank.

David was speechless with fear. He simply stood open-mouthed, praying he did not have a panic attack. He would be finished if the men became suspicious, looked inside the bag and found the clothing. He had read about genetic finger-printing and how bloodstains could be tied with almost unerring accuracy to particular individuals.

'What were you dumping, anyway? A dead body?' The voice was theatrically inquisitive.

David sensed his legs grow faint and gave up all thoughts of sprinting away to safety.

The policeman stepped into the light, his face at last visible, lips drawn back in a grin. His colleague began snorting with laughter. 'Don't worry, sir. I was just winding you up a little bit. But just bear in mind what I said – these aren't public rubbish tips but private ones.' He cocked his head back as he chuckled. 'Go on, off you go. The way you look almost makes me think you *did* have a body in that plastic bag.'

Stammering a goodnight, David turned away and ordered first his right foot and then his left to go in front of the other – left, right, left, right – as calmly as possible so as not to arouse suspicion. Left, right, left, right. It seemed to take an hour to reach the pavement. He heard no shouts behind him. Nothing but the murmur of the city, the clatter of his own feet and distant laughter.

Once out of earshot of the policemen, he started to run. He revved up the car and roared away. In the rear-view mirror he kept catching the glance of a man wide-eyed with fear, his own face glittering with sweat.

David swallowed two huge gin and tonics when he reached home. He wanted to relieve the tortured tenseness that afflicted his body. As he climbed the stairs to his study, the sense of exhilaration returned, and with it a feeling of invulnerability. If destiny, God, justice – David did not know how to describe it – believed him guilty and worthy of punishment, the policemen would have arrested him that night. Instead, he escaped. It was a decree of providence. As he considered this, his eyes lighted on the letter from Patricia Hoskin. He would not after all rip it up into tiny squares and flush them down the lavatory. He would keep the letter as a talisman, symbolic of his good luck. David carefully placed the letter in a drawer of his desk.

'Where *have* you been, darling?' When the phone shrieked David guessed it might be Pamela. 'I tried to ring you earlier but there was no reply.'

'Sorry. I – er – just popped out to the corner shop to get some milk.'

'It took you long enough. I phoned first about half an hour ago.'

'No, well, having got the milk I went for a little walk.' Her probing, her desire to know what he was doing every minute of the day, irritated him.

'Anyway, *talking* of shopping, that's *just* why I'm phoning actually. It was to remind you of your promise to go to the supermarket tomorrow morning and do the shopping.'

What shopping? What promise? David squeezed his brain to recollect what she meant.

Pamela groaned. 'Don't say you've forgotten? I'm having the Pearsons and the Theobalds round for dinner tomorrow night. You said you'd do the shopping for me first thing on Saturday morning.'

David remembered. It was the fact he was not looking forward to the meal that made the dinner party slip from his memory: the hesitant small talk over preprandial drinks; the polite enquiries about children, holidays, and work; the clatter of knives and forks against Pamela's best china; his fiancée's tipsy chatter; the stifled yawns as he focussed his eyes in a mask of interest. Even now, in his thirties, David felt uncomfortable at social events. His shyness encouraged his eyes to stray round the table, observing faces and reactions. After a few glasses of wine, however, he liked to amuse himself by flirting with Pamela's female friends, fixing an attractive one with his smile and imagining how she would react if he slid his hand onto her thigh under the table. He never did. It was only a game. When David relaxed he could be witty in his cynical way and some women were flattered by his attentions. Pamela's blistering glances only sharpened his pleasure.

None of her attractive friends would be there tomorrow night, only a horsey housewife and her slow-witted lawyer husband and a nondescript couple from Fulham. David groaned inwardly but agreed to pick up the shopping list the next morning.

Pamela paused. She had caught the distraction in his voice. 'Are you alright, darling?'

David sighed with irritation, his eyes drawn by the dark coils in the terrarium. 'Yeah, fine. I'll see you in the morning.'

He walked over to the glass cage to admire the python. His eyes brimmed with the same pride as a father worshipping his sleeping child.

# 8

Blanche gazed out of the window of her temporary office. The glass was coated with a dark film, the dust and grit of a choking city. Away towards the east, in the direction of Streatham and Dulwich, the wash of grey cloud that formed the sky was stained paler by an invisible sun. Ranks of houses stretched away into the distance like waves breaking on a rocky shore, their slate roofs glistening. Immediately below, beyond the police car park, was a street of substantial Victorian villas. Although it was already half past nine in the morning, Blanche could still see several windows where lighted bulbs singed the gloom. One room was a reception strewn with children's toys, another a bed-sit with an Indian lampshade, yet another the frosted glass of a bathroom. She could almost sense London stretching itself, preparing for another day. Somewhere, behind one of the tens of millions of windows that watched over the city, was the person she sought, the murderer of Patricia Hoskin.

The body had been discovered almost thirty-six hours ago. Spittals had already phoned that morning for a progress report. When she told him no one had been arrested his only reaction was a grunt of disappointment. He seemed to cheer up when she mentioned the former boyfriend. The newspaper John Hebden worked for had told Dexter the journalist was on holiday and gave out his address in Acton. When two constables had rapped on the front door of the house at seven o'clock that morning, their knocks had echoed through an empty house. Neighbours said the Hebden family had gone off for a break in the country but no one knew where. Blanche ordered her men to camp in the road for a few hours.

As the superintendent's heavily-lidded eyes scoured the horizon, a flurry of rain pattered against the window and dribbled down the glass. She turned round to face the incident room, reminded of how much she hated winter.

Blanche had taken over the incident room at Clapham police station for her Murder Squad. The duty sergeant had drawn the key and shown her the room at the end of the corridor: it was characterless when she first saw it bare of furniture, their shoes squeaking on the linoleum floor. Within hours the superintendent had finalised details of the officers from the local area who would be attached to her investigation. And by clubbing her superiors with irate phone calls, the superintendent had won a number of concessions: the requisition of phone lines, a fax machine and office furniture, and the provision of two HOLMES computer terminals. The initials stood for Home Office Large Major Enquiry System and the name still brought a smile to Blanche's lips as a rare example in her profession of nature imitating art. Blanche had wanted five terminals but the computer section had only chuckled with amusement. The engineers had just arrived to install them under the gaze of the police civil staff, women of motley ages united only by their eager expressions. Blanche was always cheered by such local enthusiasm and efficiency. It was inspired partly by altruism – the desire to deploy skills that threatened to grow rusty from disuse; and partly by self-interest – much valuable overtime was at stake and nobody at local level would want to be seen rocking the boat.

Her own office was no more than a slab of carpet marked off by padded screens. It was too young yet to be cluttered with the usual cascade of files and papers. Blanche loved tidiness but had come to recognise that she was too busy to achieve it – either in the office or in love.

The hour and a half since she arrived in the incident room had been gnawed away by routine paperwork. It was only now that she could apply her mind to the murder enquiry. She plucked the top document from the desk, regarding her battered fingernails with a groan, and vowed to manicure them tomorrow night. As a police officer she had to fight a continuous battle to maintain her femininity. The document was a statement from the old lady who took her Alsatian for nocturnal strolls in the area of the murder.

The woman had been brought to the police station with her dog the previous evening and declared she had seen a man come out of the front door of Patricia Hoskin's flat some time between a quarter and half past eleven. She said it was a matter of luck that she saw him because her Alsatian happened to be 'caught short' and had squatted in the gutter. Her description of the man – in his thirties or forties, of medium height, dressed in a gaberdine – was applicable to thousands. But she said she would 'definitely' recognise the man should she meet him again.

The rectangle of light where the two screens almost met suddenly darkened. Dexter lounged in, sucked the last goodness from his cigarette and stubbed out the butt in Blanche's wastepaper bin. He slid three photocopied pages onto the desk as if placing a bet in a game of poker. 'Well, that Colin guy was right. The girl has got a musical ear – although I don't see where it's gonna get us.' The sergeant had been to visit the couple who lived downstairs from the murdered girl. The photocopies were the libretto from Bach's *St Matthew Passion*. 'I marked the bit she remembered hearing.' His languid forefinger, the skin like wrinkled milk chocolate, stabbed towards a chorale he had outlined in red. He tapped out another cigarette from the packet and lit it with his gold-plated lighter while Blanche read.

> Be near me, Lord, when dying,
> O part not Thou from me!
> And to my succour flying,
> Come, Lord, and set me free!
> And when my heart must languish
> In death's last awful throe,
> Release me from mine anguish,
> By Thine own pain and woe.

'Cheerful stuff, eh?' Dexter commented, moving his weight from one foot to the other with restless energy and flicking ash from his grey cotton trousers.

Blanche glanced up. 'I don't think Bach intended it to reach the Top Ten.' There were three versions running across the page: in French, English and the original in

German. The superintendent had studied German at school and found it depressing to discover how much she had forgotten, how useless academic knowledge had proved in the battle against crooks and thugs.

The words of the chorale awoke memories of her private school: December sunshine tumbling through the stained glass and weaving patterns on the tiles while the girls sang to the accompaniment of a wheezy organ. In those distant days she believed in Jesus, God and the Resurrection. As she grew older and came to know the world her faith began to fade. Until one day when she was seventeen, she found her belief had melted away with her dreams, never to return.

"Scuse me.' Another man entered Blanche's pen: stumpy and overweight, prematurely balding and sporting a brown jacket. Detective Sergeant Wootton was an old drinking acquaintance of Spittals from Manchester who had been imposed on Blanche a couple of months before. He strutted about the office on his flat feet and smiled too much. The superintendent did not trust him a millimetre: she had heard he was spreading rumours that she was a 'lesbo'.

Wootton nodded at Dexter with a fake smile of friendliness. Dexter simply yawned. 'One of the DCs over at Hebden's place is on the phone. Apparently some neighbour has just come back from doing a nightshift who knows Hebden pretty well and says he's up in Derbyshire all week, staying in his cottage.'

Blanche strode out of her partitioned office into the quiet hum of the incident room and pressed the switch on the telephone console. The sergeants followed like obedient page-boys with her train. She scribbled down the address of Hebden's holiday home in her crabbed but fluent handwriting.

'The other thing we've found out, ma'am,' continued the constable over the phone, 'is that Hebden hasn't been up in Derbyshire all week. This neighbour said he happened to see Hebden on Tuesday night, parking his car and going into the house about seven o'clock.'

Blanche dropped the receiver back in its cradle with thoughtful precision. Dexter lounged on a mahogany-veneered desk, a flamboyant silk tie rippling across the front of his white shirt.

The other sergeant stood with arms akimbo, eyes musing on a pretty woman police constable on the other side of the room who had just joined the Murder Squad.

Blanche leant forward and whispered in his ear. 'Enjoying the scenery, sergeant?'

He spun round, and smiled wanly by way of a reply. His breath smelt of antiseptic mouthwash.

'Come on, Dexter,' yelled the superintendent, 'get your coat on. I could do with some fresh country air.'

Matlock sank away behind them as the unmarked police car threaded to the top of the narrow road. It jostled between the houses of an exposed hamlet and Blanche glimpsed the hill on the far side of the valley scud up to form the Heights of Abraham. They crested a last hillock bathed in wintry sunlight and plunged into a tunnel of gloom. The trees had woven such a dense canopy over the road that Dexter was temporarily blinded by the darkness and his right foot leapt to the brake. It was fortunate that he did because otherwise the superintendent might have missed the turning on the right, discreetly hidden in a murky thicket. The car bumped up the unmetalled drive, clambering towards the sunlight again. They passed a detached house on the brow of a hill to the left and finally squelched to a stop in a farmyard, deserted except for a mangy dog that snapped at the tyres of their car with rabid enthusiasm.

Eighty yards ahead Hebden's house looked down at them, trapped in a loop of the road as it cricked to the right and disappeared into a copse of trees. The building oozed a melancholy yet defiant air, cornered by an unforgiving landscape with which it refused to make any compromises. To Blanche its four front windows – lozenges of deep blue reflecting the sky – seemed to follow every movement of her body, like the eyes of prisoners gazing through the bars of their cells. The superintendent, through politeness and self-interest, had phoned the local collator at Matlock to check out Hebden's address. The journalist was not known to the local CID and did not have a shotgun certificate.

Dexter parked in the lee of a mouldering barn, the roof

83

speckled by the blue of the sky where the corrugated iron had rusted away to air. The dog, its hair knotted with mud, continued to bark at them with surprising ferocity. 'Shut up,' hissed the sergeant with a grim smile, 'or I'll sell you to the nearest Indian restaurant.'

The dog either understood the threat or concluded its barking was having no effect, for it scampered away to an enamel bath stranded in the middle of a neighbouring field. On the other side of the valley the land heaved upwards, drystone wall upon drystone wall, curve interlocking into curve, until the slope broke into a crest of bare trees. The air was cloyed by so much moisture that even the November grass was green and lush. The Derbyshire stone from which the houses had been built did not seem to bathe in the wintry sunlight but swallow it up. Blanche shivered.

John Hebden's wife flung open the front door so heartily that the superintendent supposed she was expecting some- one else. The smile melted from the fat, plain face when Blanche introduced herself. Mrs Hebden said her husband was out walking but would be back 'any minute'.

'What is it you want to talk to him about?' she asked nerv- ously, leading them into the cluttered sitting-room.

There was a twee nostalgia lurking among the pot-pourris, dried flowers and mezzotint scenes of country life on the walls that did not appeal to the superintendent. 'A girl called Patricia Hoskin.'

A protective look flared in Mrs Hebden's face. 'John's got nothing to do with that terrible murder, if that's what you're thinking. He finished with her several months before she was killed you know.' It was not, Blanche reflected, a particularly attractive face. Susan Hebden had eyes that were sewn like buttons on either side of a prominent nose; lank, black hair that was already streaked with grey, and pinched lips. There was not a speck of make-up discernible on her skin and she was overweight, rolling her barrel of a body around the house with a frenetic air. Although her woollen dress was scarlet it nonetheless appeared drab.

The affair between her husband and Patricia Hoskin, she told them, had lasted for about a year. She had known about it for some time but allowed it to continue, thinking that John would see sense and finish with his mistress. 'And that's precisely what happened,' she added with a smile of self-satisfaction. 'The girl put pressure on him to choose between her and us and he chose us. It's as simple as that.' Looking into her stare, Blanche guessed that things were *not* as simple as that. Susan Hebden's eyes looked bruised from sleepless nights, still puffed from shedding the tears of the betrayed. She looked every second of her forty-one years.

'Why did your husband go back to London on Tuesday, by the way?' Dexter prodded with exaggerated casualness. He lounged by the window, his eyes caressing the roadway for any sign of Hebden's return.

'He had work to do. A couple of interviews,' she snapped with a certain smugness.

Blanche could tell the woman was desperate to hide her concern: her voice had slid up a semi-tone. 'Did he contact you at all on Tuesday night or Wednesday morning?'

She looked up with renewed hope in her eyes. 'Yes, he did actually. About nine o'clock in the evening on Tuesday. He rang to say everything was OK and that he'd be back up here in the morning.'

Dexter waved a languid hand at Blanche as a pre-arranged signal that their quarry was in sight. The conversation stumbled on for another minute or so before two children ran past the window, their heads bobbing along the sill. A handsome man, clean-shaven and thoughtful, in a Barbour jacket meandered along after them. Blanche heard a crash as the back door was flung open, followed by whoops and screams and the scraping of furniture, and then the clatter of feet along the hall. They exploded into the room – a girl of about five with a fringe of albino-white hair and her slightly older sister. 'Mummy', was all the younger girl managed to shout before the word froze on her lips and her panting body collapsed with surprise at finding two strangers in the sitting-room. The tick of the Edwardian wall-clock bounced from wall to wall.

Another cry – breathless yet somehow imperious, Blanche considered – trumpeted from the kitchen, as though from across the valley. 'I'm ho-ome. Where aaarrree yoouu?' A second later John Hebden strode in. Although he was fit and tanned, and six feet tall with the chiselled features of a male model, he had a faintly ridiculous air because he was in his stockinged feet. He had obviously taken off his wellington boots in the kitchen and not bothered to pull on a pair of shoes. The superintendent divined from the self-conscious way he carried himself that Hebden wished he had. The sparkling white pullover and newly pressed black corduroys were designed to project an image of calm sophistication. Blanche wondered why he had married the plain woman who sat brooding beside the fireplace: probably, she thought, for that most universal of reasons, on the one side a burning love and on the other a willingness to bask in it.

Hebden narrowed his eyes. 'Who the hell are you?' His voice was classless and without a detectable regional accent, the voice of the handsome men in television advertisements.

'Metropolitan Police,' said Blanche, rising from her chair and proffering her warrant card like a box of chocolates. A twitch of concern flickered across his brow.

Galvanised suddenly, Susan Hebden jumped up and dragged the children out of the room, the youngest daughter staring open-mouthed at Dexter.

The journalist looked from one police officer to the other and asked why they had come. Blanche explained while Dexter fingered a notebook. 'I know nothing about Pat's murder,' he said simply, choosing his words with the same care he lavished on his appearance.

Blanche nodded thoughtfully. Hebden – as well as thousands of other men – fitted the description of the man seen leaving the murdered girl's flat on Tuesday night, the man described by the old lady who gave her Alsatian nocturnal walks. 'I'm sure. But could you just fill me in a bit about your relationship with her? When and why it ended for example?'

He shrugged at Dexter with a grin of supposed innocence and splayed his hands in puzzlement. 'What's this got to do with the murder?'

The sergeant smiled back, rather too warmly for Blanche's taste. She hoped he did not fancy the man they were interviewing. It might raise conflicts of interest.

'What's this got to do with the murder?' repeated Blanche. 'Everything or nothing. That's why I'm asking.'

Hebden sighed and tapped his long, slim fingers on the arm of the chair into which he had eased himself. He spoke quickly, as if reporting to a busy committee whose time was valuable. Blanche had seen the tactic deployed before by senior police officers who were trying to impress. 'Pat and I had an affair, right? We met at an office party almost a year ago. Back in August she suddenly started taking things a bit too seriously – saying she wanted me to leave Sue and the girls. Well,' he continued, instinctively but mistakenly turning to Dexter for male sympathy, 'there wasn't really a choice, was there? So I broke it off and that's all there is to say.'

'Is it?' queried Blanche, half closing one eyelid with concentration. She was irritated by his smoothness and had the same primeval desire to scratch it as a vandal has to deface a newly-painted wall. She wanted to surprise him, shock him out of his complacency. 'Is that why you phoned your wife from Pat's flat on Tuesday night then – before you murdered her?'

'How do you – ' The journalist cut himself short. His head turned accusingly towards the kitchen as he realised where the superintendent had gleaned the information. His lips tightened into a crooked smile. 'Look, er . . . ' Hebden's tongue slid across his perfect set of teeth. 'I was in London for some interviews because I had a feature to write. I phoned my wife from home around eight or nine in the evening, spent the night there and drove back up the next day.'

Dexter flicked over a page of his notebook. 'Can anyone back up your story?'

He pondered for a moment. 'No, unfortunately.'

Blanche pressed on. 'Did you see Pat when you were down in London?'

He paused again before replying, as if the question contained a hidden trap. 'No, I didn't see her.' His eyes swivelled away to the window and the bleak landscape outside, his blue eyes clouded by memories he was not willing to share. Blanche thought once again how much easier her police work would be if she could see into people's minds, slot their thoughts like a videotape into a machine and play them on a screen, cut through their evasions and hypocrisy and go straight to the truth. He stood up abruptly. 'Now if you'd care to leave I'd be most grateful.'

Blanche glued on a conciliatory smile and did not move. 'I'm afraid we can't go yet. We need your fingerprints, Mr Hebden, and I'd also like to ask you some more questions.'

The journalist moved towards the door. 'Well, you can't do that until my solicitor's here. I'm not answering any more of your questions. Thanks for coming all the way up from London to disturb my holiday.' He smiled, the fake smile of a man used to talking his way out of tight corners.

Blanche rose and picked up her handbag, her neck cricked and one eye squinting with concentration. Hebden's smile widened to a smirk with the relief of victory: the superintendent was about to leave.

Only then did Blanche draw herself up to her full five feet ten inches and arrest him. The journalist blinked at her for a few seconds before his tanned face collapsed, reminding Blanche of one of her unsuccessful soufflés. She gave him five minutes to pack an overnight bag under Dexter's supervision and say farewell to his family.

In Matlock, the superintendent stopped the car first at a record shop to buy some music tapes for the journey. From a garage on the ascent out of the town she phoned the incident room. She ordered Detective Sergeant Wootton to prepare a certificate to authorise the search of Hebden's house she would make that night, and to organise an identity parade tomorrow morning with the old lady who saw the man leave Patricia Hoskin's flat.

By the time the unmarked police car was thumping down the motorway to London, the sun teetered on the horizon. The dark landscape had started to exhale a mist which rolled across the service lane and tugged a white curtain across the margins of their vision. Above the tarmac endless blurs of sodium lights receded into the distance. Blanche settled in her back seat next to Hebden and unwrapped the music cassettes she had bought in Matlock. She tossed one onto the front seat next to Dexter and asked him to play it.

The majesty of the opening bars of the *St Matthew Passion* swelled to fill the car. Dexter grimaced and raised his eyes to the sun visor. 'Not this load of old tat again,' he groaned,

88

leaving one ring-laden hand on the steering-wheel of the hurtling car while tapping a cigarette from its packet.

'Not to your taste, sergeant?' enquired Blanche with mock politeness.

'Give me a bit of Motown or soul rather than this crap any day.' The car's cigarette lighter popped out and the sergeant raised the glowing red metal to his lips. 'I'll probably fall asleep at the wheel.'

'Just shut up and listen, Dexter. It's good for your education,' sighed Blanche good-naturedly. 'If you start nodding off I'll just hit you over the head with my handbag.'

Dexter exhaled smoke with a snort of discontent.

Blanche turned to Hebden, who sat slumped in the corner of the seat, staring out into the gathering night. He had said nothing since he hugged his children goodbye and the car had bumped down the drive to the main road. 'Does this music mean anything to you, Mr Hebden?' She almost had to shout over the roar of the engine and the volume of the music.

He did not move. He seemed to be listening to the undulating, sad richness of the music or else to his own thoughts and regrets. Blanche waited. There was something attentive about the way the journalist sat that made her sure he had heard. He finally turned to her, shook his head slowly from side to side and swung back to contemplate the dusk. In those brief moments, by the brindled light, Blanche saw that his eyes glittered with tears.

# 9

The voices began early on Saturday morning. Although David was not sure whether they woke him or whether he simply became aware of them when he prised his eyes open at twenty-three minutes past six, the important point was that the voices existed. The bedroom was dark, the heavy curtains drawn against a sun that still had to heave itself into the winter sky. Once he had established the time from the digits on the radio alarm clock, David yanked his eyelids together again. Outside in the road he detected a chilled car-engine being hounded into life. Inside the room he could distinctly hear his own breathing – the sharp intake of air, followed by the slower exhalation. But he was not alone. Voices were murmuring in the fitted wardrobes at the foot of his double bed. They were indistinct at first, like the hum of conversation at a drinks party. As he listened in his self-imposed darkness, David became able to distil certain words, certain phrases, that were repeated over and over again like a Buddhist mantra. 'Something eat something body,' they chanted, 'something something something.' The relentless beat of the words swung like the clapper of a bell against the inside of his skull.

Thinking he was sunk in a dream and that the voice would be stilled as soon as he awoke, David grasped for the switch of his bedside lamp. An oval of light flashed onto the ceiling, sending out an elongated shadow from the lampshade in the centre. By his bed was the same spy thriller, still open at the page where he had left it. The chair was the same ghost beneath the pile of clothes he had smothered it under seven hours before. Ahead of him, sitting up in bed, reflected in the mirrors on the front of all the fitted wardrobes, was David – his eyes deep-set, brown hair tousled, with a look of apprehension on his face. From the wardrobe the mysterious

90

incantation rippled. 'Something eat something body, something something something.' David was convinced someone was playing a trick on him. Perhaps his neighbour, a salesman with a penchant for the latest electronic gadgets, had drilled through the wall and pushed through a loudspeaker like some loathsome weed which manages to sprout even through concrete. He had read of the British intelligence services installing microphones in just this way.

David threw back the bedclothes. The voices still issued from the wardrobe, juggling the words that he found incomprehensible yet fascinating, comforting yet disturbing. As he crawled down the bed towards his own reflection, the sounds focussed slightly. 'Something eat something body something something saved.' David edged towards the mirrors, his breathing hoarse with expectation, and grasped two knobs on the wardrobe doors, one in each hand. 'Something eat something body something something saved.' He slung the doors back. The voices were cut off as suddenly as the squeaks of a mouse were stifled by the lightning grip of his python.

As much through frustration as curiosity, David dumped suits, shirts, jackets and trousers on the bed while he searched through the wardrobe, ever more frantic, until finally he dropped to his knees to examine the floor, tossing shoes over his shoulder.

He found nothing. No tape recorders. No loudspeakers. No microphones. Nothing. David sat on the carpet in his silk pyjamas, contemplating his image in the mirrors and the silence in his room, wondering if he was going mad. The disappearance of the voices had bequeathed him a gnawing sense of loss, as though a vision of unimaginable beauty had faded, leaving behind nothing except the memory.

The voices returned later that morning when he went shopping for Pamela. David parked near Finchley Road and was walking up the hill towards the supermarket. A voice called to him from under the eaves of a house – four-storey and built of brick. It seemed familiar, a woman's voice, but David could not make out what she was saying. He stared at the wooden, carved eaves intently, straining his ears to catch the sense. But the voice was too far away. He gazed upwards until

91

a lace curtain flicked back and he realised an elderly woman with white hair was studying him suspiciously. He flushed with embarrassment and turned away.

More voices began to call and gibber from other houses, and everywhere he saw signs that the familiar world was disintegrating. Subsidence and decay multiplied while he watched – garden walls buckled, cracks in buildings widened, the uneven pavement heaved like a living sea. A frieze of patterned terracotta tiles ran round the houses at the level of the first floor and the flower motif throbbed in the wintry sunlight. The pattern, he remembered, echoed the one on the tiles of Patricia Hoskin's house in Clapham. David leant against an abandoned supermarket trolley and closed his eyes while he counted to thirty. The voices slowly faded. He heard a car drive by.

When he opened his eyes again, the street and its noises were back to normal – the colours, the solidity, the sounds. But he rubbed his forefinger guiltily against his top lip while he pondered the implications of a new insight. The woman's voice calling to him from the eaves, he realised, was that of his dead mother.

David was swept into the Saturday morning rush at the supermarket, sucked past the line of cashiers and corralled by the metal rail guiding customers into the store. The vegetable section was straight ahead. A man in a green nylon jacket was stacking up apples. David took out the list Pamela had given him and skimmed through the columns of neat, rounded handwriting. He smiled to himself. He felt better, normal again.

As if to prove it, his eyes were snared by a girl dressed in an outfit made of pink towelling. It was a jump suit which stretched from just below the knees to her neck but so tight that it clung to every hillock and crevice of her body. David was mesmerised by her buttocks, the material clenched between the cheeks like a second skin, while the pornographic effect was heightened by cream stiletto heels and the bracelet that glistened round her left ankle.

She was selecting mushrooms but David hardly glanced at her face – it was a blur of auburn hair and cosmetics. He tried to imagine what it would be like to peel off the outfit from the girl, dragging it down softly from her shoulders, to disclose the tender flesh beneath. He wished a girl like this had replied to his advert.

He loped across in his shy, shambling way, flicking his eyes across to her. He was dressed neatly in grey flannel trousers, jacket and blue striped shirt, his hair still glistening from the shower. He plucked a couple of plastic bags from the roll above the shelf and filled them with broccoli and cabbage: another thing David did not like about Pamela was her conservatism as a cook. His eyes slithered across the bewildering array of other vegetables – the clutches of garlic, dwarf custard marrow, sugar peas, semi-dried prunes, hazelnut kernels, pecan nut halves – and he wondered how they would taste on his tongue. His gaze moved along steadily until it rested on the mushrooms – chestnut mushrooms, shiitake mushrooms, field mushrooms. The girl had gone.

She queued by the weighing counter now with a pout of arrogance. A sullen Indian, his face cratered by acne, was taking plastic bags from the customers and placing them one by one on the automatic scales. The girl's throat was white and soft and David's fingers tingled with the fantasy of caressing it gently and then watching her expression as they suddenly clamped like a vice. That would make the little tart look less sure of herself, David thought. The girl caught David's stare and he turned away, scalded by her glance.

In front of him now were Galia melons, their skin veined like a hand. He squeezed one and his fingers sank into the soft flesh. With an inward smile he remembered the crude connection often made between melons and women's breasts, and he tossed the fruit he held into his trolley. David passed by the lemons and babaco. Pamela wanted some kiwi fruit. He selected some daintily, repelled by their hairy skin.

The girl had left the weighing counter. How could he approach her? Could he knock his trolley into hers? Pretend to recognise her as a client? Or should he just go over and invite her out?

Clementines, Dan Ben Hannah grapes, sturmer apples, red plums – his eyes passed over them all, glazed with other thoughts. David pushed his trolley frantically along the aisles, bustling with lust to see the girl again. He passed the conserves, tinned vegetables, pasta, snacks and chilled meals without even a glance at the displays. They were all a motley blur of colours. He shouldered past one woman with a screaming baby propped up in the back of a trolley, and knocked into an elderly man with a walking-stick who cursed him through ill-fitting dentures. Then, in a gap between a display of Indian pickles and frozen Black Forest gateau – he even noticed and remembered this bizarre detail – he glimpsed the pink outfit like a beacon. He stood transfixed, a voyeur feasting on the swell of the girl's buttocks and the erotic shadow that marked the edge of her panties.

She was standing at the meat shelf, scanning the plastic packets. David decided to approach her more directly this time. He pushed his trolley round the end of his aisle and stopped. The girl had been joined by a tall man in his forties, wearing an expensive olive-green sweater and a look of mean thuggery, and together they walked away.

David felt angry and betrayed. He told himself he had no rights over the girl and that he should have realised before that she had a husband or boyfriend. The disappointment burned nonetheless. He picked up one of the packets of boneless chicken breasts she had handled and examined the mottled, creamy-purple skin and the raw, pink blotch where the knife had cut the bone. Through the smooth plastic, it was impossible to feel the texture of the meat, only sense its chillness. How unlike the flesh of a certain girl . . . But as soon as his mind conjured the memory of Patricia Hoskin lying dead before him, his hands exploring the still warm flesh of her half-naked body, David switched off the projector in his brain. He forced his attention back onto the chicken legs, the chicken quarters, and then the thighs – smaller, neater, trussed – all in lines, then the skinned chicken breasts lying on display like flayed saints or Marsyas, the chops, quiet, each slab of pink meat edged with creamy fat, a dash of red near the chopped bone, then the catalogue of beef boneless leg roasts trussed with string lamb cutlets smaller neater osso bucco with little veins of white fat the bone in the centre pink with marrow and finally the beef whose blood oozed onto David's hands blood he could not wipe off sticky blood drying on his hands like paint the meat red and succulent the

94

blood on his fingers and suddenly all went black.

'Are you alright, young man?' The woman knelt beside him, her voice thick with the accent of middle Europe. Her words seemed to be filtered through water: David felt he was lying at the bottom of a pond with her gazing down at him from the fresh air above. Under a cardigan, she wore a thick dress seeded with red, pink and blue flowers. 'You must have fainted all of a sudden, because I heard a sort of crumpling sound, turned round and found you on the floor.' Instinctively, she rested her calloused palm on his forehead. David felt too enervated to resist. He coldly noted the blur of the moustache above her upper lip, the helmet of permed hair and her winged spectacles. He lay on his back next to the meat counter, staring up at the ceiling.

A shop assistant wearing a white coat scurried into the circle of his vision. She wore pearl ear-rings and had brown, blow-dried hair and a bad complexion. 'Manager'll be 'ere in a sec,' she mumbled, wiping her pale hands on her coat.

'Can you sit up now?' asked the elderly lady with grey hair. 'Come on, don't just stand there, give me a hand,' she barked at the shop assistant.

Just as they propped David up against the side of the display counter, the manager strode self-importantly along the aisle. A small crowd had gathered, craning their necks towards David, and muttering. The manager was a tall, thin man with a harassed expression on his pale face. 'How are you feeling now then, sir? Can we call you an ambulance?'

A dull ache throbbed at the back of David's head. He rubbed it gingerly and wondered whether his skull had cracked against the tiled floor when he fell. But he could feel no bump and when he brought his hand back into view, the only blood he saw was stained into his palms. It was not his gore. He vaguely recalled blood leaking from a pack of liver or beef which he had picked up. 'Sorry?' he asked vaguely, absorbed in his own thoughts.

'I said can we call an ambulance for you, sir?'

David shook his head. He looked from face to face with a sense of panic. All he wanted to do was wash his hands thoroughly in hot water and be left alone. He hated being the object of public attention and ridicule like some fairground mountebank. On the other hand he did not want to attract even more notice by being rude. The throbbing in his brain slowly subsided and the solicitor staggered to his feet. 'No, thank you. I'm OK again now. It happens sometimes,' he lied. 'I really don't want an ambulance.' His trolley stood forlornly a few yards away, crammed with food for the dinner party. It reminded him of why he was there. David smiled inwardly. Although he was concerned by his collapse, it might be useful. He could exploit it as a reason to avoid the looming dinner party at Pamela's. 'I'd be grateful if you could do me a favour though.'

The manager adjusted his spectacles with a solicitous nod.

David pointed to the trolley. 'I wondered if you could organise a taxi to take these things over to my fiancée. She lives quite close. I just want to go straight home, you see.'

David refused the invitation to go to the manager's office for a cup of tea. All he wanted to do was escape from the people observing him. He scribbled out Pamela's address on a scrap of paper and an open cheque to cover the cost of the groceries and the taxi. 'Tell the driver to tell Pamela I'll give her a ring when I get home.'

He felt normal again now except for a strange urge calling him home. For reasons of diplomacy, he did not want to appear fully recovered, so he murmured some thanks and asked where he could wash his hands. David walked with theatrical slowness towards the door indicated by the manager at the back of the supermarket.

The manager started to follow but David turned on him with a convalescent scowl. 'I'd rather go by myself, thank you.' He held out his stained hands. 'I think you'd be better employed making sure your meat didn't leak blood all over your customers.'

'Oh you *poor* darling,' exclaimed Pamela, when he phoned an hour later lying on the bed. 'How are you feeling?'

'Absolutely exhausted,' he groaned truthfully. 'I don't think I'll be up to your dinner party tonight. I'm sorry.' He tried to inject as much contrition as he could into the last phrase.

'Are you *sure?*' She sounded very disappointed and David knew she was suppressing her exasperation. 'I'd arranged tonight *specially* so you could meet some more of my friends before we got married. I've already had to cancel Jenny and Henry once already.' She sighed deeply to try to win his sympathy. *'Please.'*

David turned to the grey blank of the window. Since his visit to the supermarket the sky had clouded over and now a drizzle was spotting the glass. 'No. I'm sorry, darling, I'm in bed already,' he lied. 'I'm going to spend the rest of the day here.'

'Do you think you should see a doctor?'

'Oh, no, of course not,' he snapped with a warmth that he regretted. He softened his voice. 'What I meant was . . . it was just a faint. Probably a spot of food poisoning or something. And I don't want to trouble the doctor with it. I just want to be left alone and have a quiet day in bed.'

'OK.' She paused. 'I could come over to see you this afternoon – '

'That's sweet of you. But there's no need for that. You've got to prepare for the dinner party.' He knew that she became nervous when she invited people round, fussing over minor details, and that she was offering to visit him through a sense of duty.

'Are you sure, David? I mean I'm more than happy – '

'Oh, no, no. You stay at home and get things ready for tonight.'

With a gasp of relief, he replaced the receiver. He *did* feel tired but the prospect of a day at home alone was cheering. He was behind with his work and enjoyed sitting hunched in the warm cocoon of light from his desk lamp, the papers from a complicated case spread out before the word-processor. He would be free of the tedious social obligations and distractions of the office: small talk, silly questions from articled clerks and colleagues, the constant buzz of the telephone.

He kicked off his shoes and lay back on the bed. As soon as his eyes closed, however, a jumble of images jostled for attention: the girl in the supermarket, her buttocks swelling before him, his mother dead in her coffin, Patricia Hoskin splayed on the sofa. And with these memories the voices began softly to speak again. 'Something eat something body something something saved something eat something body something something saved.' This time they were not murmuring to him from the wardrobe but from the lower depths of the house. David flicked open his eyes. The images of female flesh disappeared. But the voices remained, still chanting their mysterious incantation. David found his lips fluttering out the words in time with the invisible chorus. 'Something eat something body something something saved.' As he spoke, his body grew taut and tense with expectation. His muscles were hard as wood, locked in a pain of waiting, waiting for a touch to release them.

As his lips joined the chorus, David found the words grow clearer. He felt himself dragged from the bed, his legs and arms quivering with restlessness. The anguish of the tension continued as he moved towards the open door. 'Come eat something body and you something be saved come eat something body and you shall be saved.' Although the words seemed a parody of a biblical quotation, David found himself profoundly moved by them. The words seemed to offer hope of escape from the agony on which he was skewered. With the stiff movements of a robot he stumbled down the stairs towards the source of the voices, his throat suddenly parched with thirst. 'Come eat of my body and you shall be saved come eat of my body and you shall be saved come eat of my body and you shall be saved.'

David entered the kitchen, all the muscles of his body tingling, as though an electric current were being passed through his skin. Embarrassingly he sensed the warm comfort of an erection in the crotch of his trousers, the first since Tuesday night in Patricia's company. He stood at the kitchen door, clenching and unclenching his fingers, listening to the voices.

Like a man who had not eaten for days, he threw open the freezer compartment of the refrigerator. A white smoke of frost rolled over his hands while they sorted frenetically through the packets of frozen vegetables, meals, chops and steaks. At the back, behind a loaf of bread frozen as hard as a plank, was the package he had been told to seek: a supermarket plastic bag folded around something the size of a paperback book. The bag was encrusted with ice which splintered to the floor as David unfolded it with trembling fingers. He was ravenous, saliva already slopping in his mouth, his stomach quaking with hunger. He stood for a moment, cradling the frozen flesh in his hand, knowing it was to provide his salvation from guilt and escape from his own core of darkness.

As he gorged himself on the grilled meat, David sensed the tension and panic ebb from his limbs. The girl's flesh tasted little different from that of other animals but the effects on David were deep. He experienced release and happiness for the first time since October. He no longer felt responsible for the death of his mother: it was fate, she was destined to die. The same was true for Patricia Hoskin.

A drowsiness stole over him. David just managed to stagger up the stairs before collapsing onto the bed. He curled into a ball, and tumbled into a profound sleep.

# 10

When Blanche entered the interview room with Dexter, the woman was sitting alone. She cradled a polystyrene cup of tea in her left hand while her right held a cheap filter cigarette between her fore and middle fingers in a gesture of surprising delicacy. The elderly lady looked up through her miasma of smoke and pinched her face into a tight little smile. The superintendent held out her hand and introduced herself and Dexter.

'Nice to meet ya,' the woman replied, before nodding towards the sergeant. 'I've already met the spade. Seems a nice lad.'

'That's what they all say, Mrs Jones,' Dexter grinned. "Til they get to know the real me.'

She flicked on her nervous smile again in lieu of a reply. Blanche concluded the lady who sat in front of her, the lady who saw a man leave Patricia Hoskin's house on the night of the murder, was not used to dealing with authority. She distrusted words as tools of the rich and clever, and with that objectivity that comes more easily to the old, she thought of herself as neither. Her clothes, the superintendent noticed, were cheap, ill-matched and threadbare, as if she had bought them at a jumble sale: a mock-sheepskin coat, unbuttoned at the front to reveal a pea-green cardigan over a blouse whose neck was fraying, and a pair of blue nylon slacks. The outfit was the sartorial equivalent of the patterned carpets that shrieked at Blanche from a shabby store in Northfields where she sometimes did her shopping. But the clothes were all clean and neat. Mrs Jones, Blanche reflected with approval, might have little money but she issued from that generation that believed in personal cleanliness. Since her husband had died fifteen years before the old lady had rented a floor of a house in Clapham as a sitting tenant, eking out her seventy years on a state pension.

Blanche, whose enjoyment in wearing elegant clothes was matched only by resentment at their ludicrous cost, suddenly felt over-dressed. Her own suit in a fine check of grey-brown and cream was now five years old, the fruit of a sweaty and expensive dash round the January sales to celebrate her promotion to inspector. Although sporting a designer label and of classic design, the jacket was now starting to show the ineluctable signs of age: the cut was no longer high fashion and the fine woollen material was burred at the neck and wrist where it was beginning to fray.

Mrs Jones had obviously made an effort to dress up for the occasion. The lines on her high forehead and the broken blood vessels on her cheeks were partially hidden under a veil of face powder, and she had dragged a bright red lipstick around her mouth. Her newly permed hair was wispy and dyed blonde. But Blanche noticed Mrs Jones's tiny eyes, almost concealed among the wrinkles of powdered skin, shone with intelligence: she was nobody's fool.

'The sergeant has explained how the identity parade will work, has he, Mrs Jones?'

She smiled again in reply, her face dimpling.

The uniformed inspector who was in charge of the ID parade appeared a few moments later to pick up Mrs Jones. He was clutching the twenty-page booklet, known as Form 6/20, which had to be filled in at each stage of the identity parade to ensure the correct procedures were followed. He was tall, clean-shaven and softly spoken, with a ready smile to put Mrs Jones at ease. Blanche had seen him about the station before and trusted him. As the young inspector shepherded the old lady away down the corridor towards the snooker room, Blanche knew there was nothing more she could do but wait. The law stated that she could not be directly involved with the identity parade. If she stood and watched there was always the risk Hebden's solicitor might suggest she had interfered with the witness, and, if Mrs Jones were to give a positive identification, her evidence was too valuable to risk simply to satisfy Blanche's curiosity. Rather than fret in the interview room, the superintendent wandered back to her office to do some paperwork. 'Call me when you've got a result will you please, Dexter?'

The chairs in the snooker room had been cleared to one end and ten men stood in a straggly line near the left-hand wall. Hebden was the fourth from the end. Although there were three slit-like windows high up near the ceiling behind them, most of the illumination came from six strip-lights caged behind boxes of frosted glass. The walls were painted cream, the plaster pitted and flaking where it had been knocked by the chairs. The snooker table stood, dark and forlorn, in the centre of the room.

The men garnered from the streets of Clapham for the identity parade stirred when the old lady walked in, like a herd of sheep scenting a dog enter their field. They were a motley crowd, united only by their fleeting resemblance to the description of the man seen leaving the house. A couple were dressed in suits, some in leather jackets, some in pullovers. The inspector led Mrs Jones over to the start of the line and reminded her that she did not need to hurry and should only identify someone if she was absolutely certain that it was the man she saw on Tuesday night. Some of the men coughed and instinctively drew themselves to attention. One of the youngest, dressed in a black leather jacket with a stud in his left ear, continued to smoke his cigarette, cradling his right elbow in the palm of his left hand. On the floor, in front of each man, was a small square of white, laminated plastic. Each bore a number printed in black.

Hebden looked ahead impassively while the old lady made her pass along the line. The only sounds in the room were the shuffling of the old lady's feet over the plastic tiles and the hum of an electric clock. Mrs Jones lingered frequently to peer at the faces. Most of the men preferred to avoid her glance, either gazing round the room or studying their shoes with intense interest. She stopped for a moment in front of Hebden, whose nose crinkled into a sneer, before pushing her stiff limbs on to the next man. A night in police cells had scraped Hebden's smoothness: his sandy hair was no longer so immaculately styled, four black spots of dried blood showed where he had nicked himself while shaving, and his clothes were crumpled.

When Mrs Jones shuffled across to the inspector, her face was benign and placid, impossible to read. She flashed her false teeth apologetically. 'Can I 'ave another look, please? Just to make sure?'

Hebden's solicitor, who sat at the back of the room, struggled to suppress a yawn.

The old lady hobbled along the line again, pausing almost for half a minute each in front of a besuited man and the slovenly individual with the studded ear. The uniformed sergeant coughed and from the corner of his eye the inspector saw him surreptitiously scratch his testicles through his trouser pockets. Hebden's face had collapsed back into a mask of indifference and Mrs Jones shuffled past him without a second glance.

Hebden's solicitor stalked across the room. By law any identification must be made out loud. 'Well?' asked the inspector.

A glitter of certainty twinkled in Mrs Jones's eyes. 'Oh, 'e's there alright. Number seven, the fourth one from the end,' she said, glancing towards Hebden. 'Wouldn't think 'e was a murdering bastard, would yer?'

Hebden refused to breach his silence after the identity parade. He also refused to comment on two things that Blanche had found when searching his house on the way down from Derbyshire: a key to Patricia Hoskin's flat and a lock of hair of the same colour as the dead girl's. The hair looked as though it were smeared with dried blood. Apart from protesting his innocence, Hebden had said nothing of importance since the drive down to London. Blanche abandoned her interrogatory monologue after an hour and wandered back to the incident room with Dexter, her sergeant whining about how hard he had been forced to work recently, so hard that he had been unable to complete the planting of his bulbs and write off for the winter seed catalogues – Dexter's only obsession apart from handsome men, whom he preferred, as he described it himself, 'blond, clean and legal', was his roof terrace.

The incident room hummed with the pleasing sound of industry. Girls now sat at the computer terminals, tapping intermittently with glum looks on their faces. The few detectives who were not out making enquiries sat or stood around the office, some on the telephone, some making notes, others simply chatting. Blanche noted with a little pride – she had a lot but preferred to ration her deployment of it – that even some of the tasks allocated for that day on the action boards screwed to the walls had been fulfilled.

Sergeant Wootton waddled over to acknowledge Blanche, his thighs almost splitting the trousers of his suit. His wide-rimmed spectacles always looked to her as if vaseline had been wiped over the lenses and the fact that his tiny eyes were always blurred gave him an even greater conspiratorial air. He wiped the sweat from his wide brow and hitched his belt up over his nascent paunch. 'No news yet from forensic on the stuff you found at Hebden's house, ma'am,' he mumbled, pausing slightly before the last word to imbue it with ironic emphasis. Blanche scrutinised his round, bland face for any sign of insubordination but all she saw was a mask of ill-shaven skin.

Blanche was about to plunge into her impromptu office when her attention was snagged by a gold-fish bowl on Dexter's desk. Inside a fish hung motionless in the water, its fins ruffled by an invisible current. On the bottom of the bowl on a bed of gravel was an artificial rock in the form of a skull, the brain cavity hollow so that the fish could swim in and out through the eye sockets and the open jaw. 'What's the idea of this, Dexter?' she asked with mock seriousness. 'I thought this was a Murder Squad, not a zoo.'

The sergeant lifted an admonitory finger, the palm of his hand much paler than the rest of his skin, the counterfeit Rolex watch on his wrist coming into view as the immaculate white cuff slipped back. 'Ah,' he said, 'there's much more to this fish than meets the eye. You see he's a computer aid.'

Blanche hoisted her left eyebrow. 'Really?'

'You see, when we've got a tricky problem that the computer can't solve, or more to the point that *we* can't solve, we call on Gregory here.' He pointed to the fish and smiled.

Knowing Dexter as she did, the superintendent guessed there was a good reason for the choice of name, probably connected with Catholic theology. And she was right. The sergeant treated his faith with serious frivolity. Their conversation was gathering a small crowd. Blanche did not mind: a Murder Squad could not afford to be serious all the time.

'I decided to call him Gregory, after the saint. Not Gregory the Enlightener,' and as he enumerated the saints, Dexter counted them off on his long fingers, 'Gregory the Great, Gregory the Seventh, Gregory of Nazianzus, Gregory of Nyssa, Gregory of Sinai, Gregory of Tours, or Gregory of Utrecht.'

'Which fuckin' Gregory was it then, sergeant?' asked one of the constables.

'Gregory the Wonderworker of course, famed for his miracles and the first recorded person to whom the Virgin Mary appeared in a vision. I think we're going to need a few miracles on this case.'

Blanche could tell that the sergeant had prepared his routine like one of the costermongers selling useless gadgets along the Portobello Road and smiled indulgently. He had already reached into a drawer and pulled out two index cards. On one was written 'YES' and on the other 'NO' – both in Dexter's rather childlike hand. 'It's simple. You put a card on either side of the gold-fish bowl and whichever one Greg swims towards is the right answer.' He held out his long arms with a broad smile: the costermonger thought the customers had been convinced by his *spiel*. 'Gregory the Wonderworker.'

'Let's try him out then shall we?' suggested Blanche.

'Sure,' drawled the sergeant, placing a card on either side of the bowl. 'What's the question?'

The superintendent crouched down so that her nose was almost pressing against the glass. There were hundreds of questions she would like to ask the piscine sibyl if she had faith in the power of prophecy. Would she ever find a man who loved and understood her? Would she ever have children? What would she be doing in ten, twenty, forty years time? But Blanche only had faith in herself – that sometimes glimmering like a distant star – and faith in the power of reason. There were too many false prophets in the world already without relying on gold-fish. But she had allowed the game to go too far now to retreat, and it was, she told herself, only a game. She smiled at the faces clustered round to show she meant the whole event to be treated as a joke but nonetheless a hush fell while she asked the question in her clipped, aristocratic voice. 'Did John Hebden murder Patricia Hoskin?'

The fish seemed to stare at her with its bulbous eyes, occasionally flicking a fin to retain its balance. Blanche's breath misted the side of the bowl, her lipstick leaving a smudge on the glass. Suddenly, as if he had pondered long enough on Hebden's guilt, Gregory whipped his tail and disappeared into the skull – half way between the two cards.

The gnomic reply to Blanche's question led to an outburst of laughter and the knot of men broke up and drifted back to work. When the superintendent stood up she saw Wootton standing a few yards away. He was regarding Dexter and the gold-fish bowl with disdain.

Dexter glanced at the fish bowl. Gregory had still not emerged. 'What with the positive ID and the lock of hair we found last night, I don't see why Greg needed to hedge his bets.'

Blanche stood thoughtfully in the centre of the office. Nothing had been confirmed yet, of course, but the evidence was certainly accumulating against Hebden. He had been identified by Mrs Jones and now it appeared he had the means to enter Patricia Hoskin's flat and could have sliced the lock of hair from the dead girl's head – the scissor cut that Ruxton had spotted. Much of the evidence was circumstantial though and Blanche decided to wait until tomorrow before charging the journalist with the murder. By then, with luck, she would have heard from SO3, the Fingerprint Branch, as to whether any of the prints discovered in the flat matched Hebden's.

She thanked Wootton and ordered Dexter to ignore his gold-fish for a couple of hours and harry the Fingerprint Branch and forensic instead. Back in the dubious privacy of her office, she brewed a cup of strong black coffee in a percolator brought from home and slumped in her chair. Her eyelids were raw from lack of sleep and her calves throbbed with fatigue: the hours she had worked since Wednesday were ludicrous.

106

'Ma'am.' The call was gentle. 'Ma'am.' The voice was louder now as if someone were approaching her step by step. Through the daze of sleepiness Blanche made out a black profile etched across the slab of light that was the entrance to her office. 'Ma'am.' The superintendent shivered and tugged back her heavy eyelids to wake herself up. She had dozed off in her chair: stale saliva rotted on her tongue and her cheeks prickled with unaccustomed heat.

A young constable coughed with embarrassment. Blanche glanced at her watch and sighed with relief: she had only been asleep for a couple of minutes. She stifled a yawn and straightened her skirt as she sat up. 'What is it?' she snapped with a roughness she did not intend.

At that moment Dexter swaggered up behind the constable to find out what was happening.

'Sorry to trouble you, ma'am,' the constable stammered. His eyes were shy and flickered away from hers. 'But a girl's just phoned in.' Blanche sighed to control her impatience with the man's indirectness. He was a promising young officer but sometimes she wondered in her sourer moments how he would cope if he were cornered down a dark alley by a group of knife-wielding thugs and had to talk himself out of trouble. 'She says she's a waitress at an Italian restaurant in Battersea and she served Patricia Hoskin the night she was murdered.'

Blanche lifted her face – the features somewhat masculine but handsome – to the constable's. The sleep was snatched from her eyes like a cobweb ripped down by a child. 'Was she alone?'

'No. She was eating there with a man. The girl's at this address.'

The constable stood bemused as Blanche loped past him with a groan of fatigue, taking the scrap of paper he proffered. 'Come on Dexter,' she shouted over her shoulder, shrugging on her raincoat, 'it's time for a *cappuccino*.'

The waitress dumped the two coffees on the table unceremoniously like place-mats. 'That's three pound please,' she demanded, tossing the till receipt onto the plastic table-cloth.

'Bloody hell,' whined Dexter, 'three quid! Did you pick the

coffee beans yourself?'

She smiled an apology and dragged her fingers through her spiky hair. 'That's what they charge here . . . I sometimes wonder how they get away with it.' As Dexter searched through some loose change for three one-pound coins, Blanche wondered how recently the girl had moved down from Birmingham: through clamped jaws she spoke the nasal and flat accent of the West Midlands.

The superintendent and Dexter had arrived at the restaurant a few minutes before. It had been empty except for another girl in a striped blue jersey who was swabbing the tiled floor with a mop ready for the lunch-time customers. Her face pouted at them resentfully when Blanche asked if she was Sharon Philips. 'No. Sharon's out the back. I'll get her.' The girl dumped her mop in the can and slouched past the lines of brightly coloured tables to the bar and cash-till at the back of the narrow room. She disappeared through a door hidden in the penumbra and a moment later Sharon scurried out.

The waitress held out a limp hand to Blanche, nervously rocking from one foot to the other. 'You took long enough to come. I only put the phone down ten minutes ago.' Blanche sensed the waitress trying to conceal her nerves behind a façade of brassiness. She was of medium height with small, rounded features that she tried to render more impressive by make-up: scarlet lipstick to make her mouth pout and lines of kohl to widen her eyes. Silver triangles jangled from her ears, made all the more prominent because Sharon had chosen to crop her brown hair short and layer it back like the quills of a porcupine. She was dressed in tight jeans and a loose white pullover. The waitress sat down and flicked a defiant look over her shoulder at the other girl, who had since reappeared and stood over by the cash-till. Dexter pulled a packet of cigarettes from his leather blouson and offered her one. She took it thoughtfully like someone choosing a straw when drawing lots.

From her handbag Blanche took out a colour photograph of Patricia Hoskin. It was the most recent one available, taken in June by a girlfriend with whom she had gone on holiday to Italy. The photograph showed her in the Campo in Siena,

108

sitting on the cobbles, her blonde hair shimmering, eyes screwed up against the sun. Blanche slid the photograph across the plastic table-cloth and asked if she was the same woman Sharon had served on Tuesday night. The waitress drew on her cigarette and studied the photograph intently. After a few seconds she nodded vigorously. 'Yeah. That's the woman. I'm sure of it.'

Dexter groaned and shifted back in his chair, rolling his eyes up to the ceiling. 'So why did you wait two days before you decided to tell us, for Christ's sake?' His tone was sharp with genuine anger.

Blanche kicked him in the shin with her left shoe. She was as annoyed with the girl as her sergeant but had decided years ago it was futile, if not dangerous, to show impatience with the public. After all the public – that simple word to encompass the rich and poor of humanity, the evil and the good – paid her salary and also had its reasons to hinder a police investigation. They were usually simple enough: ignorance, forgetfulness, fear. Emotions that Blanche considered had been with man since his misty inception and would go with him to his grave. Besides, the superintendent knew only too well that the public usually played a central role in clearing up the few crimes that were solved. One should be grateful for any help received rather than carp at its paucity.

To Blanche's relief, Sharon did not seem offended by Dexter's remark. She blew smoke out through her nostrils. 'Linda said I shouldn't tell the police 'cos I'd get involved.' The waitress shrugged and glanced towards the other girl who was returning to her mop and bucket. 'I thought about it last night and changed my mind. It's as simple as that.'

While Dexter surreptitiously massaged his shin, Blanche asked the girl to describe what happened on Tuesday night. She said Patricia Hoskin – whom she had seen a couple of times in the restaurant before – arrived around nine o'clock with a man who was in his mid to late thirties. She could not remember much about him except that he was clean-shaven, conservatively dressed in a jacket and tie, of medium build, wore spectacles and had brown hair. The description seemed close enough to Hebden to make Blanche feel mildly excited.

Blanche was coming round to liking Sharon. The waitress had the courage to ignore her timid friend and telephone the police – not always easy, the superintendent reflected, when you are seventeen – and she also had enough respect for the truth not to embroider her recollections.

Having recovered his good temper, Dexter entered the conversation. He patiently took Sharon through every detail of the meal – asking what Patricia and the man ordered, how they acted towards each other – in a vain attempt to release any other useful clues trapped in the girl's memory. When he was not in an impatient mood, Blanche knew Dexter was brilliant at this sort of interrogation, conducting it with great sensitivity. The only thing of interest to emerge was that Sharon had the impression the couple did not seem to know each other very well. When asked by Dexter she said she did not know why.

'Did they look into each other's eyes much?' asked the sergeant, with the tender interest of the practised seducer. 'Hold hands? Touch finger-tips?'

Sharon giggled to hide her embarrassment. 'You make it sound like one of those crappy romance books me mum reads.'

'Well, did they?' pressed Dexter.

'Not that I can remember.'

The restaurant had grown darker. Outside the wintry sun-light had been stifled by cloud and Blanche saw pedestrians begin to walk past with glistening umbrellas. Suddenly some of the wall lights around the restaurant were switched on. 'Better hurry up, Sharon,' shouted the other girl from a table at the back. 'Manager'll back in a minute and we're open in 'alf an hour.'

'OK Linda. Be along in a sec,' replied the waitress.

The superintendent had one last hope for a quick identification of the man who dined with the murdered girl. 'I don't suppose the man paid by credit card, did he?'

'No,' said Sharon, rising from the table.

'You sound very definite about it.'

Sharon's pale blue eyes fixed on the superintendent. 'I am. You see,' and she stubbed out her cigarette as if to focus the memory, 'I remember thinkin' how rare it is that the custom-

110

ers pay with cash these days. Most of them fish out a credit card, others write a cheque. But this guy paid in cash.' The waitress turned and glanced nervously at the door. Blanche guessed she was worried about the manager returning to find her gossiping with the police. 'I suppose the bill was for fifty odd quid. I remember him pushing the little silver tray towards me with the notes in. He had strange eyes . . . ' She waved a hand in front of her face like a non-smoker wafting away cigarette smoke. 'They jumped all over the place, didn't seem to rest on you.'

The superintendent needed a statement immediately from Sharon and insisted that she went back with them to the police station. The other waitress whined about the increased work when Sharon explained what was happening but Blanche silenced her with a steely glare.

Blanche stood outside on the pavement under the restaurant's yellow awning and mused on what the girl had told her. The rain fell steadily now, transforming the tarmac of the road into a mirror reflecting the leaden sky, a mirror that melted and re-formed as cars and cabs hissed over its surface. Rain-drops like pearls clung in a line to the wooden slat at the bottom of the awning.

The description of the man given by Sharon was so vague it could fit Hebden but Blanche was unconvinced. Hebden's gaze was cool and fixed, a seducer's glance. The waitress trotting along beside her had seemed unsettled by the other man's eyes. Blanche noted, without consciously thinking it through, that she was already describing him as 'the other man'. She would wait until after the identity parade with Sharon for the final proof, but Blanche was convinced she had stumbled across the phantom Michael Drayton, the man referred to in Patricia Hoskin's diary.

With renewed vigour in her stride, Blanche erected her black umbrella over Sharon and strode back towards the car. Dexter opened his umbrella too, a golf umbrella made up of triangles of eidetic colour, coaxing it to blossom like a flower on his roof terrace. The superintendent watched the street uncoil beside her: the Olde Worlde snooker club with its perspex sign, an expensive French restaurant cheek by jowl with a derelict menswear shop, a tramp who shambled along

111

the pavement grasping a bottle of meths and a plastic bag. Blanche thought once again what a mess London was. The unholy triumvirate of developer, planner and architect had maimed it forever in the sixties and seventies. Cars were suffocating the roads like weeds. Buses and underground trains were so expensive that it was no longer accurate to regard them as *public* transport. The schools were dreadful. London was heading towards the twenty-first century without pride or confidence. 'Why do we carry on living here, Sharon? You know, here in London?' she asked suddenly.

The waitress looked up, puzzled by the question. She thought for a moment and blew her breath out over her lips. "Cos we ain't got any bloody choice. Besides, it's a good laugh sometimes.'

Blanche chuckled and her good mood endured until she walked back into the incident room. She was met by Wootton who handed her a message with an unreadable smile. She had been summoned urgently to New Scotland Yard to see her boss, Commander Brian Spittals.

# 11

Unease fluttered through Blanche and she was irritated by its presence. After all, she repeated to herself, the summons had only been to see Spittals, not an Assistant Commissioner. To the best of her knowledge she had done nothing particularly cretinous. The murder investigation was proceeding smoothly, a suspect had been arrested and there was a fair amount of circumstantial evidence against him. So far the case had not proved the 'sticker' Blanche had feared. But still the superintendent could not rid herself of the sense of unease.

Blanche kneaded her brains for an explanation of the summons. Spittals' secretary had refused to give one when Blanche had phoned and asked for a postponement, pleading that she needed to organise an important identity parade later that Saturday afternoon. The line had fallen dead for a minute or so while the secretary consulted Spittals. 'No, I'm sorry, Blanche. But the Commander says he's got to see you this afternoon at three.'

Blanche sucked in her lips. She knew the secretary from long ago − a sweet, anodyne girl of great efficiency and prominent teeth. 'Ruth, can you give me some idea of what it's all about?' Without meaning to do so, the superintendent dropped her voice to a conspiratorial whisper.

The secretary thought for a moment. 'Sorry, I can't tell you anything, superintendent,' she replied. 'The Commander told me it's confidential.'

It was like being back at school and called to see the head-mistress, Blanche thought, as the police car slipped onto Chelsea Bridge. There was the same surge of self-examination, the same fear of criticism. Behind the Thirties' iron-work of the bridge she made out the Thames, its grey surface lashed by the wind into scudding waves. The river reminded

Blanche of how her mother used to ice birthday and Christmas cakes, flicking the surface of the icing sugar into dancing points. Her mother had been dead for several years now, a memory of sad happiness rekindled by associations like the sight of a wind-whipped river. The superintendent remembered the famous passage from Proust that she had read years ago at school about a man who dunks a *madeleine* in some tea on a winter's day. But with a smile she dismissed it from her mind as irrelevant: Proust was no *vade-mecum* to the mind of Commander Brian Spittals.

Although it was only a quarter to three in the afternoon, many cars streaming over the bridge towards them had switched on their headlights. Refracted through the windows of the police car they shattered into blazing jewels set in the gloom of twilight. The warm fug of the car heater made Blanche drowsy and her eyelids seemed to turn to lead as the police driver swung right onto the embankment. The looming majesty of Battersea power station, the bare and shivering trees that lined the pavement, Dolphin Square, the Tate Gallery – all slid by in the wintry mist before the car deposited her outside the inscrutable tower of New Scotland Yard.

'Sorry to drag you across to the Yard at such short notice,' murmured Spittals, advancing towards her with what was intended to be a hearty smile of welcome. One hand was already rubbing against the palm of the other, the susurration of skin whispering under his voice. He was about an inch shorter than Blanche and the superintendent always had the impression that the Commander tried to stand on his toes in her presence so that he did not feel over-awed. Blanche noticed he was wearing a new suit – one of the set he had bought to mark his promotion a year ago. The old ones, too tight and all in various shades of grey and brown, had been discarded. The new ones, although better cut and made of more expensive material, could still not conceal the growing paunch which tugged at the buttons of his white shirt. Spittals stopped about three yards away from her, as if suddenly remembering something, and gestured with a ruddy hand towards the sofa in the corner of his office.

Blanche sensed his tiny eyes dart over her buttocks as she

114

turned and walked over. She always felt half-naked when he looked at her, as if his eyes were able to peel away her clothes. He never dared proposition her of course, let alone touch her. Although Blanche sensed sexual frustration burn in those black eyes, she knew that the brain behind them valued his career before everything else. Spittals would not have sacrificed his steady advance up the ranks of the Metropolitan Police for a snatched caress. He was also sensible enough to realise that if he made a sexual advance to Blanche she would slap him across his stubbly moustache.

'I wanted a word with you about the Hoskin murder case,' he began, his eyes flickering across Blanche's breasts. 'Find out how much progress you're making.' He rested his forearms on his knees and continued to rub his palms together.

Blanche could not believe this was the real reason for her summons. She had already prepared one written report for Spittals because she knew he was a stickler for paperwork. 'We're making good progress, sir,' she answered warily, crossing her arms as a sign of discontent.

He continued to stare at her for a moment as if expecting something more. 'Good. Good. You obviously know how important it is, lass,' and he raised a forefinger to scratch his moustache, 'to solve this case as soon as possible?' Blanche noticed that yellow pouches were starting to sag from under his thin eyelids. Although burly and keen to give the impression of bustling energy, the superintendent had always guessed that much of her boss's drive was aroused by fear.

'Of course, sir. *All* murderers should be caught as soon as possible.' Having referred obliquely to the personal interest that certain people at the top of the Met had shown in the case, Blanche decided to plunge in. 'But, er, if there's any other reason why you feel this case needs to be cleared up more urgently than it is, perhaps you could tell me now.'

The superintendent watched his angular face crack into a smile, revealing a set of regular but yellowing teeth. 'That's just what I meant. We've got to show we're efficient these days, you know. It's no good just bleating on about the rising tide of crime to get money out of the government. They want results. I don't want any "grief" from this case.' From her twelve years in the Met, Blanche knew he did not mean

115

simple sorrow or distress. 'Grief' had a peculiar resonance for policemen: it meant trouble with the hierarchy, the public or politicians. His eyes swivelled over to the window as if he had said something he should not, and focussed on the spots of rain that dotted the glass. 'Tell me about this man, Hebden, you've pulled in,' he added quickly. 'Got an admission yet?' On the last word, he turned back to her, his eyes narrowed.

Blanche sensed an ambush but, like a helpless traveller stumbling through a wood at night, she had no idea where it might be. 'No. Hebden hasn't said a thing. Except to deny any involvement.'

The Commander nodded thoughtfully. 'There's quite a bit of evidence against him though, isn't there?'

Blanche squinted at him with concentration. How could Spittals know exactly how much evidence she had accumulated against Hebden? She had told his office late last night that the journalist had been arrested but nothing since. 'Some,' she hedged. 'But not enough.'

Spittals tugged at the knees of his trousers and began to rub his palms together again, this time more slowly, as if he were rolling a rod of plasticine between them. 'You've got rather more than you think, haven't you?'

'What do you mean, sir?' Blanche decided to feign stupidity so that the Commander could patronise her and she might discover how and why Spittals had been looking into her investigation behind her back.

It was a mistake. Blanche knew it as soon as the words dropped from her lips. It was always a mistake to underestimate Spittals. A stubby finger poked towards her, glistening with an enormous signet ring. His voice dropped to a hoarse whisper. 'Don't play silly games with me. I may not be one of these graduate high-flyers in the Met like you are with a Cambridge degree and a lah-di-dah accent to match, but that doesn't mean my head isn't screwed on the right way.' He pulled himself upright on the sofa and shuffled inside his clothes as if they were sticking to his skin.

He infused his voice with what he intended to be seductive charm. 'I called the incident room this morning to check with you whether things were moving with this Hebden character. And who should pick up the phone but an old friend of mine from Manchester, DS Wootton.'

Blanche wondered whether the truth was somewhat different, and Wootton had called Spittals' office. 'And what happened, sir?'

'He told me what the score was. Positive ID by the old lady at the parade this morning. Key to the girl's flat at Hebden's house. Even a lock of hair with some bloodstains on it that Wootton said might well have come from the girl.' Spittals' eyes did not blink, their pupils pin-pricks of black. For some foolish reason, Blanche found her attention fixed on some flecks of dandruff that had fallen from the Commander's mud-brown hair and now shimmered round the collar of his suit. 'I was just wondering when you were planning to charge him?'

'When I thought the time was right, sir.' Blanche was irritated that she had been placed on the defensive. 'You see, I wanted the full forensic results on those things found in Hebden's house as well as a check on his fingerprints.'

'But you've got enough to charge him, haven't you?'

It was Blanche's turn to glance towards the window. A pulsing blue light in the sky marked the silent progress of a jet as it cut through the gloom. 'I've got a few doubts, sir. That's all.'

'What doubts?' he challenged aggressively, as if he had personal knowledge of Hebden's guilt.

The superintendent sighed and tightened the muscles in her cheeks to indicate difficulty in articulating them. 'Well just before lunch I found a waitress who remembered serving Patricia Hoskin on the night she died.'

'So?'

'Well, she was with a man whose description doesn't fit Hebden very well. In other words it looks – and I won't know definitely until the identity parade with the waitress later this afternoon – that Pat Hoskin was with another man earlier in the evening. A man who wasn't Hebden.'

'That doesn't mean she wasn't with him later for Christ's sake. Hebden was actually seen leaving the house at about the time of the murder.' The Commander sighed and ran an impatient hand through the curls of his hair, eyes scurrying over Blanche's stockinged knees.

117

Uneasily, the superintendent adjusted her shirt. She realised just how obvious it was that Hebden had some
involvement with the murder. Blanche knew the strength of
the evidence against the journalist. But equally it was her case
and she resented Spittals' interference. When she spoke it
was with calm deliberation. 'I just don't want to be hurried,
sir. The forensic and fingerprint results will be back tonight
or tomorrow and I can charge Hebden then.'

Spittals stared at her for a moment and then wandered
over to the window. He turned, leant back against the wall
and crossed his arms. 'Tomorrow's too late. I want him
charged tonight.'

Blanche sensed her anger rumble in the distance like
approaching thunder. 'Why?' she exclaimed, her cheeks
burning. 'I'm the officer in charge of the case. Surely I'm
better able to decide when to charge a suspect than anyone
else?'

'Not necessarily.' Spittals' voice was gruff and cold, his face
impassive. Blanche sensed the tension in his body, the
clenched muscles. He had something else to tell her. He
pulled back the sleeve of his suit to glance at his watch. 'We
better get a move on.' He pointed to a telephone on his desk.
'Now if you'd be kind enough to phone up DS Wootton and
order him to charge Hebden . . . ' he tugged his face into an
edgy smile. ' . . . we can go along to the press conference.'

The superintendent jumped up with amazement. 'Press
conference? What press conference? I haven't called one.'

'I know. *I* have.'

'I would rather wait until tomorrow, sir, if it's all the same
to you.' Blanche tried to dampen the anger in her voice.
Although she knew there was a risk of prejudicing the trial
through the press conference, it was not that that annoyed
her. It was Spittals' high-handed manner, his failure to consult her.

The Commander twitched on another smile, this time a
patronising smirk. 'I'm afraid it's *not* all the same to me,
superintendent. I want Hebden charged this afternoon and I
want the press conference this afternoon.'

It was a smile Blanche had met before during her career in
the police, a smile of masonic superiority, a smile that pro-

118

claimed its owner willing to disregard the strict letter of the law in the cause of true justice. Blanche had even used it herself on occasions. But as she loped reluctantly behind Spittals onto the raised podium, shielding her eyes from the scorching white of the television lights, aware of an expectant murmur from faces she could not see, her lips were set in a pout of discontent. She hated the flummery of public relations, and during the press conference she only glanced up twice to give uninformative answers to prying questions. She passed most of the time glowering at the desk and doodling so fiercely on her note-pad that the pen cut through the paper like a scalpel.

When David woke up it was still dark. His sleep-crammed eyes clambered across to the bedside clock and widened when they read it was five fifteen in the morning. He had slept solidly for about fifteen hours, something he had not done since childhood. He felt somehow different and shut his eyes again to try to discover the cause.

The answer came quickly. For when he checked through the inventory of pain that his body had become over the past weeks David found nothing. His hands were not clamouring to be washed, his muscles were not panting with anxiety, the agony of restlessness had disappeared. No voices gibbered at him from dark corners. He felt relaxed in a way he had not experienced since before his mother's death, cleansed and refreshed, as though able to begin his life again. He lay in bed and relished the pleasure of happiness, tweaking his fingers and toes with joy.

David padded up to his study. He prised the curtains apart and looked out onto a London still waiting for the dawn. Overnight the cloud had been whisked away and a full moon hovered in the sky, drenching the rooftops with pale silver. When his eyes had adjusted to the darkness, he distinguished the pulsing glimmer of the stars above the glare of the streetlights. David turned round and looked in wonder at his black, amorphous shadow cast by the light of the moon which led from his feet to the terrarium. David knelt beside the glass cage and by the light from the stairwell he watched the python slide effortlessly among the rocks, its head rising occasionally to sniff the warm, animal-scented air. David suddenly felt very hungry.

He prepared a *cafetière* of black coffee and a breakfast of scrambled eggs and bacon. By the time he had finished it was only half past six and he still had half an hour to wait until the local newsagent opened. So he took a leisurely bath and started work on some papers he had brought home on Friday.

The morning air was crisp and clean when he closed the front door soon after seven thirty. The street was deserted with blinds and curtains drawn. In the gutter and against railings caches of autumn leaves were turning black with rot, a reminder of the distant summer. The moon still hung in the sky but was no more now than a white stain. At the corner David turned right and two streets further on arrived at the frontier between the middle-class enclave he inhabited and the council estate. The blocks of council flats crouched like some terrified animal, square and damp, the window-frames made of cast iron and the paint peeling. Most of the cars parked in the road opposite were battered and rusty, their bodywork too exhausted to reflect even a glimmer of the sunshine. Away in the distance the Lloyds Building rose into the morning light, a stump of polished flint. The newsagent stood next to the bookmakers in a parade of dingy shops. The windows cowered behind a wire grill and were dotted with advertisements scrawled out on postcards.

When David first caught sight of the newspaper headline on the board outside he shook himself with wonder. But the words printed in bold, black letters were clear enough: 'Clapham Strangler – Man Charged'. David stared at the words open-mouthed, his eyes tracing the line of each letter, fearful that he was the subject of some cruel practical joke. He strode in through the open door and picked up a copy of every newspaper from the piles on the floor. To David's relief, the Asian man behind the counter displayed no surprise or curiosity at his yearning for newsprint and simply took the money with an enigmatic smile.

In his systematic, legal way, David scoured each newspaper for an article on the murder. Most carried one and they all agreed on the essential facts: a journalist called John Hebden

120

had been charged with the murder of Patricia Hoskin, the daughter of the Home Office minister, whose strangled body had been found in her Clapham flat late on Wednesday night. The quality newspapers treated the story in a few paragraphs. The tabloids however devoted much more space, several printing photographs of a triumphant Commander Brian Spittals presiding over the press conference.

Perhaps he had not strangled the girl after all, David ruminated. The police must have evidence against this man, Hebden, good reasons to believe he was responsible for the murder. The events of the past few days had been no more than a dream from which he had just woken. But David knew he was deceiving himself. Only the day before – and it seemed aeons ago, not a matter of a few hours – his teeth had chewed the girl's flesh. No. He *had* killed the girl, but destiny, God, Jesus Christ – whatever or whoever it was who guided his life – had decided he should escape punishment. The act was sanctified.

David respired deeply to quieten his euphoria. Not only did he feel the burden of guilt and physical anguish had been lifted from him by feasting on the dead girl's body, but David sensed fate had decided to be his friend. He was safe, invulnerable.

Only one worry creased his forehead. Two of the newspapers said the murder enquiry was headed by a Detective Superintendent Blanche Hampton. The name woke a forgotten and embarrassing memory. There was no photograph of her, just one of a female profile out of focus behind Commander Spittals. David scrutinised the picture, as if intense study would bring it alive and add a third dimension. After a few moments he shook his head decisively. He rejected the idea as fantasy, a coincidence too distant to be credible. It could not be the same woman.

# 12

Three weeks later David halted at the end of the concourse leading out of Liverpool Street station. A chill breeze prickled his face as he watched the flood of commuters disgorge into the streets with the inexhaustible power of a lava flow. The heavy rain had stopped a few minutes before and thousands of feet splashed through the puddles. He stopped because he thought he had heard a voice call to him from the structure that stood outside the station. It had been erected several years before and was supposed to be a piece of sculpture. David abhorred it, comparing the sheets of rusting iron to a rocket that had crashed in the centre of the City whose tail-fin was the only part that remained visible. He listened but heard nothing more, only the rumble of traffic, the clatter of a pneumatic drill and the click of shoes on the marble floor of the concourse. With a sigh he plunged into the glistening maze of stairways and gridded windows that made up the Broadgate Centre. The plants that had been cultivated to soften the harsh edges of grey stone were flailed by the wind but the buildings with smoked windows and faced with pink marble seemed impervious to the weather.

David had noticed the return of worrying symptoms in the previous few days. He had felt wonderful – relaxed and in control – after the Meal and news of Hebden being charged with the murder. He called it the Meal to distinguish its importance from all others, although in retrospect the act of eating human flesh did not seem very remarkable. The flesh was tender but not particularly flavoursome. It was the peace and power gained by consuming the meat that was important. In recent days, however, David sensed the return of the obsessional need to wash his hands. He had also had a panic attack at work, quite a spectacular one, in front of the articled clerk with whom he shared his office. The lawyer believed his colleagues had begun to whisper about him behind his back. Two days before he had decided to attend one of the regular partnership lunches. David arrived early at the boardroom and surprised the head of the Tax Department and another senior partner. The words on their lips faded for a second when they saw who it was, before Douglas Ferguson, the senior tax partner, had taken up the conversation again with exaggerated gusto.

David walked through the lobby of the office building and took the lift to the third floor: one of three occupied by Whitlock, Cameron and Collins. As he approached his office, anxiety began to gnaw at his innards because in recent days David had found his concentration more and more fragmented. He had promised just before his mother died to write an article for *Taxation* about company tax structures and had not yet begun. He had tried to begin the research several times but on each occasion found his mind tripping from thought to thought. The pile of work on David's desk — plotting the tax arrangements for a merger between two oil companies, setting up a handful of overseas funds, and advising on the tax implications for a consortium involved in a take-over bid — seemed to swell rather than diminish. Several times he had ambushed himself staring into space, or found the gaze of the articled clerk glued to his face as though he could read his thoughts. In case he could, David had struggled to censor them, skimming off any memories of Patricia Hoskin as soon as they bubbled to the surface of his mind.

David placed his briefcase on the floor delicately and sat at his desk with his back to the window. On his right, built into the wall, were two filing cabinets, one containing pink and orange folders, the other lever arch files, each neatly labelled. A number of text-books lolled in a bookcase. On the floor slumbered other boxes crammed with more files. Opposite to David's desk stood a smaller one occupied by the articled clerk. To David's relief, he had not yet arrived. David wanted to revel for a few minutes in the peace and reassurance of being in his office, a womb against the world. But instead of relaxing, his muscles tensed. The flanks of his hands itched with imagined dirt. He imagined his fingers out in front of

123

him, gripping the neck of Patricia Hoskin, her eyes bursting from their sockets, her tongue lolling like a slice of liver, and the dribble of blood trailing from her ear.

He looked up and found the articled clerk, Nick, standing in the open door gazing at him with muddied eyes. 'Are you alright, David?' he said.

David was sure that the slim, blond figure advancing towards him could decipher his mind. He brought down the shutters on the image of the dying girl with a crash, stood up and spun round to gaze out of the window. The hand that flew to his brow dipped itself in a varnish of sweat. Nick had to move out of the office. It was as simple as that, David decided. The lawyer could not face the prospect of guarding his wayward mind throughout the day to ensure that no foul imagining appeared that Nick could latch on to and use against him.

Later that morning, David decided to go to the company's law library. It was partly to escape from Nick and partly to consult a legal journal. Standing by one of the teak-veneered bookshelves was Douglas Ferguson, the senior tax partner. He was a shy and clever Scot, who was twirling his half-moon spectacles in one hand while asking the librarian for a copy of a particular newspaper. He turned to David with a nervous smile. 'Morning, David.'

'Morning,' David replied vacantly, waiting for a pause in the conversation so that he could ask for a brief word with the senior partner about changing his articled clerk.

Ferguson slipped the spectacles back on his nose. He always dressed in a dapper way for a man in his fifties and his breath was redolent with mint. 'I was wondering whether I could have a brief word with you some time this morning?'

'Of course, Douglas, yes. In fact I was going to ask you for the same thing.'

Ferguson tossed a mysterious look over his spectacles. 'Oh, really? Well, let's pop along to my office now.'

David always looked about Douglas Ferguson's office with a quiver of jealousy. It was spacious, panelled with stained mahogany and well-furnished. He also did not have to share it with anyone. The room however always looked as though a burglar had just rifled through it with papers strewn over the carpet and tumbling out of cupboards. Ferguson asked David how his work was going.

'Fine. Fine,' replied David with as much confidence as he could muster. 'The oil company merger's going well. The overseas funds I'm setting up have got a few snags but are making progress. I had to save the conveyancers' bacon again the other day over a property deal. But, yes', he mumbled, 'things are going OK.'

The senior partner smiled from behind his desk. David had a reputation within the firm for his mild but regular whines that he was forever getting other lawyers out of scrapes created by their lazy drafting of documents. 'So it wasn't about work that you wanted a word with me?'

David scraped the skin on the back of his hand. 'No, it wasn't really, Douglas.' David hesitated. He could not express his real fear about Nick, that he could read this thoughts. 'It's about Nick.'

'Problems?' Douglas Ferguson raised his eyebrows in surprise.

'Er, no . . . not from the point of view of his work.' David gulped. 'It's just that, well, I don't know how to put it really. I don't feel comfortable with him any more in the same office.'

'Really?' The senior partner nodded as though David's comments confirmed a long-held suspicion. His blue eyes narrowed to shrewd slits. 'That's unfortunate. You see . . . Nick had a word with me yesterday and said much the same thing.' He paused. 'It's difficult for me to say this, David, and it's not just me, but the partners as a whole have become quite concerned about you in the past few weeks.'

'What do you mean, concerned?' snapped David defensively.

Douglas held up his well-scrubbed hands in a gesture of conciliation. 'Don't misunderstand me, David. We're not criticising or attacking you. It's just that, well . . . you've seemed rather, how shall we say, disturbed in recent weeks.'

David's cheeks were singed with embarrassment. He squirmed in his chair. He had always hated being the butt of criticism. 'Have clients been complaining about my work?'

Douglas breathed out deeply. 'Well, a couple of them have made some comments as a matter of fact. And so have some of your colleagues. They've said you don't seem to be your old self at the moment.'

David sat stunned. This had never happened before. He knew within the partnership that he had a reputation as a 'tax boffin', a learned lawyer, whose strength was unravelling tortuous tax problems and proposing brilliant solutions. His weakness, and David recognised it as well as the other partners, was his dislike of long and tedious meetings with clients, the social aspect of being a City lawyer, netting business for the firm. But, except over minor matters, the quality of his work had never been questioned before. David thought of spluttering with anger. It seemed pointless because he still had enough pride in his work to know that the criticisms were just: since his mother had died, he had no longer been his old self.

'Look, what I'm proposing is that you take a holiday.'

'But what about all the work I've got on?' David almost screamed in a panic. He had never trusted others to do work as well as he did. 'I can't just drop it and buzz off.'

Douglas lifted his hands again in propitiation. He spoke with the calm confidence of a priest. 'Don't worry, David. That's up to me to sort out. You just take a holiday. We'll cover for you.' He breathed in deeply again over his thin lips. 'You might care to consider having a brief word with the firm's doctor by the way. His consultations are free and his rooms are close by.'

The prospect of the 'holiday' did not appeal to David at all in the beginning. He had always respired his work with the same primal need that his body sought oxygen. He realised however that Douglas Ferguson was speaking for the whole partnership and that it was foolish to resist. Besides, he told himself, ever since he had joined Whitlock, Cameron and Collins as a callow articled clerk straight out of law school, he had always resisted taking his full quota of holiday. On reflection, David thought it was almost as though he had been running a race all his life and only now been forced to stop, catch his breath and look round at the scenery for the first time.

David decided not to visit the firm's doctor. He did not

believe there was anything wrong with him that could not be cured by a good rest. The newspapers were always full of the dangers of stress for people who worked too hard and he had perhaps been overdoing it. He must learn to relax more, not be racked by the tortured tenseness that had afflicted him for the past weeks. Besides, the doctor might refer him to some psychiatrist or psychoanalyst – one of those strange, earnest men he had seen in films who pried into people's minds. David had always treated them with a superior curl of the lip. They were for other people, mad people, not for people like himself – professional, respectable and, despite certain eccentricities which everyone had, normal.

Pamela called round to see David on the first night. He lied to her about the company doctor, saying he had seen him that afternoon and that the doctor had advised a complete rest for a fortnight because he had been overworking.

'I'm so relieved you saw him, you know, David.' Pamela smiled and reached out one hand to cover his. They had just finished supper. David noticed the mole on the side of her nose and how the powder was caked on her face. 'I've been *terribly* worried about you recently you know. But now you've seen the doctor everything will be OK, won't it?' She poured out a smile that reminded David of weak tea.

He patted her hand in a gesture that seemed to be expected of him. 'Of course it will. Everything will be alright now.'

The next day David decided to book a week's holiday in the sun. The girl in the travel agency reluctantly interrupted a conversation she was having with a friend of hers over the telephone. 'Just 'ave a look over there, luv. Take your pick of the brochures and pop back to me when you're ready.'

The Canary Islands did not appeal to him: endless photographs of teeming bodies grilling in the sun. Greece did appeal to him: renewing his links with the classical world out of season when the great sites would be deserted. But the girl, after wrestling with a computer for several minutes, said there was no convenient flight at the weekend. All the flights were charter and left at seven o'clock in the morning from Gatwick. Since David lived in north London and abhorred rising early, he grunted and asked for another destination.

'What about Cyprus?' asked the girl with a flick of her dyed hair. David noticed that her cheeks were almost a pale mauve from the over-enthusiastic application of cheek blusher. She was wearing a gold-plated bracelet in the form of a heart. 'Goin' by yourself are you, sir?' she said enigmatically.

'Yes,' said David. 'Probably.'

The girl flicked open the brochure with a scarlet finger-nail. 'Lots of 'istory on Cyprus. Pretty upmarket destination, you know. You don't get many yobs.' She slid the leaflet across the formica and lit a cigarette.

Too impatient to search further, David booked the holi-day.

When he returned home there was one letter for him with a postmark from Ipswich. It was from his mother's solicitor asking for instructions about her bungalow: whether or not he wished to sell it. With a listless, wintry day in Islington crawling in through his windows, and nothing planned to fill the day ahead, David decided to make up his mind after one last visit.

The bungalow huddled under the wide Suffolk sky. The clouds above were one flat, unbroken plate of lead. No sigh of wind brushed David's cheek in the silence. As soon as he left the car he sensed the air to be damper and colder than in London, musty with the scent of the distant North Sea, whose breakers were grinding the beach a few miles away at Felix-stowe.

Something had changed about the bungalow. As he walked towards it, treading warily to avoid the puddles, he remem-bered the magnificent sky on the evening when he had ar-rived to stay with his mother for the last time. The sun had just set and the clouds were splashed with a variety of peach, orange and red, as though the sky were a child's painting exercise. That October evening had seemed, for the minute he stood transfixed outside, so joyful and carefree. At the front window, however, in the space between the drawn curtains, was a black figure, staring out into the night, watching. It was his mother. It was always his mother, looking out for him, correcting him, accusing him. And the next morning she was dead.

With a jolt, the lawyer realised what had changed. When he had finally left the bungalow after the funeral several weeks before, David had drawn all the curtains. It seemed a mark of respect for the dead. But now the curtains were open. As far as David knew, no one else had a key. A cold weight suddenly slid down his back, and his hair prickled. There was no sign of anyone. All was still.

The light in the front room flashed on. He could see the battered standard lamp, the mirror, the dowdy wallpaper. And in the window stood once again, black and accusing, his mother. She was no more than an ebony profile against the cream oblong of light. But she was there. David watched with unblinking eyes as the figure pulled the curtains shut. He edged forward in a trance and, as he did so, the light in the room was switched off.

The darkness of winter twilight was roosting on the land. Already the pines on a distant tumulus away to the right were melting into one indistinguishable mass. David pressed himself against the wall of the bungalow, his heart leaping. He listened to the silence. Footsteps clicked on the concrete path that led along the side of the bungalow. He could not draw himself to walk to the end of the wall in case he confronted the ghost of his mother. He pressed his face deeper and deeper into the bricks, sensing their roughness on his cheek. He wanted to sink into them like drops of rain, disappear, forget his mother. Yet she would not let go of him. Even from beyond the grave she tortured him.

'David, what are you doing here? Cor, you didn't half give me a fright!' Mrs Goddard stood trembling in front of him, clutching her handbag.

'Oh! It's you,' murmured David, pulling himself away from the wall. 'I thought . . . ' His words drained away into the approaching night.

Mrs Goddard chuckled. 'You thought I was a burglar.'

David was angry. He had been scared out of his wits by this old fool, a friend of his mother's. How on earth could he have thought she was his mother watching from the window? He stood pale and shaking. 'I didn't have the faintest idea who it was,' said David waspishly. 'But one thing I do know is that I

don't like the idea of you creeping around inside the bungalow while I'm away.'

'But, but . . . ' Mrs Goddard's mouth flopped open with
surprise. 'All I was doing was keeping a watch over it for you,
David. Make sure it weren't vandalised. I thought I was being
helpful.'

David had recovered his self-possession by now. He had
never liked Mrs Goddard and now saw a chance to be finally
rid of her. 'Thank you for keeping an eye out while I've been
away. But now I'd be grateful if you'd give me back the key.'

David noticed the blur of moustache above her lips quiver.
'But, David, I was only . . . '

'I know what you were doing, Mrs Goddard, and I'm very
grateful.' He held out a hand for the key.

With a bustle of irritation, she unzipped her bag. She
hesitated and finally held out the key.

'Thank you, Mrs Goddard, and goodbye.'

Her eyes hard as pebbles, she grunted and bustled off.

David moved through the bungalow from front to back.
The electricity supply had not been cut off and nor had the
telephone. He remembered that he had told the solicitor to
ensure that they remained available just in case he made any
visits. Mrs Goddard had obviously appointed herself an
honorary caretaker. David wondered whether she had ex-
ploited the opportunity to telephone her relatives, even sit in
front of the television huddled next to the electric fan heater.

As he entered each room and disturbed the faint powder-
ing of dust that had settled there, he also awoke memories
that he had thought long forgotten. His father, tall and thin,
sitting in the lounge on a Saturday afternoon watching wrestling on the television, his shirtsleeves rolled up above the
elbow in the old-fashioned way. The perfumed tobacco from
his pipe filled the room. Dad would call to him with a broad
smile and offer some of his cake. David also remembered his
father taking him to the old outdoor swimming baths at
Piper's Vale in Ipswich and the two of them gambolling
together in the water, and the den that Dad made for him in
the tree at the bottom of the garden.

John Parker, David's father, had been a compositor at a
large printing works in Ipswich. He was from a family of

130

farm labourers who had worked the Suffolk land for centuries. From that perhaps had come his calmness, his unwillingness to be hurried. Sometimes Dad's relaxed approach to life exasperated David's mother but she adored him nonetheless. David could read it from her smiles.

David would never forget the day it happened, a chill day in February, February the thirteenth, when he was nine years old. The fields he could see from the window of Kirsham primary school rustled with winter wheat. The headmaster appeared at the frosted glass of the door. He whispered to the teacher and called David out of the classroom. Their footsteps echoed down the bare corridor. 'Your mum's come to pick you up from school early, David. She's got some bad news.'

He said nothing more, but just showed David into his study. Mum was slumped in a chair, glass-eyed, her face mottled by tears. David walked over and stood by her. She said nothing at first but suddenly seemed to notice him. 'Dad's dead,' she sobbed. He stood there, numb, for several seconds before he realised what had happened and burst into tears. He remembered even now that he had thrown his arms round her legs, craving comfort, and sensing her above him, cold and wrapped in her own grief, indifferent to his.

He only learned the next day that his father had died from a sudden heart attack while at work. It was completely unexpected, for John Parker was only forty-two and until then had been the very image of good health.

His death, however, was only the beginning of David's pain. His mother's aloofness on the day she heard the terrible news turned to a kind of mistrust, even hatred, as though she blamed David in some bizarre way for the death of her husband. Like many human beings she could not accept the injustice of suffering, that it strikes alike the good and the evil with supreme indifference. There had to be a reason for her pain. And since John Parker's death could not be God's fault because He was perfect, it had to be the fault of either herself or her son. It was their sin that had caused the death of John Parker. Although David was completely innocent, Mrs Parker felt guilt for the death and transferred the guilt to her son. 'Why,' she even shouted once during a quarrel in his

131

teens, 'did God kill your father and let you live?'

At least this was the explanation for his mother's behaviour that David invented when he became old enough to understand that his relationship with her was abnormal. What annoyed David was the realisation that his mother had succeeded in making him feel a totally illogical guilt for the death of his father. At least he had been burdened by it until his mother died. Her body alone was not buried in the grave at Kirsham church but, David thought, much of his guilt with it.

And then there was the garden shed and what his mother had done to him . . . David had reached the kitchen in his walk round the bungalow. From the window he could see the shed, a dark creosoted rectangle in the twilight, stirring a memory too painful to recall.

He hurried back to the lounge to decide whether or not to keep the bungalow. The disadvantages were clear enough. He would not visit it very often and so the building would be expensive to maintain. It was poorly decorated. The scenery was not particularly attractive. If he wanted a property in the country, he could always sell the cottage and buy something else. On the other hand, there were advantages. If he sold in the middle of winter, he would not get a good price. The bungalow was fully furnished and equipped. Like many bachelors, David hated frittering time away on interior decoration. He knew and liked east Suffolk and the bungalow was convenient from London, a useful and isolated retreat he thought suddenly. Not only from Pamela but also perhaps from the police.

David was confident the police had no evidence to connect him with the murder otherwise they would have arrested him by now. Instead they had charged the journalist Hebden. With a sigh of relief he recalled how lucky he was on the night he disposed of the clothes in the skip. His escape was an act of destiny. David sensed Patricia's flesh was imbued with magical powers and eating it had given him some measure of invulnerability. It was of course not complete. The heroes of myth all had some point of weakness: Samson his hair, Achilles his heel. David suddenly thought of the reference to Detective Superintendent Blanche Hampton and the photo-

132

graph of the police press conference. The woman who was supposed to be hunting him seemed all the more dangerous because her face had been hidden in the photograph. He had no visual image of her, only the name. Blanche Hampton. David wondered again with a surge of ancient bitterness if it really *could* be the same woman.

David decided he would keep the bungalow but tell anyone who asked that it was sold. He would retain it as a secret retreat – from life, Pamela and even possibly the Hampton woman.

# 13

Children were everywhere. Some whooped and yelped like savages, others lounged in corners staring wistfully at toys they could never afford. Their hands – podgy, thin, freckled or pale – touched everything, prodding, caressing, tickling, squeezing. They had no concept of private property. The toy shop was one huge playroom where everything was owned in common. Piled in boxes were guns to maim creatures from outer space, miniature tractors, dolls who could manage every bodily function with ease, bricks of all sizes and colours, jigsaw puzzles of cartoon characters so ephemeral Blanche did not even know their names. Books cowered in a corner, tapes and videos flirted, model aircraft swooped down from the ceiling entangling their propellers in the superintendent's hair, model dinosaurs roared with a viciousness matched only by some of the children. Swarming over them like ants were the infant consumers, catching up in their flow the odd adult like Blanche who invariably wore an expression of harassed fatigue. She remembered shopping for Christmas with her mother twenty-five years before, she and her brother buttoned up in their Sunday best. If they had so much as breathed on a toy their mother would have slapped them firmly.

Detectable above the hubbub was the relentless throb of Christmas carols. Blanche had been forced to spend so long in the store, shouldering her way through the seething mass of children to buy Christmas presents for her nephews and niece, that she found she was listening to 'O, Come all Ye Faithful' for the fourth time.

As she staggered out, hardly visible under boxes and plastic bags, into Oxford Street and a freezing drizzle, she cast a jaundiced eye at the Christmas decorations. Strung between the lamp-posts like gelatine they were devoid of nocturnal magic in the middle of a winter day. The crowd tramped past, collars drawn up and heads bowed against the chill. Unable to face the prospect of travelling on a bus, Blanche finally managed to hail a cab. 'Where to?' barked the driver through the open window.

'Ealing please.' Blanche had to shout above the din of a bus that was accelerating past.'Sorry, luv,' he said. 'I'm goin' 'ome.' The driver, a fat, wheezing man in his fifties with leaky eyes, turned back to the steering-wheel.

Blanche did not often like to exploit the special knowledge she had gained as a police officer but occasionally, when the demands of combining police and a civilian life became unbearable, her self-restraint snapped. She dropped her parcels and thrust one arm through the window. 'You know the law as well as I do. You've stopped and spoken to me. You're refusing a lawful hiring.'

When the driver swung his head to face her, he shrugged and the man's features cracked into a smile of false teeth. 'I said "I'm goin' 'ome", but you didn't give me time to explain I live out Ealing way, so it'd be just on me route.'

Blanche sank into the back seat with a sigh and let west London roll over her curious, mahogany eyes: the bustle of Oxford Street melted into the bleakness of Hyde Park; the shabbiness of Notting Hill into the gentility of Holland Park; the aridity of the Westway as the cab hammered through Acton finally sank into the spacious suburbia of Ealing. When the superintendent staggered through the front door of the maisonette she did not notice the flashing light on her answerphone.

She filled the Italian percolator with Mocha coffee and through the kitchen window examined her overgrown garden with a sneer – it had received minimal care since her husband had walked out on her a couple of years before. Once Blanche heard the snort of the percolator and her nostrils pricked with the scent of newly minted coffee, she poured herself a cup and slumped into her Harrods sofa in the sitting-room.

With only one more Saturday before Christmas, the evidence had accumulated with a slow inevitability against Hebden. Forensic tests showed that a fingerprint on the

135

inside of the door to Patricia Hoskin's flat was Hebden's and made in the dead girl's blood while the lock of hair found in his house had been cut from Patricia's head. A stain on Hebden's raincoat was also discovered to be the murdered girl's blood. Without doubt, Hebden had been in Patricia Hoskin's flat on the night of the murder. Yet the journalist still refused to answer any questions from the police. To Blanche's intense annoyance Spittals was triumphant, jigging along the corridors of New Scotland Yard with the excited smile of a dog which has just scented a bitch on heat.

Reclining on the sofa, the superintendent wondered once again why Spittals was so desperate to have the murder case cleared up. It was partly a matter of the friendship between a minor government minister and a senior officer of the Metropolitan Police. But Blanche was convinced that was not all: the Commander was concealing other reasons to explain his decision to overrule her.

Her relationship with Spittals had become increasingly prickly in the previous few weeks. He wanted Blanche to delegate the work of preparing the case against Hebden and move on to other work. 'It's all over bar the shouting,' he had said the day before in his office. 'Hebden's as guilty as sin. I don't see why you're still wasting your time looking into other possibilities.'

Blanche decided to be non-committal. 'Don't worry, sir. The work I'm doing is just tying up a few loose ends in the evidence against him.'

'Just make sure they are tied up, Blanche, and bloody well. I don't want this case to unravel in court. It'll make us look a right couple of Charlies.'

The superintendent pondered whether a direct assault would release the truth. She decided she had nothing to lose. 'You know I didn't approve of that press conference, sir.'

'I know. You made it all too apparent.'

'It was in my view a possible contempt of court – '

Spittals raised his eyes to the ceiling with a look of bewilderment. 'Look, lass, we're here as policemen, not lawyers. Our job is to nick the villains, not defend them.' He dabbed nervously at his moustache and pursed his lips thoughtfully. 'Go on, you're leading on to something. What is it?'

136

'Well . . . I've been wondering, sir, what with the press conference and so forth whether there was something else about Hebden I should know.'

'What do you mean?'

'Well . . . everyone seems very convinced of his guilt. And –'

'Come on,' said the Commander incredulously. 'He's seen coming out of the flat at about the right time, he's got a key, his fingerprint is found in the blood of the girl he's murdered, he cuts off a lock of her hair as a memento. What more do you want – a video of the strangling?' He chuckled at his own joke.

Blanche smiled with her lips and not her eyes. 'It's just that we've found no trace of the . . . ,' the superintendent paused to find the right word, 'flesh that was cut from the body. And although Hebden and the dead girl had broken up, why should he come back and kill her that particular night?' She knew she was struggling. 'Besides, there's Bach.'

'Who's he? Some witness.'

'The composer.'

'He's been dead for years for Christ's sake. What the hell's he got to do with it?'

'There was a record of his on the stereo turntable in the girl's flat.' Blanche let her voice trail away. She could tell the signs when Brian Spittals' patience was wearing thin: his hands began to rub together frantically and his eyes wandered towards the bowls trophies in the display cupboard.

The Commander sprang up from his desk, shaking his head. 'Bach? My God, lass, you're not at Oxford or Cambridge any more you know, doing some useless course on classical music. You're in the Met.'

Blanche paused by the door and squeezed into her sweetest, dolly-bird smile. Spittals' eyes slithered from the superintendent's chest and up to her eyes. 'Just why *are* you so keen to have Hebden put away, sir?'

Brian Spittals chuckled. 'Good morning, superintendent.' He walked back to his desk and Blanche knew she was dismissed.

So much, thought Blanche, for flirting with the lascivious old devil. She had learnt nothing. What irked her more than anything else was that Spittals was probably right. All the evidence pointed towards Hebden's guilt. Perhaps her diligent persistence pursuing other leads was no more than a pig-headed attempt to prove her boss wrong.

The tape on the answerphone whirred back and crackled into life. The first message was from her brother asking her to confirm that she was spending Christmas with him in Somerset. The second was from Dexter: Dinah Lynn had rung the Murder Squad office and said she wanted to speak to the superintendent urgently.

Dinah's petite figure bustled into the room and set the tray down on a low table. She passed a cup of tea to Blanche and flopped into one of the black leather sofas. 'I might have changed my mind if you hadn't returned my call quickly.' She smiled nervously, as if her lips were twitched by a thread. Her face was lively, Blanche concluded, but the melancholy still lurked beneath, lapping at the lids of her eyes. Mascara was caked round the lashes. Her frail hands picked at her dress of black, fluffy wool.

Blanche sipped her tea and waited.

'Sorry,' Dinah snorted through blocked nostrils, 'but I've got this stinking cold.' The girl tugged a handkerchief from the pocket of her dress and blew her nose. 'Look, I'm sorry to call you up but I got this through the post this morning.' She handed across a letter. It was written on rough, cream paper addressed from Brixton prison.

Dearest Dinah,

I hope you are keeping well. I am not. Ever since I arrived here at Brixton I have been ill with various minor ailments. It is partly the conditions – the overcrowding, the lack of exercise, the quality of the food.

Blanche glanced down to the foot of the letter. It was signed 'John'. There was only one John of their mutual acquaintance in Brixton prison: John Hebden.

I had read all about remand prisons in the papers but it is only when you enter one yourself that you realise how dreadful things are. But what depresses me most is that I

138

never see you. You have been down to visit me once and the memory of us holding hands over that cheap table in the middle of the room is still with me.

Blanche read the last two sentences twice and glanced up at Dinah. The girl swung her eyes to the window and flushed with guilty embarrassment.

As I said then I did not murder Patricia. I swear to you I did not kill her. The very idea is preposterous and I was overjoyed to see that you believed me. I can't say anything more than that. I just hope you continue to believe me. Everything will come out in good time.

My lawyer has been making a fuss about that dreadful press conference that the police organised but does not seem to have had much luck. The police seem to be a law unto themselves sometimes, even if it does prejudice a fair trial.

Please, please do come and visit me again soon my love.
John.

Blanche winced when she read the comments about the press conference. It was Spittals' decision, she repeated to herself once again, and useless to carry on bleating.

'So,' the superintendent sighed, 'you're also a lover of his.'

Dinah studied a dusty rubber-plant intently. Her latest set of ear-rings reminded Blanche of kebabs which had been allowed to burn over the charcoal. The girl combed her fingers through her hair before training defiant eyes on the superintendent. 'Yes. So what? It's not a criminal offence is it?'

Blanche shrugged. 'Not if you enjoy it.'

Dinah's smile held for a moment and then collapsed in on itself like a building that has been demolished by dynamite. 'That's just the trouble. I didn't enjoy it. I *don't* enjoy it.'

The detective squeezed the fresh lemon juice into her tea and savoured the sting of the hot liquid on her tongue. She was not in a hurry. The afternoon that she had intended to use to wrap Christmas presents was already dying.

The murdered girl's friend shifted in her chair, annoyed

139

by Blanche's patience. 'Well, aren't you going to ask me some questions?'

'I came to listen, not to ask. You go ahead,' encouraged the superintendent, having decided she was glad Dinah Lynn was no friend of hers.

'Well,' she said hesitantly, 'we became lovers.'

'When?'

'Four or five months ago, I suppose.'

The tea was a degree too acidic for Blanche's taste. She plopped a sugar-cube into the cup and thoughtfully watched it melt. 'Did your friend ever find out you were two-timing her?'

Dinah shook her head. 'It wasn't like that.'

'It never is.'

The kebab ear-rings quivered. The eyes smouldered. 'Look, do you want to hear what I've got to say or not?'

Blanche reached down into her handbag for a notebook. 'I've got all afternoon.'

Outside a car coughed as its owner turned the ignition. The cold and damp had penetrated to the core of the machine and the superintendent could hear the whine of the engine before it spluttered into life. The car roared away down the empty street.

'Our affair started because John felt under pressure. He said Pat was putting too much pressure on him to leave his wife. I suppose I'd fancied him for quite a while. I'd just broken up with someone else. Anyway, he offered me a lift home one night and one thing led to another.' She gulped and rubbed the ivory bangle on her wrist. 'The reason I called you here was to tell you John couldn't possibly have murdered Patricia.'

The superintendent's heavy eyelids flicked apart.

'He spent Tuesday night round here at my flat.' She gestured with her gnawed forefinger towards the door leading through to the bedroom. 'In there. In that rank, enseamèd bed.' She proffered a lop-sided, ironic smile. Blanche recalled she was an English lecturer who knew her Shakespeare.

'What did you do that Tuesday night exactly?'

'What do you mean? Which position did we adopt from the

140

*Kamasutra?*'

'All of them are impossible – so I'm told. No, I meant how you spent the evening.'

'We went out for an Indian meal in a restaurant on Shepherd's Bush Green, got back here about nine, watched television and then went to bed.'

'Did John phone anyone?'

A gouge appeared on the girl's forehead as she pondered. 'Yeah. He phoned his wife around nine o'clock, I suppose.'

'And he didn't leave the flat after that?'

'Yeah. That's right.'

Blanche watched the girl's cheek muscles tighten and how she plucked fluff from her dress with an over-deliberate calm. 'All night?'

She nodded.

'You're lying.' Dinah's face flashed up as if the superintendent had slapped it, her lips taut. 'We've got forensic evidence he was there at Patricia's flat. Why are you lying to protect him?'

The girl's shoulders flopped with disappointment that her trick had been so transparent. Her self-confidence oozed away like water trickling into sand. 'I was trying to help him. You see he *did* leave here. And he was silly not to tell you.' Tears clogged her mascara-laden eyelashes.

Blanche sipped some more tea and waited.

Dinah plucked out her handkerchief again, dabbed at her eyes and cleared her nose. She twitched out a smile 'We had a row, you see. He'd broken up with Pat but . . . he was always talking about her. He couldn't seem to get her out of his mind. Anyway, that night we had an argument. He shouted something about not being able to forget her because she might betray him in some way.' She noticed the superintendent edge forward in her chair. 'He wasn't specific. Then he left the flat around half past nine. He was very upset.'

'Do you think he then went round to Pat Hoskin's flat and murdered her?'

She shook her head calmly. 'No. He seemed angry with her for some reason but John's a wimp. He can hardly summon up the courage to squash a fly let alone murder someone.' Dinah walked self-consciously to her open-plan kitchen to

141

refill the teapot. 'I mean, you don't think he murdered Pat do you?' She tossed the question over her shoulder in such a casual way that Blanche knew she expected the reply to be portentous.

'At the moment, I think it highly likely.' The superintendent was only partly convinced by her own answer: it contradicted all her own instincts, her knowledge of Hebden. But she wanted to squeeze Dinah, make her think she was as isolated as possible. The detective stood up and walked over to the bay-window. An old woman in tattered clothes walked down the street pushing a dilapidated pram. Scuttling along beside her was a tiny dog dressed in a knitted overcoat. 'The only thing that will help John Hebden now is proving that someone else committed the murder. You tell me John was here with you until about half past nine. Assuming you're telling the truth now' – and Blanche squinted at her with all the baleful power she could muster in her eyes – 'that means Pat's mysterious Michael Drayton she might or might not have been meeting at eight o'clock couldn't have been John Hebden. So who was he?'

Dinah lay back in her armchair, her neck cricked, in a gesture of fatigue. 'All I know is that Pat was looking for another man after she broke up with John.'

Blanche raised the ball-point to her mouth and rattled it between her teeth. 'And just how hard did she look? Did she try singles bars? A computer dating agency? Marriage bureaux? Lonely hearts columns?' The detective paused before mentioning the last possibility. She was perhaps afraid of revealing her own vulnerability, for she recalled again the couple of adverts she had placed in a lonely hearts column after her husband had left her.

'She may well have done. She mentioned going to a dating agency. Pat seemed desperate enough.'

'Why didn't you mention this before?'

'It's only just come back to me.' She apologised with a shrug. 'I was so worried about John.'

The hotel in Cyprus was a rectangle of concrete. One façade of balconies faced the sea and the other looked down onto tennis courts and the dusty road threading into Limassol.

142

Tavernas, bars and discotheques crowded the pavements. After dinner in the hotel restaurant David enjoyed sidling down the road. His eyes flickered over the huge Mercedes taxis, the neon signs, the thumping music and the girls stepping high in their tight trousers. He observed from the shadows, sneering at the inanity of the night-life before him – the horse-play, neighing laughs, the pavement theatre – yet jealous that he was excluded.

David paid a supplement for the sea view and he revelled in it. Every morning he rose early and sat on the balcony in the cool air. He watched the grey-blue Mediterranean rise and fall, the gardener totter over the withered grass, and elderly couples, who formed the majority of residents in the hotel, walk stiff-legged along the mole which jutted out fifty yards into the sea. After breakfast he drove his hired car, a glistening Mercedes, out into the island. He dutifully visited all the places recommended in the *Blue Guide* but found most of them scruffy and downtrodden, admiring only the mosaics of Paphos and the undulating savagery of the Troodos mountains. David was happy to be alone, away from the office, away from Pamela, away from the voices, the anxiety, the memories that London stirred. But his relaxed mood was splintered on the fourth day.

Overnight the weather became unseasonably balmy for December and many residents of the hotel scurried to the side of the pool. David joined them and eyed a couple of unattached French women. They were both in their middle forties with plump thighs and sagging breasts smothered with suntan oil. Although one hooked David's eye a few times and even smiled once, he wanted only to observe. Two English girls in their late twenties placed their towels down beside him a few minutes later and David fell into conversation. They introduced themselves. One was a junior doctor at a London hospital with pale skin and frizzy hair. David found the other girl more attractive: long black hair framed her smiling face, lips shining with rouge, her voluptuous body heaving out of a black, one-piece bathing costume. He bought her a tomato juice from a passing waiter. As she talked, David found his eyes inexorably gliding over the curves of her body. He imagined his lips caressing her thighs, the soft skin of her neck, her breasts, her mouth.

'My name's Laura. Laura Benson. I'm a psychotherapist at the Maudsley,' she said, squinting into the sun. 'I get sent lots of routine cases. But I also do criminal work. Theft. Violence against children.'

David woke from his trance and looked at her with alarm for a moment. He feared sometimes that other people were able to read his thoughts, but because this girl sitting in front of him was a psychoanalyst he was convinced she would find it especially easy to penetrate his mind. She would know that he found her body so desirable that he wanted to eat it. 'I've even had the odd murderer. Not that you always know at the beginning,' she went on, scrutinising David's face intently. He chuckled to hide his momentary concern. 'There was one man, a junior clerk in the civil service, who was sent to me for some minor offences – I think burglary. And in the course of the treatment it came out that he'd abducted and murdered a little girl.'

David relaxed and put on his most charming manner, chatting happily to the two women for an hour or so. He was fascinated by Laura's stories of psychoanalysis and his over-enthusiastic questions almost verged on the discourteous. Having overcome his shyness, he revelled in the companion-ship. He would have liked to invite Laura for a meal or a drink but he was too shy to ask with her friend sitting only a few feet away. For the same reason he felt unable to ask for her phone number in London. Instead he stored away her name and, after an hour or so said a clumsy farewell, mouth-ing the usual platitudes about hoping to meet them again. He knew it would not be at the hotel since the two girls were flying back to London that afternoon.

David strode away, his eyes jumping over the jumble of bodies and faces by the poolside, gargoyles glistening in the sun, the image of Laura's voluptuous body pulsating in his mind, anxiety mangling his stomach. He lay heaving on the bed in his room, unable to relax in the quiet of his hotel room until two hours had passed. The girl's body floated above and around him, a teasing ghost that he had to exorcise before he returned home.

Back at the pool, the junior doctor sat up and adjusted her

sun-glasses. 'He was a funny one, going off like that, Laura. I thought he rather fancied you.'

'Oh shut up,' replied her friend good-naturedly, sipping her tomato juice. She paused and placed her glass back down on the concrete slabs that surrounded the pool. 'Did you notice his eyes?'

'Well, I noticed he was looking at you as if he wanted to gobble you up.'

Her friend chuckled. 'No, I didn't mean that. I meant how they made sort of jagged movements?' The doctor shook her head. Laura pondered on the swelling sea and opened her lips to speak. At that moment a youth sprinted past, tipped over her glass and splattered the tomato juice across the concrete.

'What was that you were saying about his eyes?' asked the doctor, as a waiter approached to mop up the red liquid.

Laura suddenly felt cold and threw the towel over her shoulders: the tomato juice reminded her of blood and of the murderer she had treated. 'Nothing. It doesn't matter.' She was going to say that she had seen the same jagged look in David's eyes as in the murderer's. But it was a silly thought and if she had told her friend she would only have laughed.

# 14

After the interview with Dinah Lynn, Blanche ordered Dexter and two detective constables to ferret in the corners of London where the literate lonely sought comfort. Not brothels and escort agencies but the plethora of clubs, dating services, lonely hearts columns and marriage bureaux where human beings, their hearts chilled by an indifferent city, hoped to find what some call love.

Blanche began by making a list of all the possibilities and had the new action plan marked up on the wall of the incident room. The superintendent thought she would start with the clubs for executives and professionals where 'friendly, presentable people' would be introduced to each other – code, she thought with a smile, for meeting members of the opposite sex. She read the advertisements in the weekly magazines and newspapers with more than professional interest, for she had wondered herself at odd times in the past couple of years whether she might find a new man by joining one of the clubs.

None of them had a record of Patricia Hoskin as a member. Blanche visited one which met in a room above a pub in Clapham on a Friday night but found the experience depressing. The organiser was an earnest man in his late twenties, prematurely balding with a hissing laugh. For Blanche the atmosphere bore no resemblance to the glamorous, fun-filled evening promised in the advertisements. It reminded her of a conference of terminally ill teetotallers. Round-shouldered men mumbled quietly to frumpy girls in spectacles or Filipino nurses who neighed dutifully at jokes they did not understand. Newcomers nursed their glass of wine on the margins of the room until they were bustled across by the earnest young man to a suspicious welcome from one of the knots of regulars. When she had finally confirmed that Patricia Hoskin had never joined the club, Blanche made an excuse and left. Her exit was hastened by the earnest young man adjusting his knitted tie and inviting her to go to the cinema with him one night.

The investigation was broken up by the Christmas holidays when Blanche drove down to Somerset to stay with her brother and his family. He was two years younger than the superintendent and worked for an insurance company. Although they had little in common, brother and sister loved each other's company. Andrew was proud of Blanche's rapid promotion in the Metropolitan Police and loved to hear her stories of crime in the corrupt city. Blanche in turn was happy to immerse herself in country life for a few days and play endless games with her two nephews. The only tension for Blanche was generated by her sister-in-law. She was short and fat with a braying voice, boasting of some new gadget for the household or bullying her husband. Blanche thought she was frightful but listened to her breathless monologues with stoic patience.

Even in the country though Blanche found her work impossible to forget. Sitting in the reception room in the evening round the wood stove – her brother watching a Christmas game show on television, her sister-in-law scanning mail-order catalogues – Blanche found snatches of conversation from the enquiry float into her mind. They were jumbled with the faces of people she had interviewed: Dinah Lynn, John Hebden, the couple who lived in the flat below Patricia Hoskin, the old lady who walked her dog . . .

On Boxing Day Blanche's curiosity overcame her distaste for hounding innocent hares to their death, and she agreed to join Andrew for a meeting of the local beagles. For the first hour, Blanche was entranced by the scene: the billowing clouds, the master of the hunt striding over the furrows and giving a blast on his silver horn, the beagles sniffing their way up and down the hills, and just occasionally a sight of their quarry, a black bullet pounding across a distant field. She was absorbed in the primitive ritual of the hunt and work was erased from her mind.

She was standing by a fence towards the end of the afternoon, her cheeks flushed by the wind, when suddenly the beagles tumbled over the brow of the hill. About thirty yards in front of her, a few of them seemed to stumble and then lunge at something. In a second the others had scampered back and jumped into the seething mass of dogs.

'Oh, damn,' said a knowing Somerset drawl. 'The dogs 'ave gone and chopped 'im.'

Blanche watched the snarling and yapping beagles with narrowed eyes before turning to Andrew.

'He means the hare decided to lie down in the middle of the field instead of running,' he explained. 'Sometimes the dogs just go right over the top and carry on. And sometimes they don't . . . that's what they call chopping the hare.'

The master and the whip ploughed into the dogs, whipping them back from the hare. The beagles reluctantly broke up into knots and scattered across the field. Blanche walked over to where the dogs had found the hare. Nothing remained. No bones. No skin. No flesh that she could see, just the pink noses of the dogs, bloodied from the hare they had eaten alive. The superintendent remembered the body of Patricia Hoskin, lying like a broken doll on the floor of the flat. Guilt plucked at her conscience. She had planned to stay until the New Year but the pink noses of the beagles sent her back to London that same Boxing Day night.

After Hebden had been charged, Blanche found her Murder Squad seep away. One by one the men were called away to other duties, and so when the superintendent returned after Christmas, she and Dexter were alone. In the following weeks, they continued to chase London's dating agencies and marriage bureaux. Dexter confided later that he used the opportunity to enrol in one for gays because he was sickened by the way his favourite night-club had changed. 'There's been a bloody take-over by the leather and rubber scene! Before it was great – cruisy, with lots of straight-acting guys who just loved the idea of a black policeman,' he drawled, glancing at his counterfeit Rolex watch before ordering another glass of wine, 'but now to get in you've got to have two Michelin tyres round your neck or pretend you're a leather handbag.'

No one had any record of a woman called Patricia Hoskin. Blanche went through all the murdered girl's papers again –

148

letters, files, magazines, cheque stubs, credit card counter-foils – but there was no sign that Patricia had tried to engineer a meeting with a man to replace John Hebden.

As February approached and the first snow of winter drizzled down on Clapham Common, Blanche began to lose hope of finding new evidence. Dexter sighed with increasing frequency when sent out to check yet another marriage bureau. The case against Hebden was still the same as it was two months before – circumstantial but strong. The other fingerprints found in the flat, including those on the stereo, could not be identified. Yet Hebden still sat silent in jail. Dinah Lynn went to visit him once or twice but all he did, so she told the superintendent, was protest his innocence.

After Christmas there were two rapes in central London which seemed to have been carried out by the same man. Blanche was given responsibility for the enquiry. Commander Spittals became increasingly annoyed by the time his superintendent devoted to following up leads on the Hoskin killing. Blanche defended herself by saying she was just tidying up the remaining loose ends. 'Stuff loose ends, lass. That bloody Murder Squad of yours can't exist forever. I'm ordering you to close it down now and redeploy yourself and Bazalgette on those rapes. That bloody management course you did at Bramshill was obviously a complete waste of time.' He sighed and paused. 'For Christ's sake, just accept this bastard Hebden did it and get on with nicking this rapist will you?' He slammed down the telephone so brusquely that Blanche feared her right eardrum might suffer permanent damage. Although angered by his intervention, she had to admit that she would probably have done the same thing in his position.

She poured herself a cup of black coffee and watched Dexter draw a red line through another dating agency which a detective constable had investigated. Blanche told him what Spittals had said and he looked at her with his brown, hard-boiled eyes. He was standing beside the gold-fish bowl, dropping pinches of food onto the surface. 'Good,' he said. 'Even Gregory the gold-fish was starting to think I was wasting my time.' The sergeant tugged at the knees of his well-cut trousers, bent down and pressed his nose against the glass of the bowl. 'What do you think of it then, eh?' With a swish of its tail, the fish plunged into the stone skull whose surface was now softened by a bloom of slime.

When Dexter stood up again, he look preoccupied. 'Something scared him.'

'Probably your ugly mug,' remarked a constable sitting at a table nearby.

The sergeant chuckled but the look of thoughtfulness clattered down again like a venetian blind. 'Something scared him,' he mumbled as he walked off to start work on the rape case.

Blanche retreated to her office to plan out the work for the coming weeks. Outside the snow was already melting on the slate roofs of the houses. In the crevices of back gardens lay patches of white slush. She picked up the morning newspaper from her desk with an automatic gesture, her eye snared by a headline, 'More money for the Met'. As she read the article beneath, Blanche squinted with concentration.

The Metropolitan Police is thought to be in line for a big budget increase so that it can employ more officers and invest in new technology, following the recommendations of a secret Home Office committee.

With an annual budget of well over one billion pounds, the Metropolitan Police is an obvious target for the government's 'value for money' programme. Last summer the Met secretly asked the government for a big increase in its budget.

To examine the merits of the police case and to discourage senior officers from going public, the Home Office set up a committee under the chairmanship of a junior minister, Paul Hoskin. Initially hostile, Mr Hoskin is believed now to be sympathetic to the demands of the Metropolitan Police.

The air in the empty incident room suddenly became heavy and oppressive. Blanche nodded slowly and ran her tongue over her lips. She knew at last why Spittals had been so keen to trumpet the arrest of John Hebden and she was not happy about it. The superintendent was just about to sink back into

150

her office chair, anger flaring in her stomach, when Dexter loped into view, the sleeves of his crisp white shirt rolled up to reveal a gold bracelet. There was something restless in the sergeant's tone and the way he held himself, his black lacquered moccasins tapping on the carpet tiles. Blanche knew he either had something exciting to tell her or else had a full bladder.

The superintendent was staring at a poster pinned up on the wall opposite by a secretary at the start of the murder investigation. It said 'I never bring my problems to work; I have enough here already.' She turned to the sergeant and cocked an eyebrow.

'There's a DI from Harlesden on the dog. Another girl's been found strangled.' His London drawl paused for a moment while he shifted his weight from one foot to the other. 'The same bits have been cut off the body.' Dexter's face glistened under the strip-lights, solemn like a mask. He turned to leave as Blanche scrambled for her sheepskin coat, murmuring over his shoulder, 'I told you that bloody goldfish knew something we didn't.'

# 15

The voices began again after Christmas.

From David's point of view the yuletide festival was excruciating. As soon as he returned from Cyprus, Pamela swept him up in a tide of concern. She attributed all his indifference towards her to the 'breakdown' – having selected the word she bandied it about with pride, for it enabled her to parade him as a medal of her tenderness. 'Poor, poor, David,' she whispered to friends, 'he just works *so* hard. In the end *something* had to give. Mind you,' she added with a cough of concern, 'the breakdown has brought us closer together than ever. Hasn't it, darling?' David would smile back at her compliantly.

He was dragged up to Yorkshire to spend Christmas and New Year with Pamela's parents. They lived in a huge house just outside Richmond which had stunning views across the moors. It had been designed at the end of the Victorian era by the son of a local lord of the manor much influenced by William Morris and the Arts and Crafts Movement, so the walls were hewn from local stone and the staircase carved exquisitely in oak. Pamela's mother and father were, however, the thrifty rich: the preprandial glass of sherry was never refilled and the radiators never reached a temperature above luke-warm. David guessed Pamela had told her parents of his problems at work, and they regarded him across the dinner table with even greater wariness than usual. On this visit, as on all the others, David was put in a separate bedroom from Pamela's. This time, however, David was relieved rather than frustrated.

At the end of the stay, on their way back down to London, Pamela seemed happy to David. 'I'm so relieved that you've made such a quick recovery. I knew it was just a holiday you wanted.'

152

David looked across to her face, slumped back in the front seat, the motorway lights strobing across the hard edge of her hair, the rounded nose, the wart on the edge of her cheek, the crisp, upturned neck of her shirt, the pale neck ringed by a necklace of pearls. 'That's right, darling, it was just a holiday I needed.' He hated her, with a cankered, shameful abhorrence. He hated her and he hated himself for not having the courage to tell her.

It was the next day that the voices began again. David woke and heard them murmuring down on the ground floor – the sound of a cocktail party. They were not menacing and David was content to lay in bed listening. For some reason he felt exhausted. His limbs were drained of all energy. All he could do was twitch the tips of his fingers and swivel his eyes around the bedroom: across the drawn curtains, down to the pile of books on his bedside table, up to the wickerwork basket that sheltered the light-bulb. He had intended to return to work that day, but now that the hour had come, David decided he could not face it. Always in the past, he had woken up with a groan but still felt driven to work, experiencing a zest for the office and the challenges it contained. That morning, at the start of January, he felt no desire except to remain in bed. Gone was the guilt he used to experience whenever he took a day off work, the fear of what errors might be committed in his absence, the anxiety about the files that would accumulate. He wanted time to think, to reassess, to be alone. The partnership had agreed to give him leave of absence for the foreseeable future, so, David reasoned, he might as well enjoy it. But he would need to maintain the impression that he was a lawyer who had disintegrated under the strain and was doing his utmost to recover as soon as possible.

He thought of the girl he had met by the side of the pool in Cyprus, Laura Benson. He recalled the undulating curves of her body, the full bosom, the black hair. David sensed his penis harden beneath the sheets but the arousal was strangely distant, as though he was experiencing the pleasure of another man. The memory of Laura gave him the idea he was looking for. He would find a psychoanalyst so that he could pretend he was seeking treatment. He decided to try

153

Laura first. David phoned her at the Maudsley Hospital and introduced himself. She sounded suspicious at first but relaxed when the lawyer explained he was seeking treatment for a recent mental breakdown and wondered if he might become one of her patients. She asked for a few personal details and said it would be fine once she received a letter from David's doctor.

David spoke to his office and explained that, although he was recovering, he needed more treatment. He surprised himself by the calmness with which he lied, although when he replaced the receiver his thin fingers were quivering.

Ten days later, David lay on the battered couch in Laura's consulting room. She explained that she hired it from a professor at a psychological institute at a cheap rent and that she preferred always to see patients outside the hospital. The room was at the back of a large house in Hackney. The french windows looked out onto a long, narrow garden dotted with children's toys, damp but vibrant in the wintry sunlight. Opposite were the elegant backs of Victorian houses, their grey bricks swelling into bow-windows, the roof-tiles glistening like wet flint.

Laura sat just in the margin of his vision, dressed demurely in a tweed business suit and white blouse. The gold-rimmed spectacles gave her a studious air. Her voice was as he recalled: gentle with a distant splash of an American accent. When she answered the front door of the house with a clipped, professional smile, David found it difficult to believe she was the same voluptuous girl he had met by the side of the pool at Limassol. But as he followed her down the hall and into the consulting room, the sway of her buttocks reminded him of the succulent flesh beneath. The difference now was in himself, not her. Laura's piercing eyes – the eyes that seemed able to read his thoughts back in Cyprus – were blunt. They could not penetrate his disguise. He was in command and she was destined to play out the role that he, as impresario, had selected for her. She was to be the psychotherapist who would confirm to the world that David was seeking treatment for a malady of the mind which did not exist. For David was convinced he was normal. He would play at being a little mad to free himself of Pamela and for entertainment.

His confidence in the face of Laura's probing eyes stemmed from the memory of his uniqueness. He had been set apart from others by his consumption of human flesh. By eating the very parts of a girl like Laura which stimulated him – her breasts, lips, and thighs – he had destroyed their power to attract him. He felt he had gained great strength as a result, the strength of controlling his own desires.

'I have strange dreams,' he told Laura.

'How do you mean "strange"?'

He stirred on the couch, wondering how close he wished to come to reality. 'I mean . . . like a couple of nights ago, I dreamt of a girl.'

'That's normal enough.'

'I know that. But I dreamt I wanted to kill her and eat her. Cut off bits of her body and eat them.'

Laura adjusted her spectacles and the leather of her chair squeaked. She was wearing black tights and David snatched a glance at where her calves stretched the material so tight that the white flesh showed through. 'Why? Do you hate women?'

'No,' he smiled in reply. 'I always thought I loved them. I adored my mother.' He stopped himself for a moment after his lips had uttered the words. He did *not* adore his mother. She had schooled him to think he adored her, to parrot to others like a poem learnt by rote in childhood that he loved her, but the truth of his affection was more complicated.

'So why did you want to eat the girl in your dream?'

'Voices told me to.'

Laura leant forward and made a note with a ball-point pen. 'And do you hear voices when you're awake – in normal life?'

There was no point in lying about this, David thought. He *did* hear voices occasionally. The voices had become a fragment of his normal existence. Schizophrenics heard voices and he was pretending to be a schizophrenic. What they uttered was illogical and nonsensical at first hearing but he was convinced it had meaning. He also told her about his anxiety attacks and obsessive hand-washing. At one level David was relieved he could at last disclose to someone else what he had been experiencing since the death of his mother,

155

but at another level he simply relished the intellectual game he was playing, observing Laura's reactions to the words he mouthed in the same way he watched his snake hunt a doomed mouse.

At the end of the consultation, Laura said it looked as if David had a mild form of schizophrenia and a mood disorder, and should continue with psychoanalysis. David acquiesced happily. She agreed it was best for him not to return to work. Just before he was about to drop his feet to the parquet floor and leave the couch, she asked David if he had ever loved a woman other than his mother.

The question took David by surprise. He looked out at a pair of starlings hopping over the lawn, their feathers ruffled by the chill breeze. Other than his mother? Well, he certainly did not love Pamela, except perhaps a little in the beginning. He had been friendly with a few girls and been obsessed with a few others, like the girl he had met a couple of years before when he had replied to her lonely hearts advert. But that was a short-lived infatuation, not love. His reply was simple. 'No,' he said. The word thudded with the same sad finality as his mother's coffin hit the bottom of her grave. David scrutinised Laura's face for a reaction. He hoped for a hint of sympathy. Her gaze was neutral, even bored. The question slipped from David's lips before he realised. 'If I carry on having treatment, will you be able to make me capable of love?'

The psychoanalyst smiled weakly. 'I'll try my best. But I can't guarantee anything.'

When David slipped the key into his door, he was already feeling guilty. Laura, he felt, had no right to make him feel guilty. She had scratched at the scab of his relationship with his mother. After all, he had loved her as best he could. And he had not wanted her to die. He experienced guilt nonetheless: guilt over the way he had treated his mother and guilt about Patricia Hoskin. He sat down in the drawing-room. The sofa was more than a sofa. It seemed to have a personality all of its own. The armchair also appeared to have its own individuality. His stomach was also trying to talk to him, burning with an unspoken hunger. David was scared. He thought he was on the threshold of some awful enlighten-

156

ment, an initiation of unimaginable pain. He lay back, respiring deeply.

After a few minutes he felt better, so he rose and walked upstairs. Under the glow of the lights, the Indian python lay coiled. The animal seemed impervious to guilt and anxiety, above the need to give or to receive love. All the creature required was warmth and food. David reminded himself that three Fridays had passed since the python had last eaten. He would need to go to the pet shop in the next few days and buy another mouse.

Kneeling by the side of the terrarium, David suddenly heard voices down below in the kitchen. They seemed to ascend the staircase and with each step they took, the babble subsided into fewer and fewer voices, although louder ones. By the time they entered David's head they had dwindled to just two, screaming at each other across the divide of his skull, one bellowing at him to 'follow the snake, do as the snake does, find peace', the other yelling at him to 'resist the flesh, resist the flesh'. The argument rose to a deafening crescendo, with David swaying in agony on his knees, until, with one mighty crash, as though of a cymbal, the voice urging the path of the snake soared triumphantly above the other, like an eagle hanging on the craggy air of a mountaintop. David collapsed to the carpet in a faint.

When he awoke a few seconds later, David felt exhausted. But his head was clear. He knew what he had to do. He sat at his desk and took out the lonely hearts advert he had placed in the magazine a few months before. He copied it onto a clean sheet of paper. He pondered for a moment and tore it up. He had to disguise the source of the new letter as much as possible.

At the head of the new letter he wrote 'Foxhall Cottage, Kirsham Road, Kirsham, near Ipswich, Suffolk.' Beneath he invented a new advertisement, falsifying his name, age and profession. He was about to write out a cheque when he remembered how easily it could be traced. Instead, he walked through the thickening twilight gloom to the local post office. It was no more than a counter at the back of an Asian supermarket. David paid in cash for a postal order and then posted the letter in the box outside.

# 16

She was waiting for him outside the main entrance to the Swiss Centre in Leicester Square. She was short, elegant and somehow vulnerable in her cream overcoat, the belt folded over itself. Her name was Elisabeth, a German girl working as a receptionist at one of the Hilton hotels in London, she had told him over the telephone. Framed by the bright lights of the entrance, she moved her weight from one leg to the other, her breath spuming on the night air. To her right, a tramp stroked a flurry of tuneless notes from a violin. He stopped occasionally and gestured towards a filthy plastic box at his feet. David waited for a moment before plunging forward, experiencing the same sense of exclusion from the bright lights and hilarity he had felt when he had prowled the road outside his hotel in Cyprus.

Elisabeth greeted him with a smile of relief, her teeth prominent beneath swollen lips. David looked at her more closely once they had established themselves at a table in the Swiss Centre café with two coffees. Her face was long and thin, framed by mousy hair which tumbled down to her shoulders. She threw off her overcoat and David noted with approval the firm line of her breasts beneath her white pullover. She would have looked less pale and tired, he reflected, if she had worn more make-up, although he did not find her unattractive. The way she spoke English appealed to David, the phrases clipped by the glottal stop, the vowels pure and clear. David discovered to his annoyance that he was becoming impatient already for the end of the evening. He tingled with the desire to caress her soft neck, feel her struggling for life beneath the grip of his fingers. He had always hated small talk. For him it was a tedious preliminary to discovering whether he had something truly in common with another human being. But he knew he had nothing in common with this girl. She told him, with Teutonic pedantry, that she had studied hotel management at a college in Munich for four years and three months, then had worked at a hotel in Berlin for one year and ten months and then at a hotel in Frankfurt for two years and one month but finally had decided that she wanted to spend some time in London. David wished he could dispense with the preliminaries and have the girl in his power as conveniently as he had purchased a mouse from the pet shop earlier that day. His impatience was sharpened by the girl's frailty. He would be able to overpower her as easily as a baby.

The conversation limped on for half an hour before David discovered to his relief that the film they were going to see was about to begin. He was thankful for the darkness of the cinema enveloping them so that he would no longer need to blather. As the titles of the film – a piece of Hollywood hocus-pocus chosen by Elisabeth – filled the auditorium with portentous music, David scrutinised the girl he wanted to kill. He needed to take her life for many reasons, some he knew and some he did not understand: to quell his guilt, to absolve himself of sin, to absorb her strength, to remain invulnerable to the police. Whatever the reasons, she was doomed. Her eyes were riveted to the screen with the troubled innocence of a child. The flickering light of the film played across her face, painting it the soft silvery-grey of a pigeon's feather. David sensed the urge to plant his lips on hers immediately and bite into the yielding flesh. But he ordered himself to wait, to have patience. 'Down, coxcomb, down,' he whispered to himself. The Shakespearian phrase echoed down to him from the shadows of his grammar school past. 'Down, coxcomb, down.'

Elisabeth seemed restless. Half an hour into the film she leant across and said she was going to the toilet. David's nostrils flickered with a whiff of her scent. She staggered along towards the aisle, stumbling over handbags and coats, the spectators rising and falling in a wave as she passed. David turned back to the film.

The heroine was beautiful – sophisticated, blonde, azure-eyed and with a body, thought David, who was a fan of Raymond Chandler, crafted like a Fabergé egg. He imagined that woman to be with him rather than Elisabeth. He wondered what it would be like to entwine her in his arms, her flesh warm and scented, so delicious it would melt, his lips slipping over the runnels of her body. David tensed in anticipation. The film only had another hour to run and then he would drive Elisabeth home.

He was drawn into the film, quietly aroused by a risible scene of love-making in a tent between the leading lady and the Australian hero. Their frantic union was disturbed by gun-toting bandits and David burst out laughing in the quiet cinema. Embarrassed, he glanced to his left. The seat next to him was vacant.

What on earth was the girl doing? Having plastic surgery? Plumbing the toilets? David twisted round and peered into the gloom. He could not distinguish her among the mooned faces. Hardly surprising, he thought. How on earth would he be able to pick her out in the gloom?

Ten slow minutes passed. Elisabeth did not return. As the truth of what had happened sank in, the metallic taste of anger soured his tongue. He grasped the arms of his seat to stop himself quivering, to stop himself screaming obscenities into the darkness. She had walked out. She had walked out of the cinema and left him.

Elisabeth had rejected *him*. She, this ignorant, pin-brained receptionist, had spurned him. The pain and the loneliness and the anger intermingled. Elisabeth had not even had the decency to explain what she was doing, to apologise. David realised he was sweating profusely, the perspiration prickling his forehead, his breathing fast yet shallow. The anger coursed through his body. He did not have her address but he had her phone number. He would phone her up and threaten her. He would track her down mercilessly. He swayed back and forth in the cinema seat.

He would do none of these things, David realised. He would sit quietly and watch the film. Why should he let her spoil his pleasure? But after five minutes David gave up. His disappointment had corroded his concentration. The lawyer stood up and shuffled out of the cinema, his shoulders sagging, his eyes glittering with the ire of an animal whose prey has been snatched from under its nose.

160

There was no reply. David respired slowly, letting the air swell in his lungs before the weight of his rib-cage forced it out. He wanted to dissipate his anger before making the next phone call. He had driven home from the cinema at a furious pace – tyres squealing, overtaking in the inside lane – determined to wreak his revenge on the girl who had rejected him. He would teach her a lesson. But not just her of course. She was a symbol of all women.

He placed her letter, typewritten on white paper and cursory, to one side. In his methodical way, he took up the next one, scrawled flamboyantly on Basildon Bond notepaper. The woman said she was an actress, although resting at the moment. 'Many of my friends call me beautiful,' she wrote.

Her voice was breathless with bonhomie when she answered the telephone, with an undertone of throatiness that David found attractive. She said she would 'love' to meet him. They haggled good-naturedly over whether it would be for a drink or a meal or a visit to the theatre. When the girl, who was called Suzy Miles, suggested the last possibility, David rejected it firmly: he wanted to keep her in sight once they had met. 'It's just that I want to meet you and talk to you – not just find someone to go to a play with,' he murmured apologetically.

He smiled to himself as he sensed Suzy soften at the excuse.

She told him she lived in the unfashionable district of Harlesden in north-west London. For David it was a blank in his mind: the name conjured no images. They agreed to meet for a meal at a Chinese restaurant he knew in Soho in three days' time, on Monday night. He said he would be busy over the weekend and he was speaking the truth: he wanted to buy a compact disc player the next day and had agreed to spend Sunday with Pamela. David considered that in one of the large, impersonal eating emporiums in Gerrard Street there would be little chance of him being recognised.

David looked across to the terrarium. Under the mellow light the python stirred. The lawyer, with his rational mind, knew that the snake could not see the cardboard box containing the mouse, let alone hear its frantic squeaks. But the serpent sensed hunger chewing at its stomach like David sensed it gnawing at his soul.

David's shadow crossing the cinema screen had only irritated those towards the back of the cinema. Those who sat five rows in front did not even notice.

Among them was a girl who had returned from the toilets to discover she had forgotten her seat number in the excitement of meeting a new man. When Elisabeth realised her mistake, she had stood up and gazed round the cinema. But the people round about hissed and told her to sit down. It was a hopeless task to identify David among so many people. She flopped down again, at the end of the row near the exit, determined that as soon as the film was over she would rush to the foyer and wait for him there. Elisabeth wrung her hands, still flushing with embarrassment, hoping David would forgive her. It was worth it, she thought. She liked him, and dreamt of his lips pressing against hers later that evening.

At precisely the same time as she waited patiently in the foyer, scanning the faces that emerged, the snake stirred as David dropped the mouse by its tail into the terrarium.

'I want to try to get to the heart of your fantasies about cannibalism.' Out of the margin of his eye, David saw Laura adjust her spectacles. He noted with covert pleasure the outline of her bra strap through the white cotton of her blouse. It was late afternoon on Monday. In four hours he was to meet Suzy, the actress. Outside, in the gloaming of January, lights seared the damp twilight: bulbs burning in kitchens and halls to keep the London winter at bay. A mist was already descending and clung to the bare branches of the trees.

David sighed. 'Go ahead.'

'I've been looking into it a bit. It seems that primitive peoples ate human flesh for broadly two reasons. First for food. In Sumatra, the Batak people sold human flesh in the market until the Dutch put a stop to it, you know.'

'Well, that hardly applies to me, does it? I could go into any restaurant in London with my gold card and eat whatever I

162

liked,' David snapped. This was just the sort of rubbish that he hated from the mouths of psychotherapists.

'Hold on a minute,' said Laura gently. 'I wasn't suggesting that in the literal sense. We're not reading a legal document now, you know.' Her chuckle annoyed David. Her comment appeared some sort of affront to his professional integrity. 'I meant a hunger in your case for something more intangible. Love perhaps.' David whipped his head round to face her. She had no right to accuse him of needing anything, of being inadequate. It was people like that German girl who were inadequate, walking out of a cinema in the middle of a film, too feeble to tell him what she was doing. 'You see, it might be related to the other reason why primitive people ate human flesh. It was to absorb the qualities of the person they'd killed – for witchcraft or something like that. It might be to get their vitality, their energy, or else – and this is the other thing – to absorb their revenge, stop the head-hunter being hunted, if you like.'

David felt uncomfortable, as though she had unknowingly touched a sensitive nerve.

'This is all linked with eating the flesh of a human being who's been sacrificed. The person who eats it thinks he receives divine life and its qualities.'

The lawyer lay back on the couch with a snort. 'And how does all this relate to my cannibalistic fantasies?'

Laura gazed out through the french windows. 'Repression. You're repressing something and it's coming out in your fantasies.'

'All a bit fanciful, isn't it?'

The psychologist said nothing for a moment, placing her hands together, finger-tip to finger-tip. 'Your mother died not too long ago. You say you loved her. Did she love *you*?'

His forehead crinkled like paper in a flame. His lips dried. Should he dare to tell her the truth? His mother would have hit him if he had said it in her presence. 'You ungrateful little worm,' she would have cried, 'how dare you!'

'Well, did she love you?'

'No. She hated me.' The words sprang out before David realised, the scream of a little boy alone in a field of swaying corn, the ears of wheat tickling his arms, tears burning cheeks whose down had not yet felt the chill touch of the razor. 'It wasn't my fault.'

'What do you mean, not your fault?'

'She never said it of course. But I knew. I knew from the way she looked at me. The way she treated me. She blamed me for the death of my dad.' In his mind he saw the poppies again, bloody wounds in the living expanse of corn, and he felt the boy's ache of loneliness. It had been his tenth birthday and he had been thrown out of the house by his mother. She had not even given him a present. 'You don't deserve it,' she had said simply.

'And do you feel guilty?'

Under his grey flannel trousers and crisp blue shirt, David's muscles tensed with alarm. He did not dare turn to face her eyes for a moment. He relaxed when he recalled he was immune to her power. She could no longer read his mind. She could not know he had killed one girl, would have murdered a second unless she had walked out on him in the cinema, and that he intended to strangle another that night. Laura was not referring to that guilt. She must mean something else. He shrugged his shoulders and waited for her to clarify her question. The only sound in the room was the tick from an Edwardian wall-clock, whose pendulum swung from side to side in an hypnotic rhythm.

'I mean did your mother succeed in making you feel guilty for the death of your father?'

'Of course not.'

The psychoanalyst pursed her lips. 'I don't believe you. Why not tell me the truth?'

David looked away coolly. His mother had made him feel guilty alright, even though he was completely innocent. Children are so vulnerable. After the death of his father, she had persecuted him towards her image of perfection. There had been no physical violence of course. She had not needed it. She had infiltrated her guilt into his soul by words and gestures alone. And all the time she thirsted for the words of love which she made the young boy recite. She was determined that he should kiss the rod that beat him.

David blinked and turned back to Laura. He could not tell her all these things. She would not understand, so he smiled

164

and murmured with a tone of finality, 'I *am* telling the truth.'

'So did she make you feel guilty about other things?'

David wanted to say, 'Yes, everything, even the fact I'm alive.' He did not need Laura to tell him he experienced guilt. He creased his face into a wan smile. 'Only about wasting money.'

'I don't believe you. You're resisting me.'

Laura had explained to him at a previous session that 'resistance' was when the patient refused to recognise and come to terms with aspects of their past. David had nodded in agreement. He knew there were dark corners of his life he did not care to explore. They imprisoned painful memories he did not want to meet again. He also believed psychoanalysts defined 'resistance' to mean when patients refused to believe the twaddle that was purveyed to them. In his days off, he had borrowed books from the library about psychoanalysis. He wanted to appear a convincing patient. None of the books adduced evidence that analysis worked. But as long as he continued to undergo treatment, David believed he could fend off Pamela and the need to return to work.

He had already found the medicine, the food, that cured. After strangling the girl and eating her flesh, his panic attacks had abated, the neurotic hand-washing had disappeared, the voices stilled. In recent days, however, and especially after the failure to trap Elisabeth, the symptoms had begun to return more frequently. When he had woken up that morning the voices were waiting, whispering out on the staircase. He glanced at his watch. He had less than four hours to wait. His fingers were already tingling.

# 17

David knew it would be difficult to park in Soho and had left home early. But the traffic was so thick that he only arrived at half past seven, the very time of his appointment with Suzy. The mist had curdled to a fog which muffled the street-lamps and reduced visibility to thirty or forty yards. As David cruised frantically through the grid of streets, pedestrians swung in and out of vision like a parade of ghosts while other cars were no more than red or white lights in the miasma. He finally found a space in Dean Street, sprinted across the clogged stream of cars in Shaftesbury Avenue, and panted up to the restaurant. The windows were opaque with condensation, blurring an assortment of fowl in various states of caramelisation. David knew Suzy had long, red hair and although he was ten minutes late there was no sign of her outside the restaurant. He looked desperately up and down the road for a woman who fitted her description. There were none. He scurried up the steps and accosted a waiter by the door to ask breathlessly if a girl had left a message for him. The man looked at David as if he were mad. The lawyer scurried back to the street, questions popping like balloons in his mind, sweat steaming in the small of his back. Had she got the wrong time? The wrong day? Had she arrived early, got fed up with waiting and gone home?

David was miserable and tense with disappointment. Why did women betray him? First there was the German girl who had despised him enough to leave him alone in the cinema and now this new one, Suzy, the girl whose body he needed to taste to save himself from a return to madness. The girl had betrayed him, like all women. His mother had hated him. Then she had died. He did not want her to die but she did nonetheless: that was the ultimate betrayal, leaving him alone in the world. Pamela had betrayed him by mocking his impo-

166

tence. Yet, he told himself, deep down he loved women. He wanted them so badly after all that he had killed one to possess her.

'You're not looking for me by any chance, are you? I'm Suzy.'

She stood in front of him, the voice huskier than he remembered from the telephone, a flirtatious smile twanging on her lips. Resting on the upper one was a small mole that David found particularly delicious. Her hair, the red of rusted iron, tumbled down over her elegant, black leather jacket. She blinked artificial eyelashes over wide, brown eyes that were smarting from the vanity of contact lenses. The skin at their margins was plucked by crow's feet and her skin looked leathery under the skilfully applied coat of make-up. She was, David concluded, trying to appear younger than she really was. But her features were small and neat, made all the more appealing for David by her pert, uplifted nose. She spoke again in the same self-assured way. 'I've just got here. I'm sorry I'm late but the bus service is terrible and it's far too far to walk to the tube.'

David grunted in a friendly way to conceal his annoyance and suggested they went into the restaurant to eat.

They were shown up a narrow staircase past a number of cheap Chinese paintings to the wide, impersonal dining-room that David remembered. It was about half full, the tables occupied by lugubrious Chinese and a variety of Europeans — some theatre-goers who were just finishing their meals, some tourists, some businessmen. David smiled inwardly as Suzy shrugged off her leather jacket to reveal a white pullover which clung with almost indecent tightness to her ample bosom. Pink corduroy jeans hugged her generous buttocks. Much more attractive than Elisabeth.

David decided to be at his most charming — attentive, intelligent and maliciously witty. Within minutes he felt in control, and as Suzy quaffed glass after glass of white wine, he sensed her eyes upon him. They were brown eyes, predatory, he sensed, but easily bruised. He watched her carefully like a laboratory specimen, noting how she began to giggle at his jokes and gaze at him vampishly through her eyelashes. He thought his witticisms were amusing but found her

167

response too extravagant. They talked about books, the theatre, cinema, where they lived, lonely hearts columns. David thought Suzy was less well-informed than she pretended but nonetheless found her company more stimulating than Pamela's with her bland unwillingness to offend. Suzy even seemed intrigued when he told her he kept a snake as a pet rather than disgusted.

Towards the end of the meal, he rested his hands on the table. Suddenly he felt one of them cupped in a warm grasp. She had boldly taken it in her right hand. He looked at the hand – pale and elegant, with prominent knuckles, the nails glistening with red varnish. He lifted his gaze and met her smouldering eyes. He felt aroused at being the subject of seduction for the first time in his life. Women, for David, were distant, creatures to be pursued, not ones to hunt themselves. 'I like you, Paul,' she murmured. 'I like you very much.'

David blinked at the name and remembered he was supposed to be a businessman called Paul Grosvenor. He supposed he ought to respond so he squeezed her hand. 'I like you too,' he said. David plied her empty glass with more wine.

'Do you know what a former boyfriend of mine used to do sometimes when we were eating out together?' Suzy giggled into her glass.

The lawyer shook his head.

A naughty smile crossed her lips and she leant forward to whisper confidentially. 'When I was wearing a dress, he used to kick his shoe off and reach out with his toe under the table.' David lifted his eyebrows as a gesture of surprise. 'He'd nuzzle it straight between my legs, right up to my panties.'

David had never been out before with a woman who talked dirty. With all the other girls he had known, sex was something alluded to with civilised diffidence rather than talked about like shopping at Sainsbury's. He was both fascinated and repelled.

'I used to wear special panties for him you know – tiny black ones with a bow at the side. He liked me to do a striptease for him before we made love.' She giggled again, her words slurred from the wine.

168

'And are you wearing them now?' David startled himself by his boldness. He sat on the front edge of his chair, a warm tautness surging through his loins.

Suzy laughed. 'No, I'm not actually. But I would have done if I'd known it turned you on.' She revolved the wine glass round and round in her hand before looking up, impaling him on her eyes. 'So what *does* turn you on? Oral sex? Stockings and suspenders?'

To his intense annoyance, he blushed. Although stimulated by her erotic talk, David was also disgusted by it. One side of him wanted her to continue, another wished her to return to the traditional ways of courtship that he knew.

She threw her head back and laughed, pressing his hand again. 'That's what I like about you. You're so funny.' Her voice suddenly seemed to grow throatier. David felt the moist heat of the restaurant press down upon him. 'You're the first man I've wanted to go to bed with in months.'

Outside in the street, David found her nuzzling up against him, her arm around his waist, the perfume of her skin and hair crackling in his nostrils. If seducing desirable women was so easy, why had he not done it before? Why had he wasted so much time with Pamela? Not that he had great respect for Suzy. David was an intellectual snob and cared that she had not been to university. In his eyes she was just a sexually attractive but unemployed actress, eking out an existence of empty glamour on a few pounds a week. She probably answered lots of advertisements to be bought a free meal, giving sex in exchange. Not that I care, David thought to himself. He just wanted her to possess her. His fingers were tingling at the prospect of clasping her neck, his tongue at tasting her flesh. The urge was so intense that as they walked back to the car, David was tempted to throw her into a dark alleyway piled with rubbish. But there were too many people on the streets, and besides he craved privacy for the fulfilment of his desires.

As they drove west along the Marylebone Road, Suzy chattered away. The fog was diluted, as if thinned by the flow of traffic. David recalled the night last November when he had travelled out to Shepherd's Bush to dispose of the clothes he had worn when he killed Patricia. Much had happened since

169

but there was no indication that the police had any evidence against him. He told himself to be doubly careful that night not to leave any clues should anything happen – not that he intended anything to happen, other than that he should make love to the girl sitting beside him in the car.

Suddenly Suzy asked if she could turn on the radio. He nodded and she leant forward to switch it on. A critic was talking pompously about the need for novels to do more than entertain the reader. She pressed the next button and the car was flooded with the crackly voice of a girl on a phone-in programme who was debating whether or not to have an abortion, now that her married lover had made it clear that he was after all going to stay with his wife and family. The third button was BBC Radio 3 and finally produced some music David recognised instantly, sounds that hit him like a slap: the distraught chorus from the *St Matthew Passion* calling down lightning and thunder to destroy those who have just betrayed Jesus on Gethsemane. He only caught a snatch of the outraged choir before Suzy settled back to listen to a pop music station. The fact that the *St Matthew Passion* was on the radio seemed like a prophetic sign to David, confirmation that the events of his life were woven together inextricably, speaking to each other in counterpoint like the notes of Bach's music. The *Passion* had been one of his mother's favourite pieces of music and had become one of his. Patricia Hoskin had played it on her stereo on the night he killed her. Just as he was about to leave her flat he had decided as a parting gesture to play the record again, leave the music to echo on in the empty flat as a requiem for the soul of the dead. And now the same piece of music was on the radio.

The relentless throb of the pop music soothed David and calmed the panic that seized his heart. Just at that moment he saw the exit from the Westway and swung off the raised carriageway. As they drove north up Scrubs Lane the fog gathered again, the bleak expanse of Wormwood Scrubs no more than a grey curtain, industrial buildings looming up like ships wrecked on the sand-banks of the night. The glitter of the street-lights on the damp tarmac was blurred by the thickening fog. Suzy directed him through a maze of Harlesden back streets, lines of terraced houses, their windows like

170

blank eyes, until they suddenly emerged on a trunk road and Suzy pointed to a block of Edwardian flats. She said she lived there and suggested David parked in a side road.

David watched her slide the key into the front door. Its brown paintwork was scratched and battered, a block of deal inserted around the lock which had recently been forced and then repaired. The door jerked to a close behind them, squeezed back by a pneumatic device screwed to the jamb. Suzy pushed a white timer switch and David's senses were so alert he caught the whirr of its clockwork mechanism. The stairway was unprepossessing, the floor made of bare concrete. Their steps echoed like the taps of a hammer as they climbed, David sliding his gloved hand up the banister, his eyes caressing Suzy's swaying buttocks. The front doors of the flats they passed had panes of frosted glass, but only one was lit to indicate someone was at home.

Suzy explained that the flat she shared was owned by a bachelor who was a chartered surveyor and spent most of his spare time playing tennis. He was out that night, she said, and would only come back very late. The flat consisted of a long, tunnel-like hall with a kitchen at the far end. All the rooms ran off it to the left. Suzy walked into the lounge and switched on a table-lamp whose shade was spotted by a coffee stain. The room, to David's experienced eyes, had all the signs of habitation by a certain type of bachelor: untidy piles of papers, tennis rackets and balls strewn everywhere, and no interest in decorating the room with objects of value or beauty. David was unsympathetic. By nature he was clean and neat. The flat seemed stifling to him, the heat dry and unrelenting. Suzy tossed her handbag and jacket on the green, battered sofa. 'Would you like a coffee?' she purred, pulling his face down to hers. David saw her brown, predatory eyes close with pleasure as he kissed her. She pushed him away playfully and whispered that they would have to wait for their coffee until later.

She led him down the hall and into her bedroom, leaving the door ajar. A slither of light illuminated a rumpled single bed, a chest of drawers, and a dressing-table glittering with jars and bottles. Suzy peeled off her white pullover. With rapid, deft movements she undid the buttons of her blouse

171

beneath to reveal a low-cut bra, swollen by her ample breasts. David watched in awe and mounting panic as she unsheathed her beauty. For he realised all he wanted to do was watch. His erection shrivelled with the fear of failure, as the prospect of making love to this woman as an idea was replaced by the sordid reality of their bodies heaving on the bed. Nausea jumped in David's throat, his cheeks burned at the possibility of this woman cackling with laughter at his impotence, like Pamela only a few months before. He saw her glance up in puzzlement and ask why he was still fully dressed. He sensed the tingling return to his fingers, the desire to love and caress this woman's body in his own way, the puzzlement in her eyes freeze to fear as his gloved hands clamped around her throat, the scream on her lips fade as suddenly as it started, her movements hampered by the jeans round her ankles, her arms flailing for his eyes, her fingernails scratching at his face, her collapse back on the bed her tongue thrust out in a silent call for mercy his fingers tightening again around her throat with the relentlessness of the python a dribble of blood from her pert nose the eyes bursting with her demonic fight to live. Then silence.

Silence. Silence and peace. No sound except the rumble of an invisible train clattering through the night. No sound except the tick from the watch on Suzy's wrist. No sound except David's hoarse breathing.

He sat back on a chair, his heart hammering. After a couple of minutes, David pulled the pink jeans from Suzy's feet and surveyed her body. His eyes tarried on the white lace of her bra, woven into a pattern of butterflies, and travelled down the sleek stomach to her panties. She was no longer a threat to him, but a source of comfort and hope. With a sigh of expectation, he rose and walked to the kitchen to search for a knife.

Sharp taps on the door suddenly reverberated around the flat. David froze, his heart racing as fast as it had been a couple of minutes before. He realised he was trapped.

The front door was unlocked. All the person had to do was turn the knob and walk in. The door to Suzy's bedroom was wide open and her partly clothed body was spreadeagled on the bed. In desperation he glanced round the kitchen for a

172

fire-escape. But his eyes had hardly begun their search before he remembered, the sweat prickling out all over his scalp: the fire-escape was reached from the window of the lounge.

The taps rattled the frosted glass again. This time they were followed by a man's voice, vigorous and fogged by an Irish brogue. 'Chris? Suzy? Are yer in?'

David caught his own reflection in a small mirror on one wall of the kitchen, his eyes wide with fear. The frame of the mirror was in the form of the arch of a proscenium stage, cut from plywood and then painted. A line of cats was dancing on the apron in front of the stage and two lines of cats, also sawed out of plywood and then glued onto the surround one above the other, made up the audience. In the mirror David saw the scratches for the first time: three gouges running down his left cheek. Only then did he experience the stinging pain.

He edged his way to the kitchen door and could see a black profile through the frosted glass. David calculated how much of a lead he would have over his pursuer if he ran through into the lounge, flung open the window and scrambled down the fire-escape. It was a huge risk. The window might stick. The fire-escape might be blocked by rubbish.

With a resigned grunt, the black shadow moved away from the door. As it did so, David's ears were suddenly filled with ringing. He whipped round to confront a set of wind-bells, hanging from the ceiling, and stirred to sound by some inexplicable breath of air.

David hovered for a moment to let his breathing return to normal. He debated with himself whether to stay and so risk capture or leave while the exit was clear. After a few seconds' hesitation, he decided to remain. The fact that the man had not come into the flat was another sign of his invulnerability, another miracle. Without the talisman of human flesh, David told himself, his guilt and madness would return. He would be caught by the police and imprisoned for life, be forced to give up all the material things he had worked so hard for and replace them with a life of institutionalised horror. And above all, he would no longer have the liberty to kill again.

David turned the key silently in the lock of the door. At a

173

measured pace, and breathing with deliberation to retain his calm, he walked back to Suzy's bedroom. From his pocket he took out a sharp knife he had found in the kitchen. He paused for a moment over the body, trying to print its beauty on his memory forever before the desecration.

# 18

'I fainted when I first saw her, you know. I never could stand the sight of blood.' The words were murmured through the man's moustache, so softly they found no echo in the interview room. Chris Tasker owned the flat where the murdered girl had lived. He was huge and lumbering, and dwarfed the chair he slumped on in Harlesden police station. Hardly, Blanche thought, the sort one expected to faint at the sight of a mutilated corpse. Yet she knew the dead touched the living in unexpected and mysterious ways.

Blanche had been driven to Harlesden police station that Tuesday afternoon by Dexter with more than his usual disregard for speed limits but, even so, she arrived too late to visit the flat before the body had been removed. It had been discovered the previous night and Dr Ruxton was to carry out the post-mortem later that day. Blanche bubbled with irritation as she prowled around Suzy's flat and watched a scenes-of-crime officer search the lounge on his hands and knees for any clues that had been missed the night before. The photographer and fingerprints man had already come and gone. A detective sergeant from the local station described what had been found as best he could but to Blanche it was all stale – the narration of an event she would rather have witnessed first-hand. It was not that Blanche was ghoulish. She simply trusted herself more than others not to miss any of the nuances of murder.

The sergeant told her Suzanne Miles was thirty-eight years old. She was born and brought up in Bradford but, after an argument with her parents in her late teens, moved down to London to try to make a career as an actress. She had failed dismally, living in the London twilight, scratching a living from small parts in fringe theatre and some voice-over work. Chris Tasker had discovered her body at one o'clock that

175

Tuesday morning after returning home late from a night out with friends at his indoor tennis club.

'Do you think Tasker could have done it?' asked Blanche, turning a tennis ball she had picked up from the floor round and round in her fingers.

The sergeant shrugged. He was a short and soft-spoken man whose face was pock-marked by acne. 'Doubt it. The pathologist reckoned she got strangled between eight and midnight last night, and Tasker's mates all stand by him for that time.'

'And did anyone see or hear anything last night?'

The sergeant slipped his hands back into the pockets of his overcoat and cast a suspicious look at Dexter who was sniffing about the flat like an inquisitive dog. 'Well, so far, we've only turned up a young Irish guy who lives a couple of floors below. He said he thought he heard voices on the stairs some time around half past ten, and then a sort of muffled scream a bit later – but nothing that couldn't be explained by an argument or some people having a good laugh.'

'Is that all?'

'Well, no. He said he'd started to make himself a cup of coffee a few minutes later and found out he'd run out of sugar. So he thought he'd ask the people up above if they had any. Apparently he was quite friendly with Tasker and the girl.'

'And?'

'Well, he tapped a couple of times and called out. He said he could see through the frosted glass that the light was on in the hall and in the kitchen. But he couldn't hear anything and he couldn't see anyone moving around inside. So he assumed no one was at home and went off.'

'Do you think this Irishman could have done it?'

'We gave him a hard time in the interview room and he didn't crack.' The sergeant's acne erupted into a cynical smile. 'Besides, we didn't find any human cutlets in his fridge.' Blanche walked through to the kitchen and gazed out through one of the windows. The air had turned chill again in the past hour and heavy flakes of snow drifted down through the gloom, vanishing as soon as they touched the damp roofs of the houses opposite. On a sports ground in the distance a group of youths, their legs chapped and bodies steaming, continued to kick a ball of grey leather through the mud. Beyond them and through the curtain of falling snow, she could just make out the ranks of gravestones that made up Willesden cemetery. Blanche smiled grimly at the juxtaposition: she could never understand the sado-masochistic part of the English temperament that revelled in the mud sports of winter. She had hated sports at school and only discovered the pleasures of walking in her twenties. She turned back to the sergeant. 'Have you found much? Fingerprints? The knife?'

He shook his head of greasy hair. 'Not much so far. The bed was a bit of a mess as you can imagine with blood and so on. But it looks as though whoever did it was pretty clean and methodical. Just cut off what was required and left it at that, taking the knife with him.'

The sergeant's tone struck Blanche once again as cold and indifferent, as though he were not describing the butchering of a human body but a wheel change on his car.

'Was the door locked when Tasker came back last night?' enquired Dexter, rejoining them after his foray round the flat.

'Yeah,' replied the sergeant wearily. 'Apparently it was quite normal for the girl to lock the door if she were by herself at night. It didn't make Tasker suspicious.'

'But presumably you didn't find her key anywhere in the flat,' stated the superintendent.

The sergeant stared at her for a second before he understood what Blanche intended. 'Yeah, that's right. We didn't find it. Presumably the murderer used it to lock the door behind him.'

'Was it in her handbag?'

'S'pose so. That wasn't here either.'

Back at Harlesden police station, Blanche agreed with the Area Commander and Spittals' office that she should take charge of the case. Detective Inspector Mitchell, who had started work on the enquiry for the Harlesden police, a lean and handsome man in his early thirties with a bulbous nose, nodded eagerly when Blanche told him of the decision and that he was to be attached to the Murder Squad.

Mitchell sat in the interview room against the wall, with Blanche and Dexter on one side of the table in the centre and Chris Tasker on the other. A woman police constable deposited four plastic cups of tea on the formica. Chris Tasker peeled the paper from two lumps of sugar with surprising delicacy for such robust fingers and dropped them into his cup. 'I've always been scared of the sight of blood, you see. I remember when I was fifteen passing out in a biology class at school when the teacher started to cut up a bull's eye.' He stirred his tea with the stick of plastic provided. 'I just passed by the door to her room. It was open, you see. And there Suzy was . . . blood all over the place.'

Blanche paused for a moment. Tasker was in his late thirties, with a flat, friendly face and short, black hair. The hair was already thinning and perhaps to compensate he had grown a luxuriant Groucho moustache which almost hid his mouth. His eyes were big and brown and as gentle as a baby's. Tasker had too easy, too vacant, a smile for Blanche's taste: the expression of a weak man. 'Have you got any idea who could have done this?' she asked him. 'It was obviously someone Suzy had let into the flat.' The superintendent tipped her head to one side and squinted with concentration.

Chris Tasker lifted his great, heavy head and shook it slowly from side to side. Blanche noticed a dark shadow round his chin. The shock of finding the corpse had made him forget to shave. The stubble contrasted with the smartness of his dress: a pinstripe suit, white shirt and paisley silk tie. 'No idea. She didn't have any enemies as far as I know. Admittedly Suzy was a flirt. She was one of these women who always needed a man and she slept around – God she slept around.'

'Did she sleep with you?' asked Blanche, as casually as if she were enquiring about his shoe size.

The two halves of the moustache pulled apart in a rueful smile like the curtain in an old theatre. 'Just once. Quite a while ago. When she was drunk.' His chuckle had a mordant undertone. 'I tried my best but . . . she wasn't interested. Said she preferred me as a kind of brother.'

Who wound you round her little finger, the superintendent thought. Blanche knew she had no alternative but to

178

scratch at the wound of his spurned affection, for it was obvious to her that Chris had been in love with Suzy. 'So, who *did* she sleep with?'

It was the first time the superintendent saw anything approaching anger fire in his gentle eyes. But the spark faded almost as soon as it appeared, to be replaced with the same stoic equanimity as before. 'Almost anyone she picked off the streets, any man she fancied. I'd always be meeting new faces round my breakfast table. None of them seemed to last very long. She led them all a merry dance, including me.'

'You make her sound like a nympho,' commented Dexter.

'She was. Randy as a bitch on heat.'

Blanche looked at the polystyrene cup of tea that the constable had brought her from the canteen. Although freshly brewed, the tea-bag was still drowning in the milky water. The superintendent flicked it into the ashtray with the plastic spoon and sipped the hot liquid. She cradled the cup between her hands. 'If she were a man, you'd just be saying she screwed round a bit wouldn't you? Not randy as a bitch on heat.' Blanche's voice was edged with irritation. Chris Tasker's tone reminded her of the whispers Wootton had been spreading about her being a lesbian. She disliked the double standards men applied to women's sexual behaviour.

Tasker was bewildered by her quiet rebuke and looked across to Inspector Mitchell and Dexter for an explanation. They both glanced at Blanche and then looked impassively back. An awkward pause swelled in the room. A drunk shouted somewhere away in the bowels of the station. Blanche continued. 'How many men are we talking about? One a month? One a week? Three a night?'

Back in familiar territory, the murdered girl's flatmate relaxed again with a sigh. 'No, nothing like that. A new man every few months perhaps. But I wasn't exaggerating, you know, when I said she was a kind of nympho sometimes. There seemed to be a compulsion about it – like collecting scalps. As soon as she'd been out with a guy a few times, he'd get possessive and jealous, there'd be a row and she'd bring back someone else. Nothing ever lasted more than a couple of months at most. Sometimes she'd have several men going at the same time. Then Suzy'd give them all the boot and she'd fall into a black depression because she was alone.'

'Sounds neurotic,' grunted Mitchell.

'No. Just a lonely woman,' said Blanche. The screams of the drunk grew louder and then faded away. 'And was she seeing a man last night?'

Tasker shrugged his burly shoulders and Blanche thought the cheap suit he was wearing might split. 'She said she was. I told the other policeman about it.' He nodded at Inspector Mitchell, who inclined his head in acknowledgment. 'I remember going out past her room on the way to the tennis club, around six or so. She was sitting at her dressing-table putting on some heavy make-up. So I asked her where she was going. She gave me one of her knowing smiles and said she was being taken out for a meal by a new man.' Tasker's cup of tea almost disappeared in his maw as he picked it up for a sip. 'I got the impression she'd been depressed for a few weeks, you know. She'd been to several auditions and not been offered anything and she didn't seem to have any men around. Then suddenly she seemed to perk up at the end of last week.'

'Because she'd met this man?'

'I suppose so, though she never said as much.' Tasker sat forward on his chair, resting his forearms on his knees.

'Any idea how she got to meet him in the first place?'

The man flopped back again with a mordant laugh. 'Probably through some lonely hearts advert. That's where she met quite a few of them.'

Blanche listened to the clatter of footsteps echo down the corridor outside and a telephone ring and ring in the distance. She saw Mitchell edge forward on his seat. 'Are you serious?'

'Yeah. She told me a few months ago. I always wondered where her constant stream of men came from. She had a bit too much to drink one night and told me whenever she got depressed, she'd answer some of the lonely hearts ads in *London Life* – you know, the magazine. She laughed out loud about it. Said she called them "file-o-fucks".'

The mortuary was in the centre of the university hospital, lit solely by artificial light, immune to the gloom and slush of the

180

London winter outdoors. It was hard to find for those unin-
itiated in the rites of death but Blanche weaved her way along
the corridors with confidence – past old people in wheel-
chairs, harassed doctors, coughing children and puddles
from melting shoes. Having ordered Dexter over to the offices of *London Life*, one of the best-known listings magazines
in the capital, Blanche had decided to talk to the pathologist
about the post-mortem.

There were two people in the mortuary when Blanche
softly closed the door behind her, Dr Ruxton and his ageing
secretary. Ruxton was holding up a specimen of urine to the
light and tossed the superintendent a friendly smile, while his
secretary set her powdered face into an expression of restrained annoyance. Ruxton's wife had died many years before and Blanche always supposed his assistant harboured
hopes of marriage to the pathologist, and that this explained
why she seemed jealous of other women in her boss's presence. 'Thanks, Margo. That's all for the moment. Perhaps
you'd be kind enough to pop off and type up the report.' The
grey assistant tugged her over-rouged lips into a smile and
bustled out.

The body lay on the shining, galvanised slab a few feet
away. Now that the dried and encrusted blood had been
cleaned from the mutilations, the wounds looked smaller
than Blanche had expected but all the more macabre for
their surgical neatness. The girl's bloody teeth grinned
through the gash that had once been covered by her lips, the
tips of her breasts had been sliced off, and there were two
ellipses of raw flesh where the insides of her thighs had been
hacked away. Blanche knew that Ruxton would have insisted
that all the bloodstains were meticulously photographed before being removed.

'I gather you're taking over this case as well, superintendent – adding it to the other one, so to speak. *Chop* logic, if
you ask me,' began the pathologist, with a broad grin at his
appalling pun. 'There's no guarantee the same man was
responsible for both murders, you know.'

'No one can give guarantees, Dr Ruxton, except shops and
factories. I certainly wouldn't ask for one from a pathologist.'

Ruxton chuckled at her spirited reply.

'It has to be a man, doesn't it,' sighed Blanche wearily. 'Women just don't seem to go around doing this kind of thing. It's neither in the genes nor the nurturing.'

Ruxton flipped his prominent right ear forward and rubbed it thoughtfully. 'Yes. These are a couple of nasty cases. But fortunately not *all* men are violent psychopaths.'

He peeled off his rubber gloves and turned to the corpse for a moment with a look of profound sympathy. 'She had wonderful long red hair you know – before we had to shave it off.' Suzy's head lay bald and fragile under the lights, her eyes closed, reminding Blanche of photographs she had seen of prisoners in concentration camps. Any sense of peace in the face was destroyed by the jagged hole around her teeth. Ruxton walked over to the sink and began to wash his big, white hands. 'She was strangled to death. The murderer used his gloved hands to do it. Just as with the other victim there's no evidence of rape – although obviously we've got to wait for the swabs to be analysed. The mutilations are very similar to the ones on the Hoskin girl, the main difference I suppose being that this time the murderer used a serrated blade rather than a straight one, and also this time he didn't cut off the tip of the girl's nose.' The pathologist led Blanche over to a stainless-steel trolley whose top was hidden by jars and bottles and various surgical implements. He indicated a pile of small plastic bags, each carefully labelled. 'Your best bet probably lies in those. I got some scrapings from under the girl's fingernails. Some of it looks like skin and blood.'

'What, from the murderer's face?'

Ruxton shrugged. 'Possibly. And there's also the odd fibre. Might be from his coat.'

The superintendent nodded. 'There was no sign of the flesh that was cut off anywhere, I suppose?'

Ruxton shook his head. 'No, not a sign of it.'

Blanche squinted at the body thoughtfully. 'You mentioned her hair. Was a lock of it cut off this time as well?'

'No. Should have mentioned that. There was no evidence of any hair being cut off recently. That's another difference from the other case, isn't it?'

The superintendent suddenly felt depressed. Perhaps the mood was triggered by the smell of antiseptic or the lack of sunlight, the experience of being imprisoned with death in that cool cell of white tiles and refrigerators. Or more likely, Blanche told herself, it was the sense of hopelessness, the recognition that evil and cruelty had always been part of humanity and always would be. She ordered herself to smile. She knew only too well the corrosive effects of hopelessness on human endeavour. 'The murderer almost certainly took her handbag. But I don't think the motive for the killing was theft. Why do you think a man would do something like this?'

Ruxton flipped his right ear forward again and wrinkled his high bald forehead. '*I* don't know. I'm only an old pathologist who's not far away from retirement. Only two people know for sure. One's God, who knows the secrets of all our hearts. And the other is the murderer.'

'Given a choice like that,' replied Blanche with a grim smile, 'I'd better get on with it and find the strangler if I want an answer.'

'I think you better had, superintendent. Or else I've got a feeling I could end up doing another of these post-mortems in a few months' time.'

Blanche flicked him a look to see if any criticism was intended. Ruxton stared her unwaveringly in the eye, a look of apprehension rather than reprimand. Blanche shared his concern. She knew she would have to wait a couple of hours to learn from Dexter how feasible it would be to trace all the shadowy men who had placed advertisements in the lonely hearts columns of *London Life*. She might even need to go to its Fulham offices herself if the editor was not cooperative and whined on about confidentiality and the need to protect the privacy of the men who placed advertisements. In the meantime, she had a visit to make.

# 19

Blanche was surprised by the lack of vigour in John Hebden's step. After three months in prison he entered the bare room listlessly, shoulders drooping. She knew that in prison time no longer holds the same sway as in the free world outside. The hours are no longer worth whipping when the only thing to be done with them is lie on a bunk and listen to the restless murmur of hundreds of caged men.

'Well you didn't waste time, did you? For once.' Hebden's arrogant gaze swung from Blanche, to her detective sergeant, to his solicitor and finally to the prison officer who stood by the door. 'I hope you're letting me out tonight.'

Blanche raised her eyebrows in polite surprise. 'What do you mean? Letting you out?'

'Well, you got my message, didn't you?'

'What message?'

The superintendent watched Hebden as he lifted his eyes to the whitewashed roof and then turn wearily to the prison officer. The solicitor adopted an expression of concerned interest. Hebden lifted his arms as though about to begin a litany of complaint but, deciding there was no point, let them flop down by his side again. 'Well, *why* you're here doesn't matter two hoots, now you *are* here. So let me give you the message personally, superintendent.' He was speaking quickly, Blanche noticed, hurried on by the adrenalin of excitement and desperation. 'I happened to be watching the evening news on television tonight and they had a report about the murder of a girl in London. I forget her name – it doesn't matter, anyway – but the point is the reporter said the police confirmed fears that this new murder was done by the same person who murdered Patricia. Now I was here – sitting in this stinking dump – last night when the poor sod was killed.' He walked towards Blanche, raising his voice and stabbing the air with a finger to emphasise his points. 'So, answer me this, how the hell could I have murdered this second girl when I was *here* on my arse in Brixton prison?'

Blanche saw the solicitor scribble a note and turn to her expectantly, his spectacles glittering in the light. The superintendent hated people shouting. Part of her upbringing was to think it was uncouth, but she had come to accept that the greater part of humanity with which she came in contact during her time in the police did not share her opinion. Her reaction was to stare at Hebden with a pained expression on her face until the journalist finished speaking and then to say quietly, articulating every single syllable, 'Would you care to take a seat, please, Mr Hebden?'

The journalist sighed and sank, deflated, into a tubular metal chair. Blanche noticed how much he had aged in the past few months. His once firm stomach was now bloated from the stodgy food and lack of exercise, his skin pale and heavy like dough. His hair, once neat and auburn, had become ill-kempt and threaded with grey.

'That item you saw on the news tonight *is* actually the reason why I'm here,' Blanche began. 'You see, the journalists – as usual – didn't quite get it right. There's only a *possibility* that the two murders were committed by the same person. No one knows it as a fact. And all the evidence I have points to you being in Patricia Hoskin's flat at about the time she was murdered.' Hebden swerved from her gaze to study the parquet floor intently, as if the herring-bone pattern of wood held some secret that he wished to penetrate. 'We found a key to her flat round at your house, as well as a lock of her hair with some of her blood on. And above all,' said the superintendent, leaning forward and slowing her speech so that the words fell from her lips like drops of water, 'your fingerprint in her blood.'

'Come off it,' flared Hebden, 'you know as well as I do that the fact I may have been there doesn't mean I murdered her. And – ' He stopped suddenly and sighed.

The only sounds were the rustle of Dexter's pen on the evidence forms and the echoing clatter from the prison outside. Ever since his arrest Hebden had refused to discuss his movements on the night Patricia Hoskin was murdered.

185

Blanche pounced on the half-admission with alacrity. 'I hope you've got that sergeant. "The fact I may have been there doesn't mean I murdered her."'

The quiet solicitor opened his mouth to intervene but, before he could, Hebden spoke again with the deliberate casualness of someone trying to conceal a mistake. 'I wasn't admitting anything then, and you know it. It was all hypothetical.'

'Just like your release from prison then,' countered the superintendent. She stood up and shrugged the sheepskin coat from her shoulders, hanging it from the hook behind the door. God, how she hated prisons, the claustrophobia, the loss of independence. If she were ever imprisoned it would drive her mad, Blanche thought. Not that there was much chance of that. Her only transgressions against the law were limited to speeding and parking offences.

All the woodwork and the unplastered brick walls up to waist height were painted a dark grey lacquer. Even though the air was warm it seemed chill on the skin, impregnated with frost from the night outside. The room was lit by fluorescent tubes above and one barred window glazed with wire-reinforced glass. She walked over to a greasy copy of the prison regulations hung on one wall. Her footsteps were little explosions of sound on the bare floor. She pretended to read it, hands sunk into the pockets of her skirt. Out of the margin of her eye, she saw Hebden shake his head, obviously wrestling with himself about what to do.

'Look,' he sighed finally, leaning back in his seat, 'I didn't do it. I didn't murder her. Can't you just believe me?'

Blanche's problem was that she did believe him. She had had her moments of doubt as the circumstantial evidence accumulated against him, but she was now convinced in her own mind that both murders had been committed by the same psychopath. As Hebden himself said, he could not be in two places at once. Equally, she had to admit to herself that the evidence against Hebden was strong and that as yet she had not found an alternative suspect. She had to use the prospect of freedom as a bait to trap the journalist into talking.

'No, I can't believe you,' she lied, clicking back to her chair.

'Why should I, until you tell me exactly what you were doing at Patricia Hoskin's flat?'

Hebden ran a hand through his ill-cut hair in a gesture of desperation. 'Look, it's not as simple as all that. Other people are involved. I can't just . . . ' His voice trailed away.

There was something in the journalist's manner that goaded Blanche's exasperation into anger. Perhaps the sense that he was trying to protect some higher ideal than people's lives, an ideal Blanche was unable to appreciate. Perhaps his indecisiveness. But when she spoke again, Blanche's voice was waspish. 'Things never *are* as simple as all that. Other people *are* always involved. Can't you get that into your stubborn skull, Mr Hebden? That while you're sitting here debating with yourself about whether to tell me the truth or not, some nutcase is roaming around out there,' and here she jabbed her arm out towards the window, 'ready to strangle some other poor girl and then butcher her body. But until you tell me anything to the contrary, I'm inclined to think that nutcase is sitting opposite me now, arguing with himself about whether to protect his own interests or whether to look after other people's for once!'

Blanche sat back in her chair, her cheeks flushing with embarrassment as Dexter and the solicitor gave her oblique looks. She did not lose her temper very often but when she did, the superintendent always regretted it. 'I don't know who you're trying to protect,' she continued, speaking softly now, 'but what you're keeping back may help me to catch the murderer and may well stop you going to jail for the rest of your life.'

Hebden crunched his eyelids together and tensed his cheek muscles as though preparing for a spasm of pain. Then he let out a great sigh. 'I'm not sure I can stand it in here any longer.' He leant back and gulped, his prominent Adam's apple rising and falling like a ball-bearing. He flickered a look towards his solicitor. 'You say if I tell you what really happened you'll get me out of here?'

'I can't promise anything. But if your explanation is a good one, you'll certainly get out of here much faster.'

The journalist paused for a moment. 'Has anyone got a cigarette?' The sergeant said he was out of them at the

187

moment and Blanche feared the magic moment of confession might melt away while someone went clattering down the corridor to beg a cigarette. But the prison officer produced a packet and Hebden lit up with evident and languorous pleasure.

'My problem was I fell in love with Patricia,' he started, his eyes pondering the grain on the top of the table. 'Things would have been a lot simpler if I hadn't. About six months ago she started to nag me about leaving Susan and the girls and marrying her. And I refused. And then she got pregnant.' He blew out the smoke through his finely chiselled nostrils and narrowed his eyes. 'I told her it didn't change things and I was going to stay with my wife. So she said she was going to have an abortion.' He looked up. 'I begged her not to. I don't know why I felt so strongly about it. I suppose men aren't always logical about these things. After all, I think I'd have done the same thing in her position.' He looked around for an ashtray and, not seeing one, flicked the ash onto the floor by one of the legs of the table. 'Then she told me it was a boy. She sort of drip-fed me with all these temptations. I've always wanted a son, you see, and she knew it. Anyway, I kept phoning her up, asking to meet her, begging her to keep the baby. She either slammed the phone down, burst into tears, sometimes said she loved me, sometimes said she hated me – but the message was always the same. "If you want me to have your son, you've got to leave your wife and marry me."'

'And where does Dinah fit into all this?'

Hebden focussed suddenly on Blanche, his eyes vulnerable. 'What do you know about me and Dinah?'

'Enough to know you started an affair with her once things got rocky with Patricia.'

Hebden nodded and closed his eyes for a moment. 'Yeah. I was a bloody fool. I think I started the affair as a kind of revenge against Pat.' He sucked on his cigarette again for comfort. 'Anyway, I came down to London from Derbyshire for some work that Tuesday – the day she got murdered. I phoned Pat several times. She was very cold and distant. Said it was all over and she didn't want to see me any more. It was only then I think I realised I was really in love with her. I decided I'd leave my wife after all and marry her. So that Tuesday night I had a meal with Dinah, phoned my wife from her place and then drove down to Clapham. I made some excuse to Dinah. I forget what it was. I wanted it to be a surprise for Pat. Make her happy.'

The last few words were edged with a throaty falsetto. Hebden suddenly started to breathe in deeply to stem his tears. 'Shit,' he whispered, wiping a hand across his eyes, his cheek muscles tight against any sobs. He gulped for air. 'I suppose I got there about a quarter past or half past eleven. The light was on in her flat behind the blinds. I let myself in with my key and tiptoed up the stairs. I remember I listened at the door. I could hear music, classical music.' He looked up. 'It sounded like that music you played in the car on the way down from Derbyshire. Anyway, I put the key in the lock as quietly as I could and walked in. I was speechless. The flat was a complete mess. I went into the bedroom first and saw all the drawers pulled out, the clothes strewn everywhere. Then I went to the lounge. And I saw her.'

He leant back in his chair, and clenched his eyes shut as if to blot out the horrifying vision, squeezing out the tears through his eyelashes like drops of blood from a wound. A shiver passed through his whole body and then he leant forward and wept, head between his knees. His hunched shoulders quivered with sobs for half a minute before he sat back and spoke again. 'You've no idea what it was like, finding her like that. God knows the loony who could do it. Killing the woman I loved, the woman who had my son inside her.'

It was typical of Hebden, Blanche thought with a cynical smile to herself, that even at that awful moment all he could think about was himself.

'Anyway I panicked. I was afraid of being found there. I'd told my wife I'd finished with Pat. There's no way I'd be able to explain how and why I was round at her flat. That really would be the end of everything – I'd not only lose Pat and her baby but I'd also lose my wife and kids. I'd be left with nothing.' He stubbed out his cigarette on the heel of his shoe and asked for another. Blanche nodded and the prison officer stepped forward with his packet again. 'Then I was afraid of being found there by the police and them thinking we'd quarrelled about something like the abortion and I'd killed her. I don't know, I just panicked. But I wanted something to remember her by, so I just picked up a pair of scissors that were lying around and cut off a lock of her hair. Then I ran out of the place as fast as I could. I just had to get away.' He sucked nervously on his new cigarette and smeared the remaining tears away with the back of his left hand. He sat musing for a second. The prison officer crossed his legs and the creak of his chair echoed round the room.

Blanche believed the journalist's story. It was so extraordinary it had to be true. Besides, his tears were genuine – one of the few genuine things about him, she thought. She had felt dislike rather than sympathy grow for him as he told his story, but not enough to make her want to twist the knife in the wound by telling him the ultimate irony. On the night Hebden decided to change his mind and offer to marry Patricia because she was bearing his baby, that precious son of his had already been aborted from her womb. He did not need the truth. No one needed to know it.

The journalist looked up beseechingly. 'So how long will it be before you can get me out of here?'

'Shouldn't be too long,' said Blanche reaching for her coat and nodding to the solicitor. 'I'll do what I can.'

'Oh, there's one last thing,' added the journalist. He rubbed his hands together with embarrassment. 'Does my wife have to know?'

Blanche remembered who Hebden reminded her of – her former husband. They were both selfish, and cowards to boot. 'Look, I'm a police officer not a marriage guidance counsellor.' She suddenly turned round in the open doorway with the hot breath of anger in her lungs. She wanted to say something else, that Hebden's life of egotism and deception disgusted her. But she tightened her lips to silence and confined her words to a bland farewell.

As Blanche feared, the editor of *London Life* – a spotty and articulate youth with a huge nose and scarlet-rimmed spectacles – was reluctant to help at first. The next morning he pleaded the need for privacy and the fear of commercial loss, in particular the fear that many of the men who had advertised in the lonely hearts columns would be so embarrassed to be contacted by the police they would never advertise again.

In reply Dexter smiled sweetly and looked round the office with an air of elegiac sadness. He said the commercial loss the editor referred to was nothing compared to that the magazine would suffer when the police told women that a sadistic murderer was using the lonely hearts column of the magazine to find his victims.

The editor gulped and murmured that perhaps he had been mistaken. If the police conducted their enquiries with discretion, he was sure the public good far outweighed the need for privacy. He took the sergeant down from his office to what he called the LHR, 'The Lonely Hearts Room'. Lining the walls from floor to ceiling and rising up from the centre of the room were pigeon-holes, grids of boxes made from varnished plywood. Each one was labelled with a box number and contained a large brown envelope. Some of the envelopes bulged with mail, others sat limply in their allocated space, flaccid from lack of correspondence. A girl with henna-dyed hair sat in the corner leafing through a pop music newspaper, a cigarette drooping from her finger. 'Sophie, would you just run off a list of all the LH advertisers for the past five months or so and give it to this gentleman please?'

The girl rose in a trance. A few minutes later Dexter watched the printer chatter out around two and a half thousand names and addresses. Almost two thousand of them were from men. The girl explained there was no easy way of linking the names to their individual adverts once the box number was reallocated, and that some of the people who advertised used false names. 'Silly, innit?' she giggled. 'But some of them get really embarrassed, you know. They like a bit of *disguise*.' She handed him a heavy pile of the most recent issues of the magazine and suggested he cross-reference the box numbers. She told him that the original letters or completed forms from advertisers were all destroyed a month after the adverts appeared. Dexter thought of possible evidence having been lost and rolled his eyes lugubriously. 'Not my fault. We'd be snowed under with paper if we

191

didn't.' The sergeant thanked her and left. 'Chiz,' said the girl, stubbing out her cigarette in a polystyrene cup.

Back in Clapham, Blanche organised part of her squad to cross-reference the adverts and begin contacting the men who had placed them. She knew the enquiries would be tedious and probably fruitless. Even if the murderer were among them, he could easily deny receiving a letter from Suzy Miles and it would then be down to how tight an alibi he possessed and whether there was any forensic evidence linking him with the murder. The team established within a day that neither Patricia Hoskin nor Suzy Miles had placed an advert and that three men – at least those with the same name and address – had placed adverts before the murder of both girls. The superintendent ordered these men to be found urgently.

Blanche gave a few more curt television interviews, voicing her horror at the murder and appealing for any information. The press were not told about the mutilations to the corpse and she refused to speculate further about whether or not she thought the same man was responsible for both stranglings.

She discussed John Hebden's story with Spittals. The Commander listened impatiently, his hands whirring like bobbins. When she had finished, he stood up and said there was no way Hebden should be released yet. The journalist's explanation of what happened on the night of the murder 'stank'. He intoned that until there was more evidence that the same killer *had* strangled both girls Hebden would just have to stay where he was, in jail. Blanche nodded agreement. The rational, conscious part of her mind told her that Spittals was right, that the evidence against Hebden was too strong to release him yet. But another part of her mind – the intuitive, unconscious part – whispered to her that Spittals seemed as reluctant to accept Hebden's innocence as he was unduly hasty in accepting his guilt.

The days after the discovery of Suzy Miles's corpse passed in a whirr of activity. Blanche worked fourteen hours a day, the weekend merging seamlessly into weekdays, chafing, prodding, interviewing, yawning. The forensic evidence dripped into the office. Scrapings from under Suzy Miles's

192

fingernails did contain enough blood to provide a genetic fingerprint of the murderer but the result would take several days. There were also grey fibres from a grey overcoat. But there were no alien fingerprints to be matched against any of those found at Patricia Hoskin's flat and no neighbours or passers-by saw anything of significance. The laborious task of contacting all the men on the list from *London Life* cranked into life. Two out of the three men who had placed adverts before both murders were found and both had excellent alibis. The third, a divorced television reporter with the BBC, was in the French Alps skiing and had left no forwarding address. He was due back in a few days and there was nothing Dexter could do but wait – something as inimical to his character as celibacy.

Exhausted and mildly depressed, as she always was when an investigation was not making rapid progress, Blanche packed her briefcase and drove home from Harlesden on the Monday night after the discovery of the body. It was February the eleventh. A sliver of moon hung in the sky, as cold as a razor. There was no wind and as she left the police station, Blanche could already sense the frost prickle her face. The roads through north Acton down to the Western Avenue were deserted, canals of empty tarmac. She swung left onto the North Circular without thinking, her fingers tapping in time to some Mozart on the radio. She felt suddenly lonely. It was the image of returning once again to her empty maisonette in Ealing. She knew what it would be like, the rooms tidy but dark, the air warm from the central heating, the bed cold as a stone. The diffident glance at the answerphone, hoping for the flickering light of a message. The hollow sound of the key in the lock. No words of welcome, just the hum of the refrigerator in the empty kitchen. Watching the television for mindless comfort, trying to blot out loneliness with an avalanche of distraction.

Such black moments descended only rarely and as she locked the door of her car and scurried across the road she told herself to snap out of it. She ordered herself to do something positive, like think ahead to the coming weekend with her brother in Somerset, phone her former husband or a girlfriend for a chat, or place a lonely hearts advertisement.

No doubt if she had been less absorbed, she would have heard the footsteps ring out into the frosty night behind her. But she did not. Until it was too late. Blanche saw the shadow first, cast on the paving-stones and on the foot of the front door, as she searched in her handbag for the key. She turned only to find her nostrils impaled on the end of a double-barrelled shotgun. A nervous voice barked at her to go to a small van parked outside her house. She obeyed instinctively, the coldness of the gun barrel chilling her skin. At that range she knew the gun would blow out her brains. It was much too risky to try to disarm the man.

'Open the doors,' the voice ordered sharply from behind her. Blanche knew this was her best chance. She stood between the two back doors and suddenly threw the left one open, prolonging the movement by swinging round her right fist. But as she did so, a crushing weight smashed across her skull. She reeled back against the van. A searing pain exploded between her ears and she sank into blackness.

# 20

David had no time to scrutinise the gouges cut into his cheek
by Suzy Miles in her death frenzy until he arrived home. He
slammed the front door, the incisions burning into his flesh
as if they had been rubbed with salt, and ran to the kitchen to
deposit the precious plastic bag he carried in the refrigerator.
Only then did he stagger up the stairs to his *en suite* bathroom
and bathe the wounds. He winced as the antiseptic bit into his
flesh, tears starting in his eyes, and the encrusted blood
melted away. There were three scratches, the worst a red
weal about three inches long running towards his mouth
from the outside of his right eye, and on either side a shal-
lower and pinker one. The pain was intense but David nonetheless breathed with relief. He had expected the scratches to
be much worse. Indeed, a part of him rather admired them,
believing them to add interest to what he had always considered a handsome but somewhat featureless face.

He was sure no one had noticed him leave the block of
flats. A much bigger problem was how to disguise the
scratches. The police might well tell the public to report
anyone who bore mysterious wounds on their face. How
would he explain them to Pamela for example? David
thought through the possibilities while he dressed the
scratches with antiseptic cream and lint. He decided he would
pretend he had tripped over a paving-stone – there were
many uneven ones in the area – and that he had been un-
lucky enough to fall on some broken glass. He would refuse
to show Pamela the wounds themselves if she became suspicious. He hoped she was not going to be too solicitous.
David was confident the two outer cuts would heal up quickly
but feared the central gouge would mark his cheek perma-
nently.

David wondered whether he should ring Pamela

immediately to tell her of his imaginary accident. He decided against it. Better to tell her the next day when he had agreed to meet her for dinner.

As he stood in the bathroom, the mirror began to shimmer and glow red hot. The walls of the room started to expand and contract like a huge lung. David looked down and his feet seemed thirty feet away, as though at the foot of a building on whose roof he was standing. His knees seemed to swell and then shrink. He was not hallucinating. He was sure. What he saw was real, containing some sort of message. Other people might hallucinate. But David Parker did not. The details were too clear, too precise. And then the voices began calling to him from the kitchen, a siren murmur summoning him down. His limbs stiffened with expectation. Saliva oozed into his mouth. He knew what he had to do to save himself. And he descended the stairs.

David enjoyed the same untroubled sleep that night after eating the flesh he had cut from Suzy Miles as he did on the previous occasion. He slept so profoundly he only woke up at ten o'clock the next morning. The events of the previous night were jumbled and distant like the blurred recollection of a dream. Only the throb from the wound on his cheek seemed real.

He bought a selection of newspapers but was unsurprised to find nothing about the murder so soon: he would have to wait until the next day or the day after. Instead the lawyer busied himself with collecting together all the clothing he had worn the night before in a black plastic bin-liner. David worked methodically upwards from his shoes, bundling his trousers, shirt, jacket, tie, leather gloves and grey overcoat into the bag. There were, he thought, remarkably few bloodstains on the garments in view of what had happened but he decided to take no chances. If he tried to dry-clean some of the clothes the shop assistant might be suspicious and besides some trace invisible to the layman's eye might remain. He decided to clean the knife he had stolen from Suzy Miles's kitchen and dispose of it and her handbag separately. As he worked, David felt distant from his movements, like an actor aware of the gestures he makes to elicit a particular response from the audience.

The fog still clung to the trees and the sun was no more than a white disc visible through the haze when David left the house. He drove north through the Victorian suburbia of Stoke Newington to a council rubbish dump in Tottenham, where he had been on odd occasions in the past to dispose of garden refuse. He remembered a pneumatic crusher operated there. The site was surrounded by a low concrete wall and a narrow flower bed planted with shrubs the council workers had retrieved from the skips. No one was there apart from two workmen in overalls who were unloading the smashed remains of kitchen units from the back of a transit van. They glanced up for a moment when David parked his car and then continued to work methodically as before. David could hear the comforting whine of the motor and the crack of splintering timber as the piston advanced to crush the rubbish. As nonchalantly as possible, he pulled the plastic bag from the boot, walked up the steps and tossed the bag into the path of the crusher. He lingered to watch the incriminating evidence disappear even though he knew it might arouse suspicion.

"Scuse me, mate,' said one of the workmen, who was waiting at the bottom of the steps, holding a drawer in each hand.

David smiled an embarrassed apology and hurried back to the car. He drove down through Clapton, hoping the workman was not suspicious by nature and would not remember the plaster on his cheek. He remembered the knife and handbag and slipped them into two skips he found in side streets.

On his return he felt so carefree and happy he decided to work. After a quarter of an hour or so furrowing through some tax papers, he started to enjoy himself. The case posed some interesting problems and David rediscovered for a couple of hours his old zest for work. Towards the end of the afternoon, however, his concentration began to falter. He could no longer read any documents and remember what they contained. David became bored and anxious without knowing why.

His nervous mood was sharpened by the evening news on television. The murder of Suzy Miles was not mentioned

197

during the national and international section but was the lead item on the local news that followed. The newsreader – a black girl wearing what David thought was a ghastly yellow jacket – read the introduction, saying that a thirty-eight-year-old woman, Suzy Miles, had been found strangled in a flat in Harlesden. There was then a videotaped report from outside the block of flats. It looked so different in the daylight, David considered, and less shabby. Over shots of policemen waiting by the main door and some wobbly pictures of what were supposed to be the windows of the flat filmed from over the garden fence at the back, the reporter said the body had been discovered in the early hours of the morning. The police were convinced the girl had been strangled on Monday night in the flat and were appealing for anyone to come forward who may have seen anything the previous evening. There was no mention of any mutilations to the body. The reporter went on to say the police were working on the theory that the same person was responsible for both the murder of Patricia Hoskin, the daughter of the Home Office minister who had been found murdered the previous November, and this latest strangling. Then the woman appeared. At the bottom of the screen the name was unmistakable, Detective Superintendent Blanche Hampton. The name and the face hit David with the force of a punch. He sat upright with a jolt, his brow knitted with concentration. It *was* the same woman.

About eighteen months ago, before he met Pamela, David had decided to reply to a couple of lonely hearts advertisements in *London Life*. One was placed by this woman, Blanche Hampton. She had phoned and suggested they met for a drink in Ealing where she lived. She had refused to let him pick her up, presumably, David thought, because she did not want him to have her address, but did give him her phone number in case he had to cancel or change the arrangements. Blanche had pretended she was in advertising and David found her charming. He kept phoning her up after their meeting and proposing they meet again but she either found an excuse or did not return the messages on her answerphone. David became obsessed with her for a few weeks, even to the extent of thinking he was in love. He had been bruised by her rejection but thought the wound had healed once he had met Pamela.

Now Blanche Hampton had returned. This time as the police officer leading the hunt to find him. He smiled faintly at the irony. She had lied to him about her profession when they met for the one and only time. She was obviously embarrassed by it. Now he had found out the truth.

David suddenly felt lonely. He found to his surprise that he was looking forward to seeing Pamela that night. So he telephoned her at home and confirmed what time he was expected. She sounded distant and preoccupied but David thought nothing of it at the time. Instead, the prospect of dinner that night mellowed his attitude towards her. Pamela was not that bad after all, he concluded. She irritated him beyond measure sometimes and was not very bright. But like her, he also craved security and conformity and companionship. She was the only woman he had ever proposed to and so far he had not found the strength to call off the marriage. He could just let things drift now, drift into marriage, drift into children, drift into middle age.

Pamela seemed abnormally quiet during the meal. She asked her usual polite questions. First about how he had come by the bandage on his face. She did not seem to pay much attention to his reply, David thought, but seemed convinced by his excuse. She also enquired how the psychotherapy was progressing. David had always pretended to her that he believed in the treatment rather than despised it and he continued the charade that night. He said he felt much better, much calmer, and that he intended to go back to work as soon as possible, part-time at first but then slowly return to normal. David asked about her work and then about how the preparations for the wedding were going.

Pamela looked away from him and down at the empty plates, smeared with the remains of a chilled moussaka from the supermarket. 'It was *that* I wanted to have a word with you about.'

David listened to the hum of the refrigerator as it switched itself on. 'Well, go on,' he said with a trace of irritation. Although often oblique himself, David disliked her belief that indirectness in conversation was somehow more civilised.

She sighed and lifted her hands up to cradle her cheeks,

making them fat like a chipmunk's. 'It's *so* difficult to say this
. . . I don't know how to do it, David . . . ' Her voice began to
crack. 'But, well, I've been thinking about it a lot recently
and – '

'And what?'

Her eyes flashed. 'Shut up and listen for once, will you?'
she snapped suddenly. 'You're always interrupting me. Just
*listen!*'

David jerked back in his chair, arms akimbo, tense with
anger. The evening was going so well until that moment, he
thought, and now she was determined to spoil it. She was
probably going to say he ought to help more with the wedding arrangements, or she was not sure where the wedding
reception should be held or what her wedding dress should
be. He hated it when she raised her voice to him, and particularly when she criticised him.

'I don't want to marry you any more.'

David blinked in astonishment. Had the words he had so
often promised to say in the past at last slipped from his lips?
Words he no longer wished to pronounce? He blinked again,
his scalp prickling with pin-points of heat, his tongue suddenly dry. 'You what?' he whispered.

'I don't want to marry you any more.'

It was she, Pamela, who had whispered the words, not him.
David sat forward in his chair. 'Why, for God's sake? You've
been going on about getting married for ages. I thought you
said you loved me.'

She nodded her head slowly. 'I know I did. And David,' she
looked up, her eyes clouded by tears, 'I *did* love you. I really
did. It's just that, well, over the past few months I felt we've
drifted apart, what with your illness and everything.'

David threw himself back in his chair, shaking with anger,
frustration and disappointment, shouting at the ceiling.
'You're fucking marvellous, aren't you!'

'Don't talk to me like that!'

'I'll talk to you how the hell I like. All I know is you really
know how to kick a guy when he's down. There I was tonight
looking forward to being better again, making really good
progress – God! I even sat down for a couple of hours this
afternoon and worked through some tax papers. Pamela, I

200

actually *enjoyed* it – and I was really looking forward to tonight. And then you let fly with this!' A terrifying thought, a disgusting thought, slithered into David's mind. He spoke through clenched teeth with the menace of controlled anger. 'There's someone else, isn't there? Another man you've met. Some man who's better than me. From a better family. A man your parents really get on with,' he sneered. Pamela said nothing. She sat with her head in her hands, shoulders quivering with sobs. 'Come on, say something. Say something for Christ's sake.' David hated shouting at her impenetrable wall of silence. He wanted her to scream back at him, tell him it was all a ghastly joke, answer his charge of betrayal, enable him to release the anger that had accumulated over years like the sediment of a river. David saw his fists clenched in front of him, balls of flesh and blood that he shook like rattles. The mute figure in front of him was yet another woman whom he had loved but had betrayed him. He would make her answer, make her understand the depth of his anger.

Suddenly she was struggling beneath him, her head thrown back, trying to wrestle his hands away from her neck. Her eyes were engorged with blood, her tongue protruding from between her teeth. David enjoyed the sensation of power. Pamela was answering him now. She was shocked into looking into his eyes with terror. For some reason, David became fascinated by the mole beside Pamela's nose. His fingers loosened and Pamela slumped back onto the floor, her lungs clawing for breath, her hands clutching her neck.

David came to himself and his anger decayed into fear. 'I'm sorry, Pamela. I'm sorry. I didn't realise what I was doing.'

Pamela crawled away from him to the kitchen, her eyes wide with horror. Through her sobbing breath, David caught the words. 'Mad . . . mad . . . you've gone mad.'

She cowered on the floor of cork tiles by the french windows, her normally immaculate hair ruffled over her eyes. His forehead shimmering with sweat, David stepped forward towards her, intending to apologise and explain. Pamela's hand snatched up a bread knife and she lunged out clumsily. 'Stop there,' she grunted, flicking the hair from her eyes. 'Don't move.'

'Pamela, you've got to let me explain,' David begged. 'I

201

didn't mean – '

'Get out,' she murmured. 'Get out of my house.'

'Pamela, look – '

'Get out and never come back. I never ever want to see you again.'

One thought began to hammer in David's mind. 'Don't tell the police, Pamela. Please.'

'Get out.' The silver blade quivered under the kitchen spotlights.

'If you promise not to tell the police, I'll go now and leave you alone.'

Pamela lunged towards him with the knife. 'Get out,' she screamed.

David drove home in a chill of fury. He expected to feel depressed, discover he had some sense of loss over the end of his relationship with Pamela. Instead, he experienced only an anguished confusion. Slumped in front of the television, his eyes registered but did not understand the flickering images on the screen. His mind was in turmoil. He told himself he had wanted to call off the wedding anyway, so that he should not be disappointed when Pamela did so. On the other hand, he did feel bitterness. But it was a bitterness over the way he had been treated, a mordant sense of grievance, rather than of grief. Over a period of half an hour or so, the vacuum of confusion was filled by panic. He feared capture by the police. David heard several car doors slam and wondered whether Pamela had already called them to his house. He even wondered if she had guessed his guilty secret and suggested to them that he might be the murderer of the two girls. After all, he had almost strangled her. Pamela might be suspicious of the scratches on his face, might know he had no solid alibi at the time of the two murders.

He was comforted by the knowledge that he had eaten human flesh, women's flesh. He had not only had his revenge for the way women had treated him but had also in a strange way been able to show his love for them by the same act. A man often says that a woman is so beautiful he could eat her. He had simply acted out the metaphor. And by doing so, he had absorbed their strength and youth. He had also been vouchsafed some rare and ineffable insights: the voices that called to him, the visual distortions that showed him reality in a new light.

After a troubled night brimming with nightmares of capture by the police, David woke early to the silence of his empty house. It was Wednesday morning. He remembered what had happened the night before at Pamela's and found the confusion of his mind had been replaced by a quiet elation. He had been a fool to think marriage to such a woman was a good idea. He was well rid of her.

David tried to forget about Pamela's rejection by following through his resolution from the day before. He phoned the psychotherapist, Laura, and explained that he wished to return to work soon. She sounded encouraging and suggested they met later that week. David also telephoned Douglas Ferguson, the senior partner at work, to tell him of his intention. He sounded relieved and said the tax department was snowed under with work at the moment: the sooner David could return the better.

Whether Pamela had called the police was not the only worry that crowded David's mind. He was also obsessed by the police investigation into Suzy Miles. It was tempting to drive over to Harlesden to see what was happening but David crushed the thought as soon as it surfaced.

Instead he bought a set of newspapers and read the lurid reports of the discovery of Suzy Miles's body. The tabloids linked the murder to that of Patricia Hoskin but the broadsheets were more circumspect. The reports also reminded David of Blanche Hampton, of how she had rejected him and how she was hunting him. In his methodical way, David searched through his papers to find the phone number she had given him eighteen months before. He found it in one of his old diaries – he always kept them for five years as a source of reference. David looked at his neat handwriting with a mixture of triumph and dread. His fingers quivered. He imagined the emotions he felt were similar to those of a spy who has uncovered a way of eavesdropping on his enemy without detection.

Whether it was at that exact moment that the idea came to him, David did not know. It was simply there, as if it had

203

always existed but he had never noticed it before. And, like his urge to murder a woman and then eat her flesh, the idea had to be obeyed. The risk did not occur to him. After all, destiny and fate were with him. He was invulnerable. No one would suspect the man who had killed Patricia Hoskin and Suzy Miles of kidnapping the policewoman leading the investigation into the murders. It was too improbable, too much of a coincidence. At one stroke he would undermine the whole police enquiry against him. If he came to kill her, and the temptation might be irresistible, so be it. On the other hand, she might come to understand him, even come to love him. The idea of exacting revenge in a more refined way on a woman who had rejected him was also appealing. He would have Blanche Hampton at his mercy to do with her what he wanted. His cheeks still stung with the memory of the innumerable times he had phoned her so many months before, the chill tone of distance in her voice, the anger of her exasperation and then finally her silence. She had no more right to treat him like that than his mother or Pamela had, he told himself. No, she would have to die in the end. She would recognise him and he could not let her escape. No one would think of looking for her body in the back garden of Foxhall Cottage. He could destroy any evidence and return to London to his usual life.

After tidying up the house – his cleanliness verged on the obsessional – David sat down to plan the kidnap. He decided the best place to carry it out would be at Blanche's home where she could be caught unawares and there would be less chance of intervention by other people. He knew police officers were given training in self-defence and David did not trust his physical strength to overcome her. He would need a weapon of some sort, a means to threaten the policewoman into his car. With a flash of inspiration, David recalled his father's double-barrelled shotgun which his mother had kept and he had locked up in Foxhall Cottage. He would also need a club to knock her unconscious so that he could tie her up – she might well attack him if he put down the gun. He had never knocked anyone unconscious before and wondered how much weight he should give to the blow without smashing her skull. Finally, he would need to transport the unconscious woman to East Anglia. David decided to buy a van. That way, Blanche would be less likely to be seen during the journey and the van could not be traced to his address.

There was undoubtedly a risk attached to the kidnap. It would be so much easier just to sit quietly and wait. There was a good chance that Pamela would not call the police and, even if she did, that they would not be suspicious of his involvement with the other killings. But another side of the lawyer spurred him on, arguing that it would only be a matter of time before someone came forward who connected him with one of the killings, or the police discovered his connection with the lonely hearts column of *London Life*.

The first major problem was to discover where exactly Blanche lived. He had her ex-directory home phone number but no address. He remembered with a flush of anger that she had changed her number because of his importuning phone calls. On the other hand, with luck Blanche would not have moved house. One way of finding out where she lived was to wait outside one of the police stations where the superintendent worked and follow her home. He knew from reading the newspapers that incident rooms had been set up in Clapham and Harlesden. But the risks were too great. He would attract attention by sitting in his car all day outside a police station and even then Blanche might not appear. The whole enterprise was too hazardous.

David thought back to his brief and only meeting with Blanche in a pub that overlooked Ealing Common. It was a balmy September evening and knots of people stood outside chatting with their glasses of beer. Blanche had given a brief and accurate description of herself and said she would be waiting by a Victorian postbox on the pavement. They met and chatted over a couple of drinks amiably enough, David thought. When the time came to say goodbye, she was pleasantly non-committal about meeting again, smiling and saying she was very busy at work. David offered to drive her home but she refused firmly, saying she was quite happy to walk. Yes, she had *walked* home. She said she was going to *walk* home. David had watched her stride purposefully down the pavement and disappear round the corner.

She could have been lying of course. Perhaps she had

brought her car and parked it in a side street. Perhaps she had even lied when she said she lived in Ealing. But assuming she had told him the truth, David thought, he had worked out a way to trace her. His heart thumping with excitement, he found an A-Z of London and turned to the page that included Ealing Common. He then passed several minutes looking for an old pair of compasses he had kept since his school-days. He sharpened the pencil in one of the legs and described a number of semi-circles centring on the public house, each slightly wider in diameter than its predecessor. He remembered that she had walked away to the south, away from the Uxbridge Road. He would start his search there. Within each segment of the concentric circles he made a note of the street names, every curve like a net within which he would trap Blanche like a helpless bird.

In the reference section of the main library in Ealing, David approached a bespectacled assistant in a shaggy jumper. He said he was looking for an old friend who lived in the borough and asked whether there was a list of electors in alphabetical order. The man looked at him suspiciously and said it could not be disclosed to members of the public. 'The normal electoral list is this,' he said with a wry smile, heaving a thick volume onto the desk. 'There are two hundred and seven thousand names on it.' The librarian rustled through some other documents and handed David a map. 'You'll find the wards marked on this. Best of luck.'

David began by unfolding the map across the desk crammed with students from the local college and drama school. His eyes trotted over the electoral wards, each rimmed with red, their names as unfamiliar as place-names from distant shires of England: Rivenor, Costons, Pits-hanger. He compared the map with his own list of roads prepared from the A-Z of London. David then turned to the electoral list. Between the hard covers, bound only with string, were booklets listing the electors ward by ward. He methodically checked off each street on his own list, scanning down the names with his fingernail. He thought he had found Blanche after only ten minutes when he saw the name Hampton. But the name was followed by the name Brian.

David pressed on with the search, his eyes dazed by the

206

endless catalogue of names, fearing that one lapse of concentration would allow his prey to escape. But half an hour later he found what he was seeking. Against Flat 3, 27 Alwold Road was the entry Hampton, Blanche C.

David made his preparations. On two nights he watched outside Blanche's flat, sitting in the darkened car and listening to the radio with the sound turned down low. The first night she returned home at half past nine, on the second her car drove up at midnight. David also scanned through the pages of *The Thames Auto Trader*, a magazine printed on cheap paper and crammed full of advertisements, to find a small van. He thought of buying one in Ipswich but decided the anonymity conferred by buying near the capital was preferable. In the end he bought a four-year-old Ford Escort from a British Rail guard who lived in Enfield. David paid him in cash and managed to persuade the man to let him have all the documentation, saying he would deal with the paperwork involved in registering his name as the new owner of the car. David was pleased with his own cleverness. He would now be able to sell the van for scrap in the man's name and so destroy all evidence of his involvement with the vehicle.

On Friday afternoon, David went to see Laura. On the way he called at a sports shop and bought a rounders bat. Made of solid wood and about eighteen inches long it seemed ideal as a weapon to silence the policewoman during the kidnap. Laura said he seemed 'very calm' and thought it was a good idea that he should return to work part-time. When she asked him whether he had heard any voices or seen any visual distortions in the past week or so — the classic symptoms of schizophrenia, she had told him — David simply lied. It had suited him well to allow her to classify him as mentally disturbed for then he could manipulate her better.

At the weekend he drove up to Kirsham and bought provisions — cans of fruit, vegetables and soup, and cartons of long-life milk. The gun and cartridges lay undisturbed where he had left them at the bottom of the locked wardrobe in his bedroom. He carefully checked the moving parts and fired the gun from close range at a piece of dilapidated fencing in the garden. The blast punched a jagged hole through the wood, peppering it with shot.

Throughout this time, David treated his preparations for the kidnap like a game – an activity beyond the realms of good and evil. It was exhilarating to plan a crime, to foresee and overcome as many hitches as possible. Once or twice he thought it was even strangely akin to drawing up legal documents, stretching the brain to conceive of every eventuality and then drawing up a clause to encompass it.

By Sunday night, when he was back home in London again, David thought he was as ready as he would ever be. He decided to wait for a few days and follow the progress of the police investigation from the newspapers. He collated all the articles he could find. Almost all of them dated from Thursday and Friday, the latter containing statements from Detective Superintendent Blanche Hampton correcting the false impression given by some parts of the media that the police were working on the theory that the Hoskin and Miles murders were carried out by the same person. David was relieved by this news and returned to the office on Monday to a warm, though watchful, welcome from his colleagues. David floated through the day with a sense of calm confidence. He returned home that night slightly tipsy, for several of the partners had invited him for a 'welcome back' drink in the office dining-room after work. The conversation was stilted because none of them felt able to ask directly about his 'illness' and David could not talk about his latest work at the office because he had only just returned. Instead he contented himself with allowing the other partners to chatter on about themselves and smiling benignly at their replies: he had learnt years ago that many people have the illusion that by talking about themselves they are being interesting.

The phone rang half an hour after David came home. He was in his study, listening to a Mozart piano concerto and stroking the Indian python. He wondered who it might be: a chastened Pamela? an angry Pamela? a colleague from work? one of his few old friends from Cambridge? He lowered the serpent back into its terrarium.

'Hello, is that David Parker?' asked the nasal, male voice, bored and apparently uninterested in the reply.

'Yes.'

'Detective Sergeant Dexter Bazalgette here, Mr Parker.'

David froze. His lungs seemed to take a full minute to expel all the stale air before filling with fresh oxygen. The pounding of his heart hammered so loudly he feared it might be audible down the telephone line. Had Pamela betrayed him to the police? 'What can I do for you, sergeant?' he asked with surprising steadiness.

'Just a routine enquiry, Mr Parker. Could you confirm you are the David Parker who put a lonely hearts advert in *London Life* magazine on . . . um.' The sergeant checked and then mentioned the date of the advert in November that had attracted a reply from Patricia Hoskin. He did not mention her name.

David confirmed the advert but then decided the best means of putting the sergeant on the defensive was to pretend outrage at the invasion of his privacy. The sergeant replied that he understood Mr Parker's feelings but that he was engaged on a murder enquiry and people's privacy had to take second place. He went on to say he wanted to organise a time when he could interview David briefly for a statement. David blurted out that he was a lawyer and just about to fly abroad on business for a few days. Dexter asked for the date of his return and David said the following Monday. They arranged for David to phone Harlesden police station on the Tuesday after his imaginary return and Dexter, gently insistent, took David's work number.

When David replaced the telephone he sat back in his chair exhausted. He sensed damp, warm patches under his armpits and a chill film of sweat on his forehead. He closed his eyes and listened to the hammering of his heart slowly quieten. He cursed his stupidity. Why had he not said come round tonight, or tomorrow night? Why had he panicked and said he was going away on business when all the police had to do was phone work and confirm that he was not? Why had he given the man his work telephone number so lamely? The police were getting closer and the only way of keeping them at bay would be to kidnap their superintendent that night. He would phone up one of the partners and Laura and say he had had a relapse and wanted to go away for a few days. With a smile, he decided to tell them he was being persecuted by the police. That would throw them off the scent! He would then return after a week, having killed the superintendent and disposed of all the evidence, and pretend he was suffering from amnesia.

He left deliberately incoherent messages on Laura's answering machine and the one at the office. Then he locked up the house, bundled all his equipment for the kidnap into the Mercedes and drove to the gentrified side street in Kentish Town where he had parked the van. He transferred the equipment across and, in the curtained darkness at the back of the van, changed into some old clothes.

In Ealing he was lucky enough to be able to park the van immediately outside Blanche's house. He did not want to make her walk further than necessary. The whirr of activity had calmed his nerves and he patted the unzipped sleeping-bag around his legs and pulled up the hood of the duffle-coat. Whenever the odd car or pedestrian passed David drew back into the shadows. As the stifling warmth from the heating began to fade, David felt the chill of the freezing night slither into the van. His breath began to spume and on the windscreen spangles of frost crackled across the glass. The only sound was the murmur from his radio which lay on the front seat. With the cold came doubts. His bladder began to ache for relief. What if he drove round the block a few times to heat up the van? But then he might miss her. What if a passer-by intervened? What if she were accompanied home by someone? What if she did not come back that night at all? He looked down for what seemed the hundredth time and checked the rounders bat which hung from his right wrist on a loop of string. His left hand gripped the gun under a blanket. The plastic Hallowe'en mask he had chosen as his disguise (he decided it would be much easier to explain away than a balaclava) was on his forehead ready to be pulled down. The rear doors hung open and loose. Would it not be easier just to drive away now and bluff the police when he was interviewed?

Suddenly she was in sight walking up the flagstones to the front door. How could he have missed her? David slipped down the mask, and swung open the van door, leaving it ajar. The chill suddenly evaporated from his body. With the forefinger of his right hand on the trigger of the gun, David walked towards her. He expected her to turn at any moment but she did not until he was only a few feet away.

When she turned, her mouth fell open in a mute scream. It was her eyes, wide and glittering, that showed the fear and it was the fear that gave him confidence. At the point of the gun he ordered her towards the van. She obeyed wordlessly. She threw open the back doors as he commanded but lunged at him in the same movement. David caught her on the side of the head with the rounders bat and she staggered back against the van. The lawyer swung again as hard as he could and hit her on the forehead. The contact of the wood against flesh and bone cracked in the silence of the night. Blanche collapsed conveniently into the van and David slammed the door shut. He heard shouts behind him as the engine fired and he skidded away through the slush into the night.

# 21

Blanche listened for a minute before attempting to open her eyes. Outside there was silence: no hum of traffic, no aeroplanes, no shouts of children in an urban playground. The air she breathed was damp and tepid, like that in a room which is only occasionally heated. Her head was a hard ball-bearing of pain: every time Blanche breathed the air entering her nostrils or mouth made her skull throb with agony. She felt as if a little drummer sat in her head insistently beating out a tattoo on the back of her eyeballs. She sensed a soft pressure under her and assumed she was lying flat on her back on a bed or sofa, her aching arms and legs drawn out tight. She felt utterly, utterly miserable.

The effort needed to prise open her eyelids seemed herculean, as if they were stuck together with superglue. She blinked tentatively because each movement, however tiny, fired a shot of pain through her head. Blanche found herself tied to an old brass bedstead. Above her hung a bulb sheltered by a dusty lampshade with pink tassels. The thin curtains were drawn against the feeble winter light – drab, gossamer wings of nylon. From the edge of her eye, Blanche could make out a man sitting in a chair in the gloom. She lifted her throbbing head to get a better view and he rustled uncomfortably.

'You,' she murmured, her voice seeming to come from anywhere apart from her throat. 'You.' She flopped back on the bed. The effort had exhausted her.

'Yes, it's me,' he replied, looking away with seeming embarrassment. 'I came to get you.'

'There are more civilised ways of doing it.' The superintendent had hardly grunted the last word before her chest muscles tautened in a fit of coughing. The shaking was agonising and, more agonising still, was her inability to lift her hand to her mouth.

'Do you realise,' David continued after a pause, 'the bed you're on was the one my mother died in?'

Blanche said nothing for a moment. There did not seem anything to say. She wanted time to think, time to squeeze her brain into yielding up what it remembered of this man: the unsettling evening in his company, the gaucheness alternating with false charm, the handsome face contrasted with what Blanche took to be a mildly neurotic mind, the mutual but vague promise to keep in contact at the end of the drink at the Ealing pub and then his nagging phone calls which only stopped when she changed her phone number. That's right, his name was Parker, David Parker. It was strange how the unconscious mind retains names the conscious one would rather forget. At least she knew her captor, she reflected wryly. That was at the heart of surviving as a hostage. 'Why did you kidnap me, David?' She pronounced the Christian name with as much intimacy as she could muster. 'What do you want?'

'You.'

For the first time, fear twitched Blanche's heart. Until then, particularly when she had woken to discover she knew her kidnapper – an inadequate, lonely man, she guessed when she had met him a year and a half or so ago – the superintendent could not treat what had happened seriously. Perhaps it was a result of the lightheadedness bequeathed by the clubbing she had received. But from his tone of voice, she knew now he was serious. Blanche assumed David wanted to rape her, act out some sordid fantasy using her body. It was common enough. And there was nothing she could do about it. She was trussed up and helpless. 'When are you going to do it to me?' she asked in as steady a voice as she could manage.

'Tomorrow.'

Blanche wondered why he was going to wait so long. Most rapes are the result of a momentary lust, obviously at odds with David Parker's calculation. 'Why wait until tomorrow?'

He looked across at her, puzzled. 'Do you really care?'

Blanche knew she had to forge some form of relationship with this man to make him realise he had a human being tied

213

to the bed and not just a human body. 'I do actually.'

'Tomorrow's the day my father died. February the thirteenth.' David obviously thought his words self-explanatory and Blanche was too tired to enquire further. He stood up and walked over to the curtains, dragging one back. Fingers of damp snow touched the window pane, and beyond Blanche distinguished an overgrown fence and a flat grey sky. David let the curtain flop back and when he turned round, he looked preoccupied.

'Do you mind leaving the curtain drawn please?' asked the superintendent. She had to repeat the question. 'It's less depressing.'

'Sorry, it's staying shut.'

Blanche wanted to irritate him by sneering, 'What, in case some neighbour comes round and sees you in the act?' But it seemed silly to risk spurring him to further violence. Instead, she said, 'There aren't many people out here in the country surely.'

'There's more than you think,' snapped her captor. 'And they're bloody nosy.'

He went off, walking in his clumsy way on the balls of his feet, to make two cups of tea. After Blanche's tea had cooled enough, David produced a straw and slid it into the cup. He offered it to her. Blanche felt humiliated to drink in this way but decided almost any humiliation was preferable to dying of thirst. She sucked up some of the tea and David, seeing the efforts she had to make, slipped another pillow under her head.

'I forgot how beautiful your eyes were,' he said suddenly. Blanche looked at him suspiciously as his jagged glance raked her body. 'I forgot how beautiful *you* were.'

Blanche closed her eyes tight and prayed to the God of her childhood that if he was going to rape her, she would find the strength to fight him off, but that if he overcame her resistance the violation would be as quick and painless as possible.

When she opened her eyes again ten seconds later he had moved away, back to his chair. She wanted to spark a conversation but was determined to avoid as long as possible the subject of their meeting a year and a half ago. She was sure one of David's motives was revenge for not responding to his

214

advances. When she spoke, Blanche tried to inject her voice with sympathy. 'I was sad to hear about your mother. Did she die long ago?'

His eyes narrowed with suspicion. 'Why are you so interested in my mother all of a sudden?'

'You made a point of telling me you'd tied me up to the bed she died on. I wanted to find out something about her.'

'Well she died in October,' David snapped. 'Painlessly, I was told. It was a combination of a weak heart and a bad dose of flu.'

'So this was her house?'

He paused. The only sound was the knocking of a radiator in another room. All other noise was swallowed up by the snow outside. 'Yes, it was her house.'

'Close to London?'

He smiled at her pathetic attempt to extract information. 'Close enough.'

Blanche sighed. 'You realise it's only a matter of time?'

'What?'

Blanche thought she would try and plant the seed of doubt in his mind. 'Before the police find out I'm here. They're very good at looking after their own you know.' David said nothing. He merely tapped a white finger on the barrel of his shotgun. 'Someone was sure to have seen what was going on and made a note of your number plate. The police across the country will be looking for us now.'

'We'll see.'

His tone struck Blanche as alarmingly confident. But she decided to press on nonetheless. 'Plus the fact I know you. Rape is a very serious offence. So is causing grievous bodily harm to a police officer. I'll be able to give evidence . . . '

Her words soaked away into the sponge of a new smile that David wore, a smirk of malice, like a schoolboy who holds a butterfly in one hand and with the other is about to snap off its wings. 'Not necessarily.'

All the moisture evaporated from Blanche's mouth. She flopped her throbbing head back on the pillow. Rape would be hell enough, but he might be planning something more. Perhaps he was going to murder her. A sad and sordid end to her life, she thought. She had always hoped to die painlessly at a ripe age, surrounded by a few friends and happy memories. People like her, she considered, should have the same rights as suicides and be able to choose the time and manner of their end once they are prepared for it. But she knew full well that death has no compunction. It grants no stay to those who wish to live. It lies in ambush for all – prepared and unprepared alike. In that fleeting moment of terror, Blanche saw in David Parker's dark and shadowy profile the angel of death.

Blanche lay still and ordered herself to calm down. Death had never been outwitted by panic. She had to escape. She would do her damnedest to die in her own bed. The superintendent decided to try a new approach. 'I'm sorry about what happened eighteen months ago.' He looked up, drawn out once again by her words from his troubled thoughts. 'I liked you,' she lied, 'but I didn't think we were suited.'

'You could have returned my phone calls at least,' he bleated. Blanche told herself she had been right. The wounds cut into his flesh eighteen months ago still bled. 'I was very angry about it at the time. And the fact you're here just brings it all back. I even thought at one stage I was . . . ' He stopped himself and rubbed his knees with his palms.

'So that's why you've kidnapped me, is it? Revenge for unreturned phone calls?'

The same smile began to spread across his face again but David cut it short as he had just done with his words. He stood up and spoke in a voice menacing in its calmness. 'Shut up. I've had enough of you wittering on. It's confusing me. I know exactly why I brought you here and that's all that counts.' He moved towards the door.

'I'd appreciate it, you know, if you could do something to help me pass the time.'

David stopped in the doorway. 'Like what?'

'Bring a radio or TV. It'll stop me getting bored.' The superintendent also hoped to find out whether a search had started for her yet.

He pondered for a moment and then chuckled to himself. 'I've got a better idea.'

Blanche heard him move about in the room next door. He appeared with the loudspeaker from an old record player and placed it carefully on the corner of the carpet just inside the door. David disappeared again. A few seconds later the crackling magnificence of the *St Matthew Passion* burst into the tiny room.

David giggled over his little joke. Not that Blanche Hampton would appreciate it. She would not know that he had appropriated this music, made it his: that it was one of his mother's favourite pieces, which she had played over and over again until the records were worn like millstones; that Patricia Hoskin had unknowingly listened to it as a harbinger of her own murder, and that he had played it again over her body as a prayer for her departed soul.

He stood at the window of the lounge at the front of the bungalow and watched the snow float down onto the wilderness at the edge of the orchard. He remembered long, long ago when it was tidy and trim, running along the paths kept clear by his father. The ferns towered up then, brushing his face rather than his knees. And he recalled the ferns from only last autumn when he walked out to the wilderness — golden-yellow in the sun, dry and dead, each a skeleton beaten down by the wind. Now they were sinking under snow.

The chill air outside seemed to cool David's desire for murder. He had come to look forward to his killings in the past but the actual taking of life had always been at the height of rage, in the grip of a passion that did not seem to belong to him. Having kidnapped Blanche, David wondered whether he could now find the anger to murder her. He certainly wanted to eat her flesh, even yearned for it. He had forgotten just how attractive she was until he had offered her that cup of tea a few minutes before: the long legs, the full breasts, those wide eyes, heavy lips. When she had lain unconscious on the bed, he had slipped his hand under her blouse and caressed her breasts. Her body was so beautiful and, asleep, she posed no threat to him. But although he enjoyed this furtive satisfaction of his lust, David was also disgusted by it. It was ignoble. Besides, as he had just seen, she was so much more attractive when awake, those brown eyes alert and probing.

But he had to kill her. He had decided. It was the only way to have the fullest possession of her body. It was too dangerous to do otherwise.

She was to be buried in the garden at the back of the bungalow. With a shudder of panic when he looked at the snowflakes again, the lawyer realised the burial might be more difficult than he had anticipated. If the snow did not melt soon, he would leave far more clues and also the partially frozen ground would be much harder to dig. Better, he thought, to start the preparations now.

He passed the open door to Blanche's room and she met his glance hungrily, as if trying to read his mind. He was disconcerted and looked away with deliberate unconcern. A furrow of anxiety suddenly ploughed its way across his forehead as he arrived in the kitchen and pulled on a warm coat and a pair of wellington boots. David recalled that his mother kept all the garden tools in the old shed. He slammed the back door. The shed seemed to stare at him from the bottom of the garden, the roof capped by snow, the windows black and fathomless, the planks splitting with age. He could always drive into Ipswich and buy a spade there. The idea calmed him. He had always found ways of not entering the shed in the past, except when he absolutely had to. The main way was to employ an old man from the village with the improbable name of Jepthah Nunn to do the gardening. But David had paid him off for the winter after his mother's death. Now if he went out to buy a proper garden spade he would only arouse suspicions. No one would dream of digging over the garden or planting anything during such filthy weather. Better to stay at the cottage under cover of the snow, venturing out only as a matter of necessity.

Besides, he *had* been into the shed several times since that awful day when he was eleven years old. His tactic had always been the same: to breathe deeply, throw open the door, and rush out with whatever he had to find as soon as possible, slamming the door behind him. But for hours afterwards he had always felt his hands were soiled. He had to wash his hands over and over again. It was the same burning obsession he had experienced after seeing his mother's body in the coffin.

218

Anyway, he needed that spade. He would have to enter the shed again.

He trudged down the garden path, his feet crunching in the fresh snow. He tried to distract his memory by studying the scene to his left, the rotting boundary posts joined by barbed wire, the dark smudge of the pine plantation beyond. Then he stood before it. Was the breathing in his ears his own or that of an eleven-year-old schoolboy, lost in innocent sexual pleasure, the August sun playing on his closed eyelids? He knew the spade was on the right next to the fork and the Ransomes lawnmower. Jepthah Nunn always left them in exactly the same place.

David sensed his heart race and his fingers tremble as they took hold of the cracked, plastic door-handle. His lungs seemed suddenly crushed by a great weight and his legs went limp. He either had to do it now or not at all. With the sweat prickling on the skin at the back of his neck, he tried the door. It did not move. In the panic of desperation, he threw his shoulder against it. The door flew back and David tumbled in to snatch up the spade.

The hammering in his ears grew deafening as he looked round for the spade, the panting and expectation in the loins of the schoolboy were wonderful, David's hand closed round the handle of the spade, the boy grunted with joy as his body shivered to a climax, the adult scrambled to get out of the shed with the spade – but there in the open door had stood his mother, a black profile against the hot sun. He still remembered her scream of animal disgust, as if she had found a slug in her bed rather than her son masturbating. All he could think of was the shame as his mother reached for the first thing that came to hand, a length of bamboo, and swung at him.

David slammed the door behind him, his breathing hoarse and strangled, and lay back against it, tortured by the past.

The blow landed on the hands that were struggling to pull up his trousers. 'Get out! You filthy brat! You disgust me! It's things like this that made God kill your father. You're just filth!' His mother was possessed with an obscene fury, hitting out at him, her face gnarled with anger. He was a sickly schoolboy who had always hated violence and could not fight back. Somehow he managed to drag up his trousers, escape her grasping hands and then run out into the garden, his pulse racing with fear. He ran so fast and so far, never looking behind him, that his lungs burned. He did not so much stop as collapse. He slept for half an hour and then spent the rest of the day rambling through the country. The day was warm and sultry. David toyed with running away from home but as hunger and night drew in he knew he had to return.

His mother greeted him coldly, as if nothing had happened, telling him to take a bath. 'Make sure you wash your hands well.' She put out a cold supper for him in the kitchen. When he appeared she dragged him to the kitchen and insisted that he scrub his hands in front of her.

'Mummy,' he asked at last, 'why did you do that to me? Why did you hit me?'

She shrugged, her face smooth as polished marble. 'You deserved it. What you were doing was disgusting. If I ever catch you doing it again, I'll do exactly the same.'

David was drawn back to the present by the touch of snowflakes on his face, so cool, so gentle. Not that the past was gone. It was still with him, still haunting him. But he had the spade. It was safe and in his hands. He had been brave once more. But with the relief blazed up a new anger. What his mother had done had blighted him. It had made him always think of sex as dirty and unclean and to think of women, who raised such thoughts in men, as cheap and degrading. And while the shed remained, a monument to his brutalised emotions, David knew he would always be reminded of what happened there.

The memory of his lost childhood filled David with cold anger. He skidded the van onto the Kirsham Road. At a garage on the outskirts of Ipswich, he bought a kerosene can and had it filled with petrol. Back at Foxhall Cottage, he snatched a packet of matches from the kitchen and stumbled up the garden path past snow-covered junk so familiar it was part of his personal landscape: boxes, pallets and rotting chicken hutches. Each had a history, each a story to tell. He hated them. All these voices from the past speaking to him. He wanted to be free of them. He wanted them to be silent.

He poured the petrol over the shed in desperate haste and threw on a match. It took fire with a whoosh and in seconds the wooden frame was ablaze, the snow melting before the heat, the orange flames magnificent in the dullness of the day, the roof sending a spiral of ebony-black smoke into the sky from which floated down little parachutes of tar. Within a few minutes the shed was no more than a hulk, only a few thicker timbers standing above the smoking ruin.

Exhausted, but with his steps somehow lighter, David picked his way back to the bungalow. He felt more indulgent towards Blanche now. Perhaps it was because he wanted to tell another human being what he had done, explain the heroism of his action. She was intelligent. She would understand. Not that he would go into all the prurient details of course. He would just say the shed was full of bad memories of his childhood. She must be thirsty. He would turn the record over and make her another cup of tea.

The house seemed unnaturally silent as he walked along the corridor towards her room. He unconsciously tightened his grip on the shotgun. It was strange how the imagination could start to play tricks. He remembered when he was at Cambridge returning after dinner to his rooms in the medieval Old Court. He would walk round the flagstones and sprint up the wooden stairs to his rooms on M staircase. And then he would become aware of a presence in his room. He was convinced there was someone or something there. In the end, he would throw open the door breathlessly and switch on all the lights, his heart thumping. And always there was nothing, nothing except the whistle and creak of the wind in the rafters. David just had time to smile indulgently at this foolishness before he stopped again, aghast, at the door to the bedroom. Blanche had disappeared.

# 22

When the opening chords of the *St Matthew Passion* limped into the bedroom, Blanche at first dismissed the choice of music as a coincidence. She was by conviction a rationalist, who preferred the natural to the supernatural and refused to be surprised by the upsets the world had to offer. When her life offered up a strange coincidence she would repeat a mathematical conundrum she had read in a book somewhere: how much human blood is there in the world? The answer – about five billion gallons – had surprised and depressed her when she first heard it, because if all that blood were poured into the Red Sea the level would rise by less than an inch. So much for the insignificance of humanity, she thought, and the efficacy of a blood transfusion for an ailing sea. She had read somewhere else that for some complex mathematical reason if you go to a party and meet there twenty-three other people, chance has it that one other person will have the same birthday as yourself.

Coincidence. It could all be explained away, she told herself. The chances of David being the murderer of Patricia Hoskin were so distant, so remote. But then she would not have thought he was capable of kidnapping a woman. And what if he had murdered Suzy Miles as well?

At that moment, David passed by the open door with his gun. She stared at him accusingly. He turned away and his footsteps retreated down the passage. A door slammed and she was alone with the music, the same music she guessed Patricia Hoskin must have heard just before her murder. Blanche knew she had to escape. She had not been left alone long enough to be able to examine how she had been tied to the bed. Her hopes rose as she examined David's knots. They were inexpert, and with her heavings on the bed over a period of hours, the bindings had become slightly loosened.

One in particular, around her right wrist, offered more play than she expected. Blanche looked around but there were no sharp edges within reach, nothing she might be able to exploit to slice into the rope. Instead, she sharpened her ears to cut through the music and listen out for any sounds beyond. She heard nothing.

She squirmed her right wrist around and around in the noose that held it. The skin against the rope was chafed raw but Blanche bit her lip to stifle the pain and worked on. Her head still throbbed and the muscles of her hand and arm began to moan with anguish. Over a period of minutes, Blanche worked her wrist deeper and deeper into the loop. Suddenly, outside, a car door slammed and a cold engine was churned into life. The vehicle revved up and the engine noise faded away. Blanche could not see what was happening: although the door to her room was open it only looked out onto a wall, blank except for a reproduction of an estuary at sunset.

Blanche assumed David had driven off somewhere. This was her best, and possibly only, chance of escape. She redoubled her efforts. The rope almost drew blood but in five minutes her wrist slid out of the noose. Blanche licked the broken skin for comfort and then began, painstakingly, to unpick the knots that held her left wrist. David had tied them tight and Blanche swore as the nail of her forefinger snapped at the quick. She gulped back in pain, working with the desperation of one who knew minutes might divide her from death. Her concentration was so intense she did not even notice when the record finished. The knots finally frayed apart but just as Blanche was about to lean forward and untie her legs, she heard the car draw up outside. 'Oh, God,' she cried to herself in agony. All this effort, all this pain, just for him to walk back in and tie her up again. She held her breath and waited.

The back door opened and slammed again. She picked furiously at the rope. The nail of her finger was raw and bleeding now and Blanche was close to tears. She cast about in desperation but there was no knife within reach to cut through the rope and speed up her escape. She listened out for his step but heard nothing. If he came back in, she decided, she would lie back on the bed in the half-light, pretend she was still tied up and hope to lash out at him at an unguarded moment. Such thoughts were born of desperation but she had to distract her mind somehow while her fingers ripped at the knots. With one last effort, Blanche pulled off the last binding and staggered to the door. The passage was empty but from the open door at the far end of the corridor to the right came a grunt and the sound of a chair scraping. David had come back in.

To her left, in the wall of the hall opposite, was a window. Through it Blanche could see a white Escort van, the windscreen scraped, the snow partially melted on the bonnet. The front entrance to the bungalow was at the end of the passage to her left, behind another door containing a large pane of frosted glass. Even further round to the left, next to where she stood, was the door to the lounge. Blanche decided she would be more likely to be seen if she took the direct route to freedom through the front door. All David Parker had to do was step into the passage and she would be visible. So she tiptoed into the lounge. She remembered little about it – a waste of old armchairs and a sofa, a standard lamp with tasselled lampshade, a swirling carpet of browns and yellows – for she heard David come out of the kitchen and walk along the passage.

Blanche saw the door on the far side of the room that led back into the vestibule. She had just reached the front door of the bungalow when she heard the reaction to her disappearance from the next room. It was not a swear word but a loud grunt of frustration.

Blanche threw back the front door and ran. To her right was a ramshackle fence of barbed wire interlaced with brambles. About fifty yards ahead at the end of the drive – marked by fresh tyre marks in the snow – was a gate. She sprinted towards it, stumbling in the furrows of the front garden, rose bushes shivering under an eiderdown of snow. She heard a shout behind her, but her panting and the slap of her feet on the snow seemed deafening. She pounded on, her feet skidding, full of regret once again that she had not donned a pair of trousers on the day she was kidnapped. The trees on the left, the gate ahead, quivered before her eyes. A deafening bang cracked the air to her right. The gate was only five yards ahead now. Beyond it was the white slab of road. The gate imprinted itself on Blanche's mind with all the hallucinatory detail of a dream: it was like a farmgate, the white paint peeling, the wooden struts held together by wire, and, for some reason, a sign saying 'Beware of the Dog' on the inside of the gate. Blanche swerved to avoid the second barrel of David's gun, threw out her left hand to grip the top bar of the gate and launched her body into the air. A second bang shook the silence. Blanche screamed. As her left foot smacked onto the ground on the far side of the gate, it slid into a deep pothole and her ankle was wrenched back on itself. Blanche felt the muscles stretched to an unnatural angle and then whip back. She sat for a second in the wet snow to regain her breath. She was only ten yards from the road now. No car was passing. She struggled upright and almost fainted when she tried to put any weight on her left leg. Wincing with the agony, she managed to hobble a few steps before she heard David's voice close behind her.

'OK, stop there,' he panted. 'Turn round and come back.' Blanche heard a car approach through the winter silence and as it passed she waved to it frantically, a blur of scarlet against the white road. In his fury David swung the butt of his gun at the small of her back and Blanche tumbled into a snowdrift. He stood over her with the gun pointing into her eyes. 'Now, get up and get back into the house before I blow your brains out.'

Leaning on a stick and with the muzzle of the gun nudging her shoulder, Blanche limped back to the bungalow. The distance she had covered so quickly a minute before now stretched before her like a desert as she laboriously hopped through the snow like an injured bird. Where she had fallen, the snow had melted through her skirt and jacket to clutch at her skin with fingers of ice. The front door, she noticed, was still open. She wanted to cry out to the empty fields round about, cry out in agony, cry out for help. She felt terribly lost and alone. No other houses were visible from the bungalow. Her only view of other habitation was when she staggered towards the road for those few brief seconds before David stopped her. Away in the distance – across the empty,

225

bleached fields, the hedgerows punctuated only by the occasional oak – was a cottage of red brick. The superintendent wondered again where she was. The landscape was too cold for the Home Counties, too flat for Surrey and Sussex. She guessed somewhere north or east of London. Perhaps Cambridgeshire, Bedfordshire, Essex, Suffolk? Snowflakes began to whisper down again, twirling on the motionless air.

David slammed the front door behind her with sullen finality. Blanche feared he might want to beat her for daring to try to escape. But he was not violent. An executioner, she meditated, is rarely violent, except to deliver the blow of death. Instead he gestured for her to sit on a chair in the centre of the bedroom. Watching over her with the gun, he untied the ropes from the bed and bound her to the chair. 'I'm not taking any chances, this time,' he grunted through his teeth, as he pulled the rope even tighter around Blanche's wrists. She groaned and asked for the ropes to be loosened but his only response was a derisive snort.

# 23

As David sat back on his chair in the bedroom and looked at the captive woman before him, joy and pride surged in his breast. Once again fate had shown itself to be on his side. He did resent her trying to escape. He was piqued, like he had been the night the German girl had walked out on him in the cinema. It was yet another rejection. But he would not repeat the same mistake. Blanche was now wholly in his power and tomorrow he would take her life and eat her flesh. It was ordained. She would not escape. She would have no chance to reject him again.

A part of him regretted that he had to kill her, and mused on the possibility of living with her in the cottage for a few days, perhaps delaying the pleasurable moment when his fingers would close around her neck and his tongue savour the taste of her body. He would be able to feed her, tend to her, even love her. She could be like a pet. But the word 'pet' caused another painful memory to surface. Long, long ago – when he was eight – his father bought him two mice one summer and built a cage for them. His mother would never allow the animals in the house. Autumn passed and winter came. Frost gripped the land and snow fell. But still his mother would not allow the mice near the bungalow. David and his father stuffed the cage with straw and once or twice the young boy remembered to fill empty medicine bottles with hot water which he placed in the cage to keep the animals warm. But one morning, when David opened the cage to change the water in the bottles, he found them frozen solid. He tore off his gloves and clawed through the straw. In a corner of the cage the two mice lay still, snuggled up against each other in a fruitless struggle to conserve their warmth, cold as the glass of the medicine bottle. David remembered that he stood there, before the open door of the cage, and wept hot tears that steamed in the frozen air. He never wanted to keep a pet again.

No, he decided, 'pet' was the wrong word to describe how he would treat Blanche. Perhaps he should treat her as a captive in war, a woman stolen from some ransacked town, a woman who with the ebb of time might come to love and understand him. Perhaps in a certain way, he was still in love with her. When they had first met eighteen months before, he had certainly been obsessed with her. He blushed at the memory of how he had pursued her. And he realised now that he had never really forgotten her – neither his attraction nor her initial rejection. Now, however, in the solitude of the bungalow both his concerns could be quietened. He could do with her as he wanted and she would not be able to resist.

He stood up and approached her. Her eyes flashed, dark brown irises suddenly unsheathed from heavy lids; she threw back her hair, now tangled and unwashed. Her features, he thought suddenly, were quite masculine. But he found her stubby nose and strong chin attractive, more interesting than Pamela's bland and painted face. Blanche's skin was of extraordinary delicacy and, without thinking, David reached out to caress her cheek. She did not move. She neither flinched away nor pressed against his hand, her eyes locked on his face. David was reminded for a moment of his snake, passive and distant. He smiled. It was the right response. If she had whipped her head away, he would have slapped her. If she had pressed up against him, he would have thought her a tart. She was clever alright. He would have to watch her carefully.

He dragged the hair away from her neck and pushed his hand round to the warm nape of her neck. His breathing became short with desire. He did not want to touch the rest of her body. It would somehow be demeaning and sordid, with those eyes looking at him and blazing with scorn. But he could see from the sweet curve of her legs how desirable she was. He had to fight back the urge to kill her there and then and gorge himself on her warm flesh. 'You're so beautiful,' he whispered.

'Then why do you want to kill me?'

He gulped. 'I don't want to. I *have* to.'

'Why do you have to? What makes you do it?' she asked quietly, her head quivering with fear.

He turned away from her and walked to the window. Why did he have to kill her? He needed to. But why? To eat the meat of her body. But why? To stop the panic attacks. To stop the anguish and the pain. To still the voices. To kill the burning need to wash his hands. To recover his potency. For forgiveness.

'Why did you kill the other women?' Blanche's voice seemed to echo in the empty room.

David wondered whether he should pretend not to hear. He brushed back the nylon curtain with the same hand that seconds before had touched her cheek. He sensed his heart quicken, sweat crackle on the back of his neck. How had she guessed that he had strangled the two women? He had told her nothing. If the police had known he was the killer why had they not arrested him in London? 'What other women?' he demanded calmly.

'One was called Patricia Hoskin, the other Suzy Miles.'

David stayed by the window, the white expanse of snow reflected in the pupils of his grey eyes. The scene was so restful, so peaceful, he wanted to gaze at it forever. And with the calm, came a desire to confess. After all, revealing what he had done to this woman would not harm him. She would die tomorrow and with her would die his confession. It would be like going into the confessional box and telling a priest of his crime, except death was a much surer way to keep secrets than reliance on a man's oath to the Church. But what if she did escape? He would have delivered himself into her hands.

David turned to her. 'Never heard of them.'

Blanche ran her tongue over her lips and looked unconvinced. David found it strange that even though this woman was tied up and helpless in front of him, she retained the power to interrogate him and make him the victim. If only he could strangle her now, she would be silent.

'Why did you play the *St Matthew Passion* to me?' She squinted at him. 'For the same reason you played it to Patricia Hoskin?'

He shrugged his shoulders as casually as he could manage. 'If you don't shut up about these other women I've never heard of, I'm going to gag you. Let's talk about something else, for God's sake.'

Blanche looked down at the floor and then up at the ceiling, fixing her gaze on the light above the bed. She looked uncomfortable, as though about to ask a favour. He was pleased. He wanted her to be beholden to him. 'I must go to the lavatory.'

David was annoyed. She had put him on the defensive again, made him embarrassed. It was perfectly natural for her of course to want to visit the toilet but he had not – despite all his careful planning – thought of the possibility. In stories of hostage-taking and kidnapping, the toilet arrangements never figured highly. Besides, most kidnappers were in gangs: two or three of them could guard someone while the hostage went to the lavatory. With David it was different. He was alone. Blanche had already made one attempt to escape. And she was also a woman.

'Can you make your mind up please, David? I don't fancy sitting here in wet underwear.'

David felt he had no choice. He remembered that the toilet only had one small, high window too small for someone to climb through and that anyway Blanche would be unable to stagger far. He unscrewed the lock from the inside of the door as a precaution and reluctantly untied her. He led her to the lavatory at the point of his gun and told her she had two minutes. He waited outside, his ear close to the door, listening to the rustle of clothes, the tinkle of urine, the flush of the toilet. He convinced himself the eavesdropping was in case she tried to escape but recognised beneath the erotic desire: the ageless vision of a dress held high, creamy thighs, and underwear tangled round shapely ankles. It was voyeurism of the ear.

It was almost one o'clock but David was so tired he felt it was evening. He offered Blanche some soup for lunch but she refused with a shake of the head. He listened to the radio and watched the television but there was no mention of the kidnap. Having checked the ropes that bound Blanche to the chair, he gagged her and put on another side of the *St Matthew Passion*. David was amused by the superintendent making the link between the *Passion* and the murder of

230

Patricia Hoskin, and wanted to tantalise her further.

Outside dusk was already gathering on the horizon, the grey blur of approaching night. A gentle wind chilled his forehead as he closed the back door and walked out to the old vegetable plot. Thank God the snow had come on suddenly, he repeated to himself, otherwise the ground might be frozen. Smoke still drifted up from the charred ruins of the shed and cheered him. He scraped away the snow and began to dig a grave. He was not physically fit and was soon sweating with the effort, but he drove himself on, digging, digging. Progress seemed so slow. The pile of soil seemed to build up much faster than the hole grew deeper. David knew he had to take a break, so he made a cup of tea and checked Blanche. She seemed to be dozing in her chair, the knots of her bindings still tight. He dragged himself outside again. The snowflakes fell thicker now and the wind gusted through the gloom. David managed to dig for only half an hour before he was exhausted. The grave lay before him, a crude black rectangle cut into the snow, about six feet long, two and a half feet wide but only two feet deep. As soon as he stopped working the wind slapped the sweat on his back like an icy hand.

David staggered into the bungalow, checked once again that Blanche's ropes were secure and slumped onto his bed. He fell asleep immediately, his shoulders and arms aching from his exertions.

When he awoke, night had fallen. His old bedroom – the veneered wardrobe, the chest of drawers with two clumsy wooden candlesticks – was painted silver by the light of a full moon. He listened to the silence of the house for a moment before he rose and cupped his face to the window. His breath smeared the glass with condensation but he gazed with awe at the glowing disc in the sky that hung above the wood. As his eyes grew accustomed to the light, more and more stars began to twinkle across the sky. No part of it was empty. He had forgotten how the lights of London stifle the beauty of the night. If only, he thought, if only . . . If only he could escape now. Live his life again. If only his father had not died. If only his mother had not blamed him unfairly for her loss. He wished to walk out into the moonlight. Travel back to

London. Go back to work. Begin again with Pamela.

A cough cracked the silence of the bungalow. David was dragged back to the present and remembered Blanche sitting in the next bedroom. He remembered the grave he had dug that afternoon and realised there could be no escape. The full moon on the eve of the anniversary of his father's death seemed yet another symbol in a world redolent of signs to which only David Parker had the key.

His exertions had made him hungry. He took his gun and looked in at Blanche. She glanced up wearily. 'Any chance of a drink, please?' Her pronunciation was clear and distinct even when she was fatigued, he noticed.

He nodded. 'I'm going to rustle up a bit of supper. Would you like some?'

'The condemned woman's last meal,' mused the superintendent, as much to the room as to David. 'Does that mean I have a right to choose what it is?'

David grew irritated with her again. She had guessed what he intended to do to her and kept reminding him of it, scratching at his intentions like a sore. He wished her to continue the pretence that she was a normal hostage and would come to no harm provided she did not try to escape again. David wished he had not told her what he intended to do but she had prised the information from him. It was the reward for her relentless curiosity. And, besides, each time Blanche reminded him of his plan to kill her, the strength to carry out the act was corroded, like a man who is regularly nagged by a partner about his impotence. 'No, you'll just have to eat what's going.'

David searched through the tins he had bought and stored in the kitchen cupboard. He decided to start the meal with Royal Game Soup. He had a yen for seafood to balance the heaviness of the soup but could only find a can of red salmon which his mother had bought. It was one of several cans of food which had simply remained in the kitchen after her death: being anonymous fruits of a production line they sparked no dangerous memories.

David held a cup of soup to Blanche's lips. The gesture comforted him: once again she was in his thrall, like an animal dependent on its master. She sipped the hot liquid with averted eyes. She refused the offer of salmon, boiled potatoes and peas, so David sat before her with his full plate and a glass of Sainsbury's Muscadet from a bottle he had chilled in the snow. He felt contented and relaxed. He was amused that he was eating salmon bought by his mother, probably a couple of years before. It was partly a matter of romance, like an archaeologist excavating a still edible meal left by a lost generation, and partly the satisfaction of further revenge. Eating the dead woman's food was another way to efface her memory, like burning down the shed.

David watched the superintendent flex her muscles and gaze round the room, occasionally glancing towards him or closing her eyes as if in prayer. The lawyer was intrigued by her calmness. 'You seem pretty relaxed for someone who's going to die tomorrow,' he commented at last, filtering the question through a mouthful of potato and salmon.

'Only on the outside,' she replied.

'What about the inside?'

She glared at him. 'That's my business.' She closed her eyes and David saw the eyeballs flicker beneath.

He decided to probe again. He was a python who for the first time had captured a mouse with the gift of speech. 'What do you think will happen to you when you die?'

She opened her eyes, tired now and bloodshot from fatigue and lack of sleep, and swung them round to him. 'The same as happened to the other women you murdered.'

David held her melancholy stare for a moment and drained his glass. She was drawing the conversation back to areas he wished to avoid. 'Would you like some wine?'

She shook her head, her gaze still pinioned against his face. 'Why did you murder them, David? Why do you want to murder me?'

He poured himself more wine and cupped the glass in his hands. 'Why do you want to know?'

Blanche pouted her lips in lieu of a shrug. 'The same reason you want to know how I feel about dying. Curiosity.'

'Curiosity killed the cat,' he said automatically, for lack of anything better to say. It was, he remembered, one of his mother's set phrases.

'It's not curiosity that's going to kill me. You are,' she

233

replied, without a smile.

David pondered. The urge to confess gripped him again. He had to tell someone, not in the indirect way he had confessed to Laura, the psychotherapist, but the whole truth. The woman he was going to kill was as good a confessor as any. Having met Blanche again, he rediscovered her attraction for him: not just her body but her intelligence, ironical humour and gentleness. The sort of woman who scared him. The sort of woman he dreamed of. In a way he supposed he was still in love with her. All the more reason to kill her, he thought. The sacrifice would be greater. Besides it was his destiny, the destiny of mankind, to murder what they loved. He shook himself to slough off the sentimentality.

He wanted to see fear in this woman's eyes, watch her squirm as she heard the footfall of death and understood that her flesh would be his salvation. 'First my mother died. Then my fiancée made me impotent. She rejected me you see. Sexually, I mean.' He saw her look away. He smiled: it was too late now for her to regret the way she had treated him. 'So I met Patricia Hoskin through a lonely hearts advert. She rejected me too. And so I killed her. I didn't intend to do it. It just happened. And having done it once, I had to do it again. The voices told me to. I needed their bodies, you see. Like I need yours.'

Blanche looked up, her eyes narrowed. He explained about the panic attacks, the obsession with washing his hands, the voices. David heard her breathing grow faster. 'You're mad, David.'

He shook his head slowly and fingered his gun for comfort. He knew he was not mad. He was different, but not mad. The voices that had tormented him, the visions he had seen, were real and not imagined. He was one of the elect and beyond morality. Women like Blanche could label him as 'mad' if they wished but it was they who were inferior, not him. 'No. You're wrong. I need to eat women to *stop* going mad.'

'Eat?' Her look of surprise and disgust pleased him. He nodded slowly. 'You mean you ate the bits of the bodies you cut off?'

He nodded again and watched. Blanche grew pale and

thoughtful, sucking in the oxygen from the room to stifle the vomit in her throat. 'You're sick.'

David rubbed his chin thoughtfully and told her how normality and happiness returned when he ate women's flesh.

He described how he had met and murdered Patricia Hoskin and Suzy Miles. When he mentioned that he had used a false name when he arranged his rendezvous with Patricia Hoskin, the superintendent nodded as if she had found confirmation of something she had already guessed. 'So you were the mysterious Michael Drayton,' she murmured. 'You were the man she had a meal with at the Italian restaurant.'

David smiled vaguely. Should he tell her about the other woman he had killed too, the one who was really the first? The one who haunted him the most? The one she would never discover unless he told her? 'There's also another one, you know. Another woman I killed in October. She was different from all the others. You might even say she caused all the others.' He paused. 'I didn't mean to do it. But it was so easy. I killed her without anyone knowing about it. Just like I'm going to kill you.'

'Who was she?'

'You'll never find out. There's no evidence left. Except up here.' He tapped his forehead.

She squinted at him with concentration, a typical gesture of hers he had noted. It made her crick her head to one side and look at him askew. He sensed her eyes boring into his mind like grubs. He felt she was able to see into him and divine the answer. 'It was your mother, wasn't it? She didn't die at all. You murdered her.'

He was alarmed for a second at someone else reading his thoughts but, as he pondered what had happened, relief soothed him like a balm. He realised he had wanted to confess all the time and was only waiting for a trigger to unstop the memory. He shivered. He not not been able to think about the truth of his mother's death since the moment the doctor had driven off into the October morning having viewed the corpse. He had repeated to himself the false, his preferred, version of history so often it had become reality. But in Blanche's presence the truth had sprung to the surface of his memory again, like a cork released from the bottom of a bucket of water. 'How did you know?'

She looked at him uncertainly. 'It doesn't matter. I worked it out.'

Pain shared is somehow pain lessened. David recounted the litany of his life: how his mother persecuted him unjustly for his father's death, his unsuccessful relationships with women, his loneliness, his obsession with work. He even told her of the incident in the garden shed. Few memories brand the soul so deep they escape the desire for a full confession. 'And then I met Pamela. I respected her. Even though she wasn't a virgin when I met her, she acted like one. We seemed to get on pretty well and so I proposed. I knew my mother hated Pamela's guts but I didn't know how much until I plucked up the courage to tell her I'd got engaged.'

Once he had begun, David hardly looked at the superintendent. She had become a piece of familiar furniture, an aid to meditation, like a crucifix or a statue of the Buddha.

His mother had had two heart attacks over the previous three years which had left her partially paralysed. On the Thursday before David's visit that weekend back in October, she caught influenza. The doctor came and friends in the village called in to keep her company. When David arrived on Friday night she had stood by the window. But she soon returned to bed and lay under the rose-patterned quilt, her hands limp on the counterpane, her face blazing with fever and discontent. She asked him to play the *St Matthew Passion* on her old record player. He obeyed and the music was the counterpoint to her catalogue of whines and gripes – her illness, the doctor, the disregard of neighbours, the failure of friends and the vicar to visit. He pretended to listen for several minutes and then told her of his engagement to Pamela. His mother lifted up her head, the eyes like scratched marbles, and opened her mouth to speak. He loved her still, this woman who had made him despise himself, yet whipped him on and on to achieve all the things she had failed to do herself. 'Go ahead if you want to. If you want to throw yourself away on a stupid girl like that. But I'll cut you out of my will.' She looked wearily across at the phone on her bedside cabinet and sighed. 'I'll call the solicitors first thing in the morning. This place is worth a pretty penny now and you won't see any of it.'

So this was it, he thought. Not even false congratulations. But yet another lash of the whip. 'Come on, Mum. Be reasonable. I'm not far off forty. I've got to get married some time.'

'Trust you to think only of yourself.' Her breath smelt of Brussels sprouts – a few still remained on the plate on her bedside cabinet. 'You don't think of me, do you? All alone here in the country. I've already had two heart attacks and I'm not getting any younger. Once you're married, you'll come up to see me even less than you do at the moment.'

'That's not true – '

''Course it's true. 'Course it's true.' Suddenly her lips curled into a sneer, her faint moustache brushed by the light from the bedside lamp. 'I suppose she trapped you into it. Let you sleep with her. *Slut*.' The sibilant whistled through her irregular teeth. 'And you were stupid enough to want to do it. You men are all the same. Like farmyard animals. Even your father.' David was amazed. His mother had never before spoken to him with such frankness. 'He could never leave me alone after you were born.' She glared at him and spoke with the quietness of genuine anger. 'You'll never know what pain I went through to give birth to you. It was hell. I told your dad I could never face having another baby. He pretended to understand but he didn't. He'd never leave me alone. He always wanted to be doing it. All the time. All over the house. And I hated it. When I said "no", he went off and abused himself. I found him once,' her face swung to David, burning with disdain, 'like I found you, abusing himself in the shed.'

He sensed the anger rumbling within him like a distant earthquake. He remembered that he warned her – although his voice emerged only as a whisper. 'That's enough, Mum. Please shut up. Please.'

But she was oblivious to his cold glare. Perhaps it was her fever that drove her on. 'I forgave your father because I loved him. But I could never forgive you because you wanted him dead.'

'Of course I didn't want him dead – '

'You wanted him dead, alright. You wanted me all to

yourself.'

'*I didn't want him dead! I didn't want him dead!*' His cry echoed round the bedroom, reverberated down the well of the past, rang against the souvenir plates on the chest of drawers, lifted a few specks of dust from the cheap, crocheted mats on the dressing-table, and was stifled by the musty clothes in the dark, veneered wardrobe. His cry was stifled by those clothes as her words were stifled by the pillow he thrust over her face. 'I didn't want him dead! I didn't want him dead!' he repeated over and over to himself as she thrashed a little under him and then lay still. All he wanted to do was make her silent, make her listen, make her understand, make her say she did not mind him marrying Pamela. He must have held the pillow for no more than thirty seconds. But it was enough. More than enough.

He didn't panic. He didn't weep. He felt nothing. She lay peaceful when he took away the pillow, her mouth slightly open, her eyes closed, as if she had just fallen asleep. David felt strangely calm. He primped up the pillows round her head, rearranged her hands under the counterpane and pulled up the bedclothes. There was no blood and no sign of violence. It was just after ten o'clock.

He had slept deep and well in his old bed. At eight o'clock he rang the family doctor at Martlesham and told him his mother had died in her sleep. The doctor sounded quite harassed and said he would be across as soon as possible. While David waited his nervousness grew. What if the doctor saw something suspicious and ordered a post-mortem? He prowled round the bedroom again, decided there was nothing more he could do and hoped the doctor interpreted his edginess as a sign of shock.

The doctor scurried in an hour and a half later with a smile of apology, explaining that his youngest son had cut himself badly with the bread knife earlier and had had to be taken to hospital in Ipswich. He was a young man, about the same age as David, with a gentle Scottish burr.

He passed on his condolences, flicked open an eyelid of the corpse and checked for a pulse. 'Yes, she must have died in her sleep,' he sighed. 'She had a weak heart and this new flu virus is very nasty indeed, especially for the old. There was nothing you could have done, Mr Parker.' He filled in a medical certificate of the cause of death and stayed to chat amiably for a couple of minutes to explain the procedures and recommend a firm of undertakers in Ipswich.

It was all so simple. And David had not shed a tear.

'So now you know about the third woman I killed.' David looked at Blanche and then at his watch. The superintendent said nothing. It was time for bed. He stood up. 'And you know why no one will ever find out.'

Blanche sat, beautiful and captive, before him. He was triumphant, cleansed by his confession. He imagined he could smell Blanche's response on the air: the sweat of fear oozing from the crevices of her body that normally only a lover would possess. Soon, tomorrow, they would be his too.

# 24

Blanche had sometimes wondered what passed through the mind of a condemned man on the night before his execution. She had always assumed it would have been thoughts of profundity: the moments of supreme happiness, the hours of sadness, the purpose of life. She remembered Dr. Johnson's saying about the approach of execution concentrating the mind of a condemned man wonderfully. But as the minutes of the night slid by she found her mind was not clear. It did not float free to a higher sphere. Instead it was fogged by terror. Thoughts and memories no sooner formed than they drifted off into incoherence. The only continuity, beating in her skull like her continuing headache, was the fragment of a children's song: the tune of a music box that belonged to one of her nephews. The box was designed to look like a radio with a dial on the front and, on the back, the picture of two terrified children wandering through a forest at night. Also on the back were some words from a song.

No one - neither Blanche's brother nor sister-in-law, nor their children - knew where the lyrics and the tune came from, which cartoon or musical comedy, Blanche discovered later they came from a musical play. The words had lodged in the detective's brain and it was their tune that jangled over and over again in her mind when facing death rather than great poetry or scripture.

On reflection it was death that terrified her more than

David's cannibalism. When he first confessed his intentions, vomit gagged Blanche's throat. The idea of him slicing off parts of her body and then eating them disgusted her. She tried to block out the image of his knife wreaking the same butchery on her body as it had done on the others. But as the minutes limped by she convinced herself that what happened to her body after death did not matter. Pain could no longer touch her. And it was pain she feared. The pain of death.

She had asked David to release her from the chair so that she could sleep more comfortably but he had refused. He said she had already tried to escape once and, now that she knew she was to die tomorrow, Blanche had nothing to lose by making another attempt. His gun no longer held any terror. Blanche pretended she wanted to go to the lavatory again but David said he would no longer release her as he had done before – her hands would have to remain tied. Blanche said she could not go to the toilet like that and her captor had twisted his unwrinkled face into a grin. In that case, he replied, she would have to stay where she was.

'Why don't you come in and watch me if it gives you a thrill?' she had said. David had paused for a moment, scouring her eyes to discover if she was serious. When he saw the disdain that blazed there he turned away. 'It's up to you,' he murmured. 'I'm not a pervert but I can't take the risk of untying you again.'

Blanche had heard him go into the lounge and listen to the late evening news on television. The sound was too blurred for her to distinguish more than the odd word. He came back into her bedroom and said, with a slimy smile, that there had been nothing on the news about the kidnap. He looked at the double bed with clouded eyes as if remembering something and said he would sleep in his own room. The superintendent assumed it was the memory of his mother's murder under the rose-patterned quilt that made him decide to sleep elsewhere.

David wished Blanche goodnight and walked out, leaving the bedside lamp to cast the only light in the room. Blanche was struck by his coolness. He said goodnight with all the calm of a host at the door of his guest's bedroom. She would not have guessed, if she had met him for the first time at that

241

moment, that he had murdered three women and intended to make her the fourth.

As night ebbed away, Blanche dipped in and out of sleep, unable to track the passing of the hours because she could not see her watch. She was tortured by cramp in her muscles but feared that if she cried out David would come and gag her.

Once she woke to find David standing at the door in his dressing-gown. He skewered her with his eyes, greedily swallowed a glass of water he held in his hand and disappeared.

Some time later, although Blanche had no idea exactly when, he brought three meat knives which he laid gleaming on the bed. Blanche felt the hairs on the back of her neck tingle as she saw them. 'Not long now,' he said. Away at the far end of the bungalow she heard the splashing of David taking a bath. She found herself paralysed, body and mind, like an animal trapped in the glare of a car's headlamps before its body is torn apart. She wanted to run and scream and fight but could do nothing.

David reappeared. He wore, incongruously, a suit and tie. He stood in front of her, considered her face for a moment as if choosing where to strike and slowly raised his white hands towards her neck. Blanche plunged forward, managed to bite the end of a finger and toppled her chair backwards. Unable to move further, she lay helpless, her own weight crushing her arms under the back of the chair. David Parker clamped his hands round her throat. His thumbs mashed her Adam's apple. She struggled and thrashed her body as hard as she could within the ropes that bound her. She wanted to vomit but knew she could not because her throat was blocked. He knelt beside her, his face puffed out with physical effort. A mist floated across her vision, an unbearable weight of pain crushed her chest and throat, and the agony ground on and on and on and on. She could not even scream to relieve the pain. Then she cared no more. She gave up the struggle and had a second of peace before the moment of death.

Someone knocked on a door to her left.

Blanche's eyes flickered open to find the room almost as she had left it. The translucent curtains were paler than

242

before and she realised time had passed. Dawn had broken and she was still alive, waiting to be murdered. So life after death, she thought, was no more than death after death: being murdered again and again by a psychopath in an isolated country bungalow. Her dream might be over but her nightmare had still to begin.

The front door was rapped again. Blanche crammed her lungs with air and screamed, sensing the muscles of her cheeks stretch, and her throat burn with her cry of despair.

David had slept well until just after five o'clock in the morning. He woke with his mouth and throat dry. He drank two glasses of water in the bathroom and walked with a third to check that Blanche was still secure. He felt tired for some reason – perhaps as a result of the excitement of the past couple of days, or else the parched throat was the precursor of a virus infection. She looked up at him balefully. He staggered back to the bathroom, swallowed a couple of aspirins and went back to bed.

His sleep was fitful and muddied by dreams. He heard his mother again, flaying her son for ingratitude and stupidity in wanting to marry Pamela. He imagined he was suffocating her, except this time, when he drew the pillow away, his mother was not dead but alive, open-eyed, with her wrinkled skin twisted into a sneer. He dreamt Blanche escaped again and that he was forced to track her footprints across windswept fields in his pyjamas. He dreamt the bungalow was surrounded by police.

When his hand stumbled out of the bedclothes for his watch and registered it was just past seven in the morning, David groaned. He felt exhausted and nauseous. His breathing was shallow, his face damp with sweat and an invisible hand stirred his intestines. He lay on his side and moaned as a sour bullet of vomit catapulted into his throat. He gagged. David staggered out of bed to the lavatory.

He felt better afterwards but so exhausted it was as if he had not slept at all. He planned to kill Blanche at precisely eleven o'clock – the hour when he had been told of his father's death. That was three and a half hours ahead. His mouth and throat were dry again so he drank more water, even though the cool liquid was painful to swallow. It was as he sat on the side of the bed and tried to shake the faint blur from his vision that he heard the first rap on the door.

Adrenalin shot through his veins. It was probably a friend of his mother's, who had seen the van in the drive and wished to be nosy under the cloak of neighbourliness. If he waited they would go away. The rapping on the front door bounded through the bungalow again. It was followed by an ear-splitting scream from his mother's bedroom: Blanche was summoning help. Electrified by fear and anger, David snatched up his tie, and stumbled into her room with the shotgun. He yanked the tie across her open mouth. The first turn had little effect but when twisted round again and tightened, the tie reduced her scream to a gurgle. Her eyes blazed with hatred.

Through the fog of panic, David heard voices outside. From near the front door a man yelled, 'Open up, police, open up!' Another walked along the windows on the corridor side of the bungalow, tapping them as he went and shouting the same order. David snatched up his shotgun, threw open a window and saw a policeman in a heavy overcoat of luminescent yellow walking away from him. As he leant out of the window to take clumsy aim over his right shoulder, the gun bumped against the wall and the shot flew harmlessly over the policeman's head. The man dived behind the wall at the end of the bungalow. David swung his gun round to the left and saw two policemen – one in uniform and one not – scramble behind the wall for safety.

'I've got a hostage,' David shouted. It was an effort with his mouth so parched and he gulped in vain for more saliva. 'I've got a hostage. I'll kill her if you try and get in. Keep away from the bungalow or I'll fire.' His words seemed to resonate on the still morning air, hanging there for a second like the white spume of his breath. No wind stirred the mist that clung around the wood in the distance. No birds were singing. The tangle of brambles and wire that constituted the boundary fence was powdered by fresh snow that had fallen overnight. Above, the sky was a sheet of leaden cloud.

David heard the crunch of snow as the man at the back of the bungalow sprinted along the other side of the building to

rejoin his colleagues at the front. 'Get away from the bungalow now, or I'll shoot the hostage,' he screamed at them. He
heard the murmur of voices and then saw the three of them
run back to the police car by the gate.

He shivered as he slammed the window shut. He realised
he was still wearing his pyjamas and dressing-gown. Back in
his room, David dressed as fast as he could, but was forced to
stop frequently because of fatigue and bouts of dizziness. He
wondered why he felt so ill. It couldn't be food poisoning. He
had had it before and the symptoms would have started
much earlier. Perhaps he had flu. If so, it could hardly have
struck at a worse time.

As he slumped down on the bed in Blanche's room, David
could sense her swelling confidence. The voice of rationality
whispered that he should keep near the superintendent in
case the police launched a sudden assault on the bungalow:
she was now more valuable to him alive than dead. But the
dark voice in his soul told him to proceed with the killing now
and eat Blanche's flesh while it was still warm. The talisman
might protect him yet.

Blanche was still secure. He decided to recuperate on his
own bed, away from her arrogant glance. After half an hour's
rest, he would return to kill her. The policemen outside
would now be calling up reinforcements. They would not try
to storm the bungalow until armed police had arrived, so he
would be safe to leave her alone for a while.

He wanted to say something to her, explain that it was
partly because he loved her that he needed to take her life –
that in his own strange way he had loved all the women he
had murdered, all the women whose flesh he had eaten. But
his jaw and tongue refused to obey his desires. They seemed
partially paralysed and the words that emerged were broken-
backed and garbled. God damn this flu or whatever it is, he
screamed to himself. He needed to rest. Blanche stared at
him, her eyes narrow, as if there were something amiss. He
wanted to ask her what it was but could not find the energy.
David picked up his gun and, cradling it like a child, slumped
on his own bed to rest.

# 25

Blanche was not as confident as David thought. Her ankle had swollen to a ball of pain and she had no idea how he would react next to the arrival of the police: he might surrender or he might strangle her immediately. And now she was gagged, Blanche lost all hope of telling her colleagues outside that David Parker was not just a gun-toting case for community care. She was at the mercy of a cannibalistic psychopath who had already murdered his mother for revenge and two women for their flesh. Now Blanche was to be his next victim. To him she was no more than a heifer waiting with soft, bulging eyes to be led to the sacrificial altar. She had never felt so helpless in her life before.

When she heard David fire his gun and scream out the threat to kill her, she knew the crucial hour had come. Armed police would be scrambled and the bungalow surrounded. It might take half an hour or it might take two at most. David Parker should not escape however – unless he committed suicide or the local police bungled the operation. The question that remained, and one she most feared to ask, was whether she would survive to see the dawn break softly again through the curtains of her own room back in London. However many times she asked herself the question, Blanche knew she would never be able to divine the answer. It would simply be handed down to her in the next couple of hours and there would be no appeal.

When David stumbled in a few minutes later, fully dressed now and no longer in his pyjamas, Blanche twitched in terror. His grey eyes were fixed in a stare, the pupils dilated. He shuffled towards her like an old man, his pale face even paler than usual, his breathing shallow and laboured. Gagged, Blanche knew it would be useless to try to scream: a waste of the vital energy she needed in the coming hour. She wished now she had accepted his offer of food the night before. It might have given her strength. He squinted at her as though through dark glass, mumbled something incoherent, and staggered out with his gun.

The bathroom and toilet stood between her room and what she guessed was his, and try as she might, Blanche heard nothing. David looked ill but she wondered if it were no more than a nervous fit brought on by the arrival of the police, a weakness from which he would soon recover and return to her room. The curtains were still drawn and the superintendent yearned for another glance at the countryside, at the sky, to orient herself. She had been trapped in this translucent coffin of a room so long she had lost track of the world outside.

She was certain the police outside had heard her scream. They would have retreated when David fired the gun, knowing that someone inside was in distress. Besides, David had also screamed that he had a hostage. They probably did not know it was her, otherwise their approach to the house would have been different. But with the knowledge that all was not well inside the bungalow, Blanche knew from her training that the police should make their move sooner rather than later.

Suddenly the silence of the bungalow cracked. Next door, in the lounge, and what seemed far away in a room down the corridor, telephones began to ring. The sound was plaintive and insistent, calling through the empty rooms. It was the old-fashioned ring, not a modern, electronic chirrup. It must be the police, Blanche thought. When a siege begins, particularly when a gunman holds a hostage, their first task is to establish contact with him. The obvious way is by telephone. Blanche waited, holding her breath to catch the faintest sound. She counted the rings . . . Fifteen, sixteen, seventeen . . . Suddenly she heard a slow creak of bedsprings. The ringing stopped and she strained out a few comprehensible words from the murmur of David's voice. 'Who's that? . . . Mrs Goddard . . . No, nothing you can do.' The phone was thrown back in its cradle with a tired curse.

A few more minutes passed in a silence broken only by the odd, muffled cough from David. The telephone rang again.

It had to be the police this time, Blanche thought. The bedsprings creaked and the ringing stopped abruptly. The superintendent heard nothing more. Silence stalked through the bungalow. Blanche wondered whether David was just listening or whether he had taken the telephone off the hook.

Police sirens ululated in the distance. A voice crackled from a loudhailer. 'You're surrounded by armed police. You can't escape. We want to talk to you.'

Blanche heard the bedsprings wince again and thought she heard a footstep. Perhaps David was coming to kill her at last, strangle her before the police had a chance to intervene. If so, she was helpless. She was gagged and would not even be able to scream when his fingers tightened round her throat.

She waited but he did not appear.

The superintendent wondered where he was, what he was doing, whether Parker was waiting in his own room because it was more comfortable, or with the hope that if the police stormed Blanche's bedroom he would have a better chance of defending himself. He was probably at his window, gun cocked, cartridges on the table, heart pounding, eyes scouring. Perhaps he had even crept to the back door, and slipped unnoticed into the trees before the police had laid their siege: she had no idea about the topography at the back of the bungalow. Perhaps he was lying ill on his bed. Perhaps he was asleep. The possibilities trotted through the superintendent's whirring mind. All whispered a reason as to why the bungalow was drowsy with silence.

A sudden anger flared in Blanche's heart. She was not willing to be a sacrificial victim, wait – like so many women for generation after generation – for a man to decide her fate. Her muscles were tense with expectation. She wanted to precipitate destiny, hurry it on its way. She could no longer bear the silence. She flexed her jaw muscles and began to loosen her gag. The tie had been hurriedly secured round her mouth and over a period of minutes the superintendent managed to slacken it so much that the silk fell round her neck.

She sharpened her ears but heard nothing. She respired deeply, sensing the weight of the rope restrict her chest. At least she would now have the right to die screaming. She thought she heard the squeak of a floorboard and imagined David advancing down the corridor with death glistening in his eyes. The loudhailer barked again outside. Blanche inhaled – so deeply she thought her lungs might crack, threw back her head, and let out a great bellow. It was a strange, piercing cry – a call for succour, and a cry of pain, terror and defiance. Blanche wanted it to escape from the room where she was imprisoned and fly out across the snow. The keening wail echoed round the bungalow. Finally her breath petered out and Blanche listened to the hum of her cry reverberate through the desolate rooms. She expected to hear the stumble of David's footsteps or the blast of his shotgun. But there was nothing. Nothing. God, she thought, he *has* escaped. Or else he has the calmness of the mad and is waiting, gun cocked, at his window. There was complete tranquillity for a moment.

Suddenly, she heard the shattering of glass by the front door, a shout outside her window, a frantic hammering of metal on wood at the back, and then the thunder of boots on the wooden floor. Three helmeted men in padded jackets rushed through her door, screaming 'Armed police!', their voices heavy with country accents, the glint of fear in their eyes. Blanche heard the same cry from down the corridor, followed by 'Don't move! Lie still!' The words were shouted again with the repetition of nervousness. Boots creaked on the floorboards. Blanche guessed one of the armed officers was approaching David, eyes wide, his heart throbbing, to frisk him for any further weapons. 'Turn over! Go on, turn over!' Blanche imagined David had been surprised still lying on his bed. The bedsprings creaked. 'It's alright,' she heard next in a hoarse whisper, 'he's dead.'

It was only then that she felt the elation of escape, the elation of having cheated death. As the armed officers worked with stubby fingers to untie her the relief poured out as tears. One of them asked her if she was Detective Superintendent Hampton from the Met. They looked pleased when she nodded. Blanche sniffed back the tears once the ropes were loosened: she did not want to appear weak in front of other, male policemen. Another enquired if she was alright. All she could murmur was, 'I don't know. I don't know.'

She asked if she could see David Parker's corpse and was introduced to the local inspector who had led the attack. He looked doubtful. But Blanche insisted, saying the least he could do was let her look at the psychopath who had wanted to murder her.

She hobbled to the door of her room, cursing her ankle. The corridor was empty, the door to the kitchen at the end open. She craned her neck into the bathroom as she passed. It was ill-maintained rather than dirty, the pink tiles cracked on the wall, one of the taps dripping into the bath, bequeathing a stain of yellow ochre to the white enamel. The door to the medicine cabinet was open, the fluorescent bulb above still blazing. Blanche staggered past the empty lavatory and caught her breath as she approached David's bedroom. When she slid her head past the door jamb, she saw him.

David Parker lay on his back on the bed, the shotgun leant up against the wall. His grey eyes were open, the pupils dilated. She touched his hand and the flesh was as cold as the barrel of the gun. No pulse throbbed beneath her fingers. He was dead and she was alive. That was all that mattered. It was only later that she cared about how or why.

Once through the front door of the bungalow, she sat down on the steps to rest her ankle. Blanche breathed the chill air into her lungs like an elixir. A few feet in front of her a clutch of crocuses had exploded through the snow, their golden bugles tremulous with the distant spring.

# 26

'Botulism,' yawned Dexter and sat back in the armchair. 'That's what killed him according to Ruxton. Botulism.'

Blanche adjusted her bandaged foot on the stool and reached out for her malt whisky. She swirled it round the glass and savoured the perfume. To help make her muscles relax at the end of the day, she adored a Laphraoig or Bowmore, always without any ice or mixer that blunted the taste. 'That's a form of food poisoning, isn't it?'

The sergeant nodded gravely. 'The worst there is apparently. Ruxton says it paralyses your nerves – going from the head downwards. The guy who did the post-mortem says Parker died in the end from respiratory failure.'

Blanche suggested Dexter made himself some more coffee.

He had called round at her flat to give her a briefing. The superintendent had hardly seen him in the two days since she had staggered to the front door of David Parker's isolated cottage and been whisked off to the Heath Road hospital in Ipswich for a check-up. Spittals had insisted on an immediate report, summarising events in the bungalow and David Parker's confession, and then ordered her to recuperate at home. Blanche had also sent her profuse thanks to the Suffolk police. Since then, Dexter had to be Blanche's source of information about developments in the case.

It had been decided, because David's mother had been buried for several months and her self-confessed murderer was already dead, not to exhume the old lady's body. Ruxton said no blame should attach to the doctor who gave the death certificate. He remembered a case of an elderly and troublesome patient in a Sussex nursing home who had been suffocated under a pillow by the matron. The doctor gave a death certificate and the truth only emerged when a nurse who had seen what happened ran to the doctor's house just before the

251

funeral and told him. The funeral was halted, Ruxton continued in his didactic way, and the post-mortem revealed the almost invisible haemorrhages in the membranes of the eye known as *petechiae* that are typical of asphyxiation. There was no other evidence of murder.

'So where did it come from then – this botulism?' Blanche shouted towards the kitchen from her armchair.

Dexter swaggered back to the doorway and slipped his hands into the pockets of his elegant black leather jacket. 'Mind if I smoke?' he asked half-heartedly.

Blanche tipped her head back and looked at him with an indulgent smile, like a parent whose child has asked a favour which he knows will not be granted. 'I'd rather you confined your filthy habits to the office, Dexter. Now where did this botulism come from?'

The sergeant shrugged his shoulders. 'Tin of salmon apparently. They found it in the dustbin. It had only just been opened, although the can itself was a couple of years old.'

Blanche tossed her head back and chuckled – the first time she had laughed in the past three days.

The sergeant looked at her bemused. 'What's so funny about a tin of salmon? If it gets a laugh this easily I'll carry one around in my pocket.'

The superintendent sighed out a last spasm of laughter. 'He offered me some, you see – and I turned it down. If I'd been my usual greedy self, I'd probably be dead as well.'

'There must be some new crap there for the Met guidelines on hostage-taking,' Dexter chuckled. He waved his right hand, glittering with rings, and mimicked the voice of a lecturer from the police college. '"Via the loudhailer, advise the hostage to go on hunger strike. Failing that, advise the hostage to accept only meals of fresh salmon."' The sergeant snorted at his own joke and Blanche smiled too.

The superintendent sipped her whisky until Dexter reappeared a minute later with another mug of coffee. 'You still haven't told me the full story by the way of how the Suffolk police found me at Foxhall Cottage. What happened exactly?'

'Sure I can't smoke?' asked Dexter with a mischievous

smile.

'Dexter, even the fact that you may have helped in some small way to save my life will never give you the right to smoke in my flat.'

The sergeant laughed good-naturedly. 'It was simple enough really. You know I rang Parker up?' Blanche nodded. 'Well, I was a bit suspicious of him. This sudden business trip and so on. He sounded . . . well, a bit on edge. So I phoned up his company a couple of days later, on the Friday I think – I had too much on my plate until then – and they said Parker had phoned in a couple of days earlier to say he was ill. The business trip was phoney. You'd gone off somewhere by then and I couldn't tell you all this.' Dexter took a swig from his coffee mug and threw a critical glance round the flat. From comments he had made in the past, Blanche knew he thought it too bare, too restrained. He preferred a frenzied busyness, the clash of bright colours. 'Of course the shit hit the fan when you got kidnapped. Some people arrived just as he was bundling you in the van but too late to get the number – we knew it was you because you dropped your handbag. Spittals ordered a media blackout and we started looking round for people who might have done it – villains you've been involved with in the past and so on. Anyway, by the end of Tuesday we were desperate for ideas. I even phoned up your ex-husband, but he had no ideas either.'

'Typical,' commented Blanche with an easy smile.

'But anyway, late on the Tuesday, out of the blue the Suffolk police phoned up to say they'd run a check on an address we'd given them just outside Ipswich that had been used for placing a lonely hearts ad in *London Life*. You know we were slowly ploughing our way through the lists?'

'Foxhall Cottage, you mean?' The superintendent adjusted her bandaged ankle again. She had torn ligaments and would be unable to walk normally again for four to six weeks. The enforced immobility had already started to make Blanche bored and fidgety.

Dexter nodded. 'And of course they said Foxhall Cottage didn't belong to anyone with the name – Paul Grosvenor, or whatever it was – Parker used in his advert but to Parker himself. Anyway, I was already a bit suspicious of him – lying to me, lying to his employers, disappearing around the very time you got picked up. So I decided to have a punt and search his house. That's when I found the letter in his desk from Patricia Hoskin.'

She squinted at him with concentration. 'What – you found the letter she sent in reply to his lonely hearts ad? And was it in the name of Helen Rowe?'

The sergeant nodded. He held his hands out in a gesture of imploration, the pale palms upwards. 'Well, that clinched it. A direct link between one of the murder victims and David Parker . . . So we put out the alert for him very early on Wednesday morning. I also managed to get hold of his ex-fiancée – a woman called Pamela – who told me he'd almost tried to strangle her when she finally gave him the boot a few days before the kidnap. And well,' he shrugged his shoulders, 'you know the rest. The Suffolk police sent round a patrol to check out the cottage. They didn't twig the importance of the van at first – bloody idiots. But they soon did when you screamed and he took a pot shot at them.'

'Where were you at this time?'

'Having a contented smoke in the incident room actually – until the Suffolk police phoned up and told us what had just happened and about the white van. Then we hit the road. But of course we arrived too late for the action. You were already at the hospital by the time we got there.' Dexter sat back in his armchair, held out the palms of his hands and shrugged. 'I just don't understand it, you see – what makes a man do such disgusting things. Did you get any idea when you were with him?'

Blanche rubbed her bottom lip thoughtfully with her fore-finger. She knew as much of David Parker's story as anyone alive. But she would never know it all and was not sure she wanted to know more about his death – how botulism caused the nerves to twitch and seize up in David's head and shoulders, how his vision blurred and became double, but his warped mind retained its clarity until the end. She would never really understand how and why a young, respectable lawyer should turn into a murderous cannibal. He was mentally ill, it was true, and that infirmity could partly be traced back to his diseased childhood. But she knew the evil she had glimpsed in his eyes was beyond explanation. Evil, she believed, was part of life itself. And, like life – from generation to generation, aeon to aeon – simply existed.

One of David's victims had had a kind of poetic vengeance however. From the land of the dead, his mother had reached back and through the botulism in the tin of salmon left in her larder, she had poisoned the son whose life she had polluted. A psychopath who had killed for the ultimate in forbidden food died through the act of eating. There was sometimes, and only sometimes, a hidden symmetry in life that struck a chord with Blanche's inner being. 'And what about John Hebden – has he been released?'

'Yeah. They let him out yesterday.' Dexter smiled mischievously and he leant forward. Blanche knew he had some interesting gossip to impart. 'And I also might have found out why Spittals seemed more inclined to think Hebden was guilty than we were.'

The superintendent raised her eyebrows to indicate interest.

Dexter sipped some more coffee. 'I overheard Wootton talking about Hebden a couple of days ago. Apparently he was a left-wing journalist up in Manchester fifteen or so years ago and kept doing knocking pieces on the police. For some reason he had it in for Spittals, hinting that he was fabricating evidence and so on. Caused him no end of grief. And according to Wootton, Spittals never forgets a face. So when Hebden came in his sights, he may have been a bit less inclined to think he was innocent than you or me.'

Blanche said nothing for a few moments. She was not surprised. It was human nature. Spittals was a good policeman at heart, honest but sometimes willing to bend the rules in the interests of what he saw as justice. Every policeman was tempted to do it. Blanche had even done it herself once or twice. She knew Spittals was not at all corrupt in the true sense of the word, but he was insecure enough, and under sufficient pressure to find the murderer quickly for political reasons, to suspend his sense of disbelief.

'So where do we go from here?' yawned Blanche, throwing her arms out to stretch the muscles. She had already read

255

three novels since arriving home and was yearning for some country air. 'I'm going off down to Somerset for a few days to stay with my brother.'

'What, to avoid the press conference and interviews that Spittals'll probably want you to do?'

'You bet,' sighed Blanche. The story of how 'The Clapham Strangler' had kidnapped the detective superintendent in charge of the investigation into his murders had leaked from the Yard and the Press Office had been inundated with requests for interviews. Blanche understood the value of publicity but abhorred being the centre of it herself. She hated the flummery of police public relations. Her hope was that interest would fade before she returned to work.

Suddenly she felt tired. She yawned again. It was only ten o'clock and her first night's sleep at home had been disturbed by dreams, a jumble of images – David Parker's dilated eyes, the silk tie tightening across her mouth, her feet pounding through the snow, the desolate hobble back to the bungalow after the vain escape, her final and desperate scream. All she wanted to do now was sleep and forget.

'I'll give you a ring before you come back to work then.' Dexter held the door open, tapping his foot nervously, ready to leave. 'By the way,' he added, lifting the dark lids of his eyes to reveal a twinkle beneath, 'do you think Spittals likes tinned salmon?'

# AUTHOR'S NOTE

Those who find David Parker's behaviour taxing their belief may care to ponder on the genuine case of Issei Sagawa,
the Japanese student who inspired "A Pound of Flesh".

Sagawa, the son of a wealthy Japanese family, came to
Paris to study French literature. In 1981 he met another
student, a Dutch woman called Renée Hartevelt, and invited her back to his flat in the rue Erlanger. When Renée
rejected his advances, Sagawa shot her dead and cut her
up into pieces with an electric meat carver, eating some of
the flesh raw and some cooked in a *shabu shabu* pot. Sagawa
was arrested as he was disposing of Renée Hartevelt's remains in the Bois de Boulogne.

He was declared insane and in 1984 sent back to Japan
by the French authorities on the condition that he would
be confined to a mental home. The Japanese complied but
after a few months Sagawa was quietly released into the
custody of his parents. He now lives in a flat near Yoko-
hama where his relationships with—mostly foreign—girls
are reported with great gusto by local scandal magazines.